"I just read Fiona Brand's *Cullen's Bride*. She's a keeper. She does a great hero, doesn't she? I'm recommending the book to all my pals."

—*New York Times* Bestselling Author
Linda Howard

Walking back into her life wasn't going to be easy.

Sam had always been as remote, as self-contained, as a cat, and sometimes just as prickly. Moving on her now went against every last shred of common sense or logic—it would be better if she was protected by someone who was uninvolved—but common sense and logic didn't come into Gray's need to get her back. He couldn't explain the urgency to claim her any more than he could explain why he still wanted her after all this time. He simply knew that he wasn't about to compound the mistake he had already made by letting the gulf between them widen any further.

Because he had never forgotten how it had been with Sam.

Dear Reader,

Once again, Silhouette Intimate Moments brings you an irresistible lineup of books, perfect for curling up with on a winter's day. Start with Sharon Sala's *A Place To Call Home*, featuring a tough city cop who gets away to the Wyoming high country looking for some peace and quiet. Instead he finds a woman in mortal danger and realizes he has to help her—because, without her, his heart will never be whole.

For all you TALL, DARK AND DANGEROUS fans, Suzanne Brockmann is back with *Identity: Unknown*. Navy SEAL Mitchell Shaw has no memory of who—or what—he is when he shows up at the Lazy 8 Ranch. And ranch manager Becca Keyes can't help him answer those questions, though she certainly raises another: How can he have a future without her in it? Judith Duncan is back with *Marriage of Agreement*, a green-card marriage story filled with wonderful characters and all the genuine emotion any romance reader could want. In *His Last Best Hope*, veteran author Susan Sizemore tells a suspenseful tale in which nothing is quite what it seems but everything turns out just the way you want. With her very first book, New Zealander Fiona Brand caught readers' attention. *Heart of Midnight* brings back Gray Lombard and reunites him with the only woman strong enough to be his partner for life. Finally, welcome Yours Truly author Karen Templeton to the line. *Anything for His Children* is an opposites-attract story featuring three irresistible kids who manage to teach both the hero and the heroine something about the nature of love.

Enjoy every one of these terrific novels, and then come back next month for six more of the best and most exciting romances around.

Yours,

Leslie J. Wainger
Executive Senior Editor

Please address questions and book requests to:
Silhouette Reader Service
U.S.: 3010 Walden Ave., P.O. Box 1325, Buffalo, NY 14269
Canadian: P.O. Box 609, Fort Erie, Ont. L2A 5X3

HEART OF
MIDNIGHT

FIONA
BRAND

Silhouette®

INTIMATE™ MOMENTS®

Published by Silhouette Books

America's Publisher of Contemporary Romance

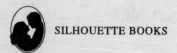 SILHOUETTE BOOKS

ISBN 0-373-07977-X

HEART OF MIDNIGHT

Visit us at www.romance.net

Printed in U.S.A.

Books by Fiona Brand

Silhouette Intimate Moments

Cullen's Bride #914
Heart of Midnight #977

FIONA BRAND

has always wanted to write. After working eight years for the New Zealand Forest Service as a clerk, she decided she could spend at least that much time trying to get a romance novel published. Luckily, it only took five years, not eight. Fiona lives with her husband and two children in a subtropical fishing and diving paradise called the Bay of Islands.

For Adrian, Tim and Simon

Chapter 1

Gray Lombard was asleep, his muscular form sprawled the length of a narrow bunk, long powerful legs clad in close-fitting fatigues, the coppery skin of his torso sheened with the moisture that hung hot and heavy in the air.

"Damn," the young NCO muttered to himself. He didn't want to disturb or surprise the man in any way. Lombard was fresh in from some long range reconnaissance mission and, like the rest of the close-mouthed, half wild band of Special Air Service troops inhabiting the base, was bound to be touchy. Just the thought of laying a hand on one of those massive shoulders made him break out in a cold sweat; he didn't have a death wish. He'd seen the way the man moved; despite his size and build, he was cat-quick and just as remorseless.

The soldier nudged the door open a little wider, wincing at the tortured whine of unoiled hinges. A slatted window shafted sunlight into the cramped prefab room that served as officers' quarters, tiger-striping the sleeping man with hot gold and inky shadow, making him seem even more savage, more untamed, and lending credence to some of the improbable stories flying around the camp.

Yet in repose, with those cold, dark eyes shut and all the grimness smoothed from his features, he looked almost approachable. Almost.

"What do you want?"

The soldier jumped at the soft demand. Lombard's eyes were open, surveying him with a slitted coolness that made him glad he hadn't advanced more than a couple of feet into the room. Even with the door wide-open at his back he felt cornered. "The Commander said—uh, he's got something you should see."

Dispassionately, Gray considered the soldier backing out of the room; he hadn't been able to conceal his fear, and Gray wondered, with a rare flash of humour, if he looked *that* bad. He had showered before he'd let himself sleep, and he'd shaved, but after weeks in the jungle he'd got used to feeling...disconnected, and definitely uncivilised.

With a grunt, he rolled to his feet, gritting his teeth against the stiffness in his shoulders, the tiredness that dragged at his muscles and made him long for a real bed, an ice-cold beer and a pizza.

Oh, baby, yeah. A pizza.

Instantly his mouth flooded with saliva, and he almost groaned aloud. After weeks of reconstituted food that tasted about as appetising as it looked, he should have known better than to think about pizza. Snagging his shirt off the end of the narrow, too-short excuse for a bed, he shrugged into it and stretched, finally allowing himself the luxury of that groan.

Ah, damn, he was getting too old for this. He was thirty-five, almost thirty-six, and if he had one lick of sense, he would leave this equatorial hellhole, and Egan Harper, to young pups like the fresh-faced soldier who had just bolted across the compound as if all the hounds of hell were after him.

Harper. The last remnants of sleep dissolved in a familiar rush of fury. Sense didn't come into the hunt for the murderous jackal. Not now, when they were this close, so close he could almost smell Egan's expensive cologne, feel the sinuous ripple of the killer's wiry, street-smart muscles twisting beneath his fingers.

No. He wouldn't be leaving Harper to fresh-faced recruits with blank innocence in their eyes. This job was his to finish, no matter the cost.

Egan Harper was his.

Raking cursory fingers through his rough mane of hair, Gray made made his way toward the shabby cluster of huts that housed the makeshift briefing room, communications centre and cafeteria of the covert and very temporary base. As he stepped through the door, he wondered what his brother, Blade, wanted that was important enough to disturb the first real sleep he'd had in almost four weeks.

Blade acknowledged him with a lift of his head. "Sorry to pull you out of the sack. Hate to interrupt your beauty sleep."

Gray's mouth twitched as he stepped over to the map table, where the documentation retrieved from their night raid was spread out. If he looked like hell, Blade came a close second. But then, Blade wanted Harper almost as badly as he did. "What have you got?"

Blade stabbed a finger at the series of black-and-white photos portraying a hi-tech office crammed with cutting-edge computer technology. "You were right, the cocaine processing plant was only a cover. The second team in found an underground facility outside the main compound. Harper is plying his terrorist trade from there—military hardware and intelligence, personnel training, aviation and ship comms. SAS Command is going to be ticked. They've been operating right beneath our noses for months.''

Gray inhaled sharply, his hunter's instincts instantly on full alert, wiping out the weariness of weeks of surveillance and miles of heavy slogging through jungle that kept its secrets shrouded in mist and rain, encased in a canopy so dense it smothered the senses, absorbing purpose as hungrily as it soaked up sunlight.

Oh, yeah, they were close. If he didn't miss his guess, they'd hit on Harper's prime residence. They didn't have him yet; somehow, with that uncanny sixth-sense for danger that he seemed to have, he'd evaded capture—*again*. But this time they had definitely hurt him.

Gray studied the photos, then systematically examined the other material on the table while Blade provided a terse commentary. His gaze skimmed over, then jerked back to a fuzzy photocopied snapshot of a woman.

The satisfaction he'd experienced at finally locating Harper's operational base was abruptly blanked out by the cold fire burning in his gut. It was fear, acrid and unmistakable. And rage. A chilling, coalescing rage that made him even calmer, even colder, than before.

He now knew why Blade had woken him. His younger brother had seen a photo of this particular woman before. Almost seven years ago, to be exact.

They'd expected to find evidence that Harper and the small time but brutally efficient Colombian drug lord who backed him, Delgado, were keeping tabs on Gray and his family. It had happened before, not because he and Blade were SAS, but because of the extremely sensitive weapons research and development business that was his own pet project and an unadvertised arm of the Lombard group of companies.

This was an abrupt escalation, a punch in the dark that brought the whispers and snippets of information Gray had picked up over the past few months into sharp focus. Harper was out for blood, revenge against Gray for the decimation of his gang and the dismantling of his family years ago. Now there could be no doubt. He was positioning himself for a strike. A very personal, very specific strike.

Sweet hell. He hadn't expected Egan to know about *her*.

She was the one person he'd been successful at hiding from almost everyone.

A shudder moved through Gray, product of the sweat cooling on his skin and another more fiercely primal reaction, an overriding need to shield and protect that which was his.

And Samantha Munro was his.

He considered the knowledge; it sat uneasily with him, yet he didn't question it. Gray knew his own nature. He was intense, single-minded; once he fixed on a goal, he didn't let up until he had achieved it. His mother and his baby sister would say he was bullheaded and probably add another few choice adjectives along the way, but that didn't change the way things were, or the way he was. Somehow, despite the passage of time and the cold fact that he had no room for emotional attachments in the life he'd chosen, he was still linked to Sam.

"It's about time," Blade murmured, as he hooked a chair close with one booted foot and sprawled in it.

"About time, what?" Gray's attention was still locked on the shadowy image. He knew Sam had never married, but now he wondered if she had a lover. The fury that rose in him at the mere thought of her lying naked beneath another man left him in no doubt as to his feelings. He was naturally possessive, and he wanted her, though he'd left her alone for seven years. *Seven years.* He felt like a sleepwalker just waking up, dazed, only now realising how much time had gone by, the magnitude of the mistake he'd made.

"About time you went and got her back."

Gray turned a narrowed glance on Blade. "How did you know I want her?"

Blade stretched and yawned, a wide grin splitting his face. "I didn't—until now. You just told me."

"I should have smothered you in the cradle when I had the chance."

"Naw. You were only two then. You couldn't reach."

"Don't bet on it. I was big for my age."

"So," Blade said softly, "why in hell does Harper have a picture of your old girlfriend?"

Gray allowed his fingertips to skim the surface of the cheap copy paper. Sam's steady gaze held him, even through the grainy matrix of the photograph. The print was black-and-white, but he didn't need colour to remind him that her eyes were a blue so clear and pure it was like looking into forever. Her hair was shorter, just past shoulder length, sleek and tailored instead of long, but it looked just as dark, just as soft. He remembered how it had felt sliding against his skin, wrapped around his hands.

Now that he'd let them in, memories he'd suppressed for years hammered him. He didn't want them, but he accepted their presence, just as he'd had to accept the presence of other memories that had settled and folded themselves darkly around his soul.

Harper had singled Sam out for attention, and there could be only one logical reason: he knew how important Sam was to Gray. Because of their past association, she was going to need protection. He silently cursed himself for not foreseeing this problem when he'd first found out she was now managing one of the Lombard hotels. It had taken him by surprise, but his mind had already been attuned to this operation, and he'd simply blocked the knowledge out. In any case, he'd been inclined to believe the name was a misprint. When Sam had disappeared on him seven years ago, he would have laid odds that she would never set foot inside a Lombard owned building, let alone *work* for Lombards, ever again. "A few months ago she took over the management of a hotel we recently purchased in Auckland. Jack okayed the appointment. He had no idea who she is."

Blade let out a low whistle. "Harper must be desperate. You haven't been near her since—"

"Since Jake died," Gray finished flatly. "I don't know what Harper is playing at. Maybe he's just compiling information. And maybe not. He knew one of the reasons I went after him seven years ago was that I thought he was holding Sam."

Blade rocked back in his chair, his expression cool and considering. "If you think the lady needs protection, we'll organise protection. Who do you want to send?"

Gray stared out through the slatted opening that served as a window, barely seeing the ragged cluster of huts, the churned mud, the glare of the noonday sun bouncing off a corrugated iron hangar. He touched the ridged scar at his throat, the ungentle reminder of his last contact with Harper, and grief and fury rose blackly in him.

He would be the one to protect Sam. There was no other option. His options had all run out seven years ago when his brother, Jake, had died at the hands of Egan Harper. Because of Gray's negligence. He had been in charge of security, and he had failed to protect his own family.

He had lost Sam then. Somewhere in the middle of that mess, she had walked, and he had let her.

Gray fixed on his brother's gaze, a gaze as dark, as grimly resolute, as his own. His mind was made up, had been the second he had accepted that he wanted Sam back. "The same guy that got her into this mess in the first place," he said in his hoarse, damaged voice. "Me."

Blade's chair landed with a thud, an earthy curse punctuating the sharp sound as he surged to his feet. "Over my dead body."

Gray gripped his brother's shoulder—a gesture meant to reassure and soothe. He could feel the tension thrumming through Blade, the passion so like his own. They were brothers, and more. He owed his life to Blade. If they had shared their mother's womb, their bond couldn't have been stronger.

He released his grip and gestured at the evidence they had collected—endless documents—while the man who had torn their family apart remained free. "I'm through with playing a defensive game," he declared bleakly. "Harper has just pushed the stakes up another notch, only this time *we're* going to call the shots. The second Harper knows Sam and I are back together, he'll move her to the top of his hit list. He won't be able to resist coming after the both of us. If we engineer the situation, we can control the outcome."

The breath hissed from between Blade's teeth. "You're going to use yourself as bait to draw Harper into a trap? Have you lost your mind?"

A trap. The word had an ugly ring to it. Gray would

take an outright confrontation any day, but in seven years, he hadn't been able to achieve that goal. He wasn't comfortable with using Sam, but he didn't see any way to avoid it. "In case you haven't noticed, the bastard seems to be stalking us. If you've got a better idea, I'm listening."

Blade silently mulled over the merits and complications of the plan. If anyone but Gray had suggested this scheme, he would have told them to take a hike, but Gray knew Harper as no one else did—knew the way the man thought, the way he operated. And Gray had carved out a reputation for himself in covert operations under various code names; his instincts were the best in the business. If he thought Samantha Munro was in danger, or that she was the key to capturing Harper, then Blade believed him.

To any other man he would have posed the question, "What makes you think the lady will have anything to do with you when she walked out on you all those years ago?"

The plain, unadorned fact was that his brother had women crawling all over him, fascinated by that cold reserve, wanting to touch his big muscles and coo over his scars. Wanting him to whisper sexy things to them in that bad ass voice of his. Gray barely gave them the time of day.

Occasionally he gave in and took one to bed, but only on his own terms. The next day the lady in question would be satisfied but bewildered at the lack of follow-up, sure he couldn't possibly have meant just *one* night. It wasn't that Gray didn't like women, he simply didn't have time for them.

If he had now found time for Samantha Munro, the lady didn't stand a chance.

Still… "She isn't going to like it."

Gray acknowledged Blade's reservations with a wry twist of his mouth. "Like" was a tame word to describe the way Sam would feel about anything. Her emotions had always run as frustratingly deep and pure as the bottomless blue of her eyes, and her trust had been, to put it mildly, elusive. The only "like" about anything was that she would likely slap his face. "I'll be taking the first transport out. Something about this whole situation gives me a cold itch up my spine. If Harper isn't here, then I want to know where in hell he is."

Gray left the makeshift operations room, stepping out into the brutal heat of the sun, his mind automatically falling into the cold, analytical cadences of problem solving.

Egan had just made a very big mistake. Up until now they had tracked him, isolated all the tendrils of his organisation, content in the knowledge that when they finally shut him down, they would destroy his entire poisonous network at the same time. But now he had threatened not only Gray's family, but his woman.

The gloves were off, figuratively, literally, any damn way you chose to look at it. The hell with finesse, they had the advantage. In his arrogance, Egan hadn't yet realised that the prey was now hunting him.

Now that he had made the decision to go after Sam, Gray was impatient to leave, but a sense of disorientation gripped him. His fierce need to claim Sam directly conflicted with his need to remain focused on bringing Harper to justice. He didn't like the sense of being split in two one little bit. The situation with Egan was both dangerous and intense. Seven years ago, Gray had made the mistake of not being prepared; this time there would be no room for error. Somehow, he would have to keep Sam separate and apart from the operation to net Harper.

Walking back into her life wasn't going to be easy. Sam had always been as remote, as self-contained, as a cat, and sometimes just as prickly. Moving on her now went against every last shred of common sense or logic—it would be better if she was protected by someone who was uninvolved—but common sense and logic didn't come into Gray's need to get her back. He couldn't explain the urgency to claim her any more than he could explain why he still wanted her after all this time. He simply knew that he wasn't about to compound the mistake he had already made by letting the gulf between them widen any further.

Immediately he began to calculate what he needed to do to get Sam back. Something inside him relaxed at the decision—a tension he hadn't known existed.

Damn. Seven years.

Gray came to an abrupt halt in the centre of the muddy square around which the huts were built, once again stunned, completely oblivious to the heavy black clouds gathering overhead, the impending violence of the deluge. Every hair on his body lifted, as if an electrical charge had just been run through his system, kicking reluctant nerve-endings to pulsing, tingling life. For years he had been shut down, closed off, focussed solely on the hunt for his brother's killer. He'd had no room for relationships beyond the obligatory family ones, and he had been damn tardy with those.

He'd had sex. A raw slaking of his physical needs. But now he wanted more than the bare mechanics of the act.

A shudder moved through him, and his loins flooded with heat, tightening on an unruly throb of anticipation. He could barely remember the last time he had made love, or the woman he had made love to.

He had never forgotten how it had been with Sam.

He wanted her now; wanted to toss her over his shoul-

der and take her somewhere dim and private and lay claim
in the most basic, primitive way there was.

He still couldn't believe he'd let so much time pass.

It was a miracle he hadn't lost her completely.

Chapter 2

The phone was ringing as Samantha Munro unlocked the front door of her private quarters. She'd heard the shrill summons all the way from the end of the hallway as she'd exited the elevator, and she was tempted to let it ring. The sheer persistence of the caller meant trouble or work. In a hotel as old-fashioned and dilapidated as the Pacific Royal, it probably meant both.

Stuffy heat engulfed her as she entered her rooms. Sam fixed the telephone with a narrow-eyed glare, briefly entertaining the cord-yanking fantasy. She was tired, she'd missed lunch, and her stomach was awash with an overload of the too-strong coffee she'd drunk as a sorry substitute for eating. All she wanted to do was have a cooling shower, then relax. Preferably in a horizontal position with her eyes closed.

She dumped her handbag, keys and briefcase down on the hall table, a part of her mind automatically running through what *could* have gone wrong. Maybe the electrics had finally failed and they had a fire? Maybe another pipe had burst and there was a flood? Maybe the Carson sisters had propagated one tropical plant too many and the whole second floor had collapsed under the weight of the potting mix they kept sneaking upstairs?

With a sigh that was half frustration, half affectionate exasperation for the foibles of the gothic old dinosaur of a hotel and some of its residents, she snatched up the receiver. Despite its many faults, the Royal was her baby. She couldn't *not* answer.

"They're here," a dramatic voice proclaimed.

Edith. Sam's mouth twitched as she used her free hand to unbutton her jacket. Judging from the sixty-plus receptionist's tone, the Devil incarnate had just signed the Royal's register. "Who's here?"

"That bunch of accountants who didn't show yesterday."

Sam's spurt of amusement flickered and died as Edith began reciting which rooms she'd assigned to the "hatchet team" sent in by Lombards to decide the hotel's ultimate fate.

So, they'd finally arrived.

Sam supposed it had been too much to hope that the new owner of the Royal had forgotten the hotel existed. Fat chance. Lombards was a large, incredibly successful group of companies. It hadn't got that way by forgetting about assets, no matter how old and insignificant they were.

"—as for Lombard, *he* doesn't look like any accountant I've ever seen."

Sam tuned in on the tail end of Edith's finishing remark. Her fingers tightened on the receiver. "Who did you say?"

''Gray Lombard. I just booked him into the Governor's Suite.''

Sam's chest contracted sharply. For long seconds she couldn't breathe. Edith had made a mistake. It had to be a mistake. ''Are you sure?''

''Of course I'm sure! That man is hard to miss. Big. Dark. Would have been handsome if he'd smiled, but those black eyes of his gave me the shivers. Can't say I like the look of any of that fancy crew he brought with him, come to that. Although, if I was forty years younger...''

''Thanks, Edith.'' Clumsily Sam set the receiver down, cutting off Edith's crusty chuckle and the graphic outline of forty-year-old seduction techniques that was sure to follow.

Gray Lombard.

Her chest squeezed tight again, and she forced herself to breathe, to *think*.

Gray couldn't be here; it didn't make sense. He wasn't involved with the hotels. She'd made sure of that months ago, before she'd taken on a job with a company she had vowed never to work for again—a job that wasn't going to do her career any favours. Before she had employed the admittedly desperate strategy of forcing herself to step back into Gray Lombard's world in order to prove to herself that she was finally over him.

Her stomach muscles knotted, and for a moment she thought she was going to be sick, as sick as she had felt months ago in the bleak aftermath of her grandfather's funeral, when she had been confronted with a past she'd thought was tucked comfortably behind her and discovered just what she had done to herself—just how she had deceived herself.

Gramps' death had rocked her. She'd stood beside his

grave at the small cemetery where he was being buried next to her parents and her baby daughter, and realised that all the people she cared about now lay deep beneath that crumbly clay soil—still, forever silent, unable to put their arms around her, to laugh or cry, to share her joy and pain.

Several days after the funeral, she had been clearing out his house when she'd picked up the business section of the newspaper she still hadn't got around to stopping. The Lombards advertisement had leaped out at her. She'd stood in the kitchen, still shaky with grief, hot and grimy and surrounded by packing boxes, staring at the bold, black print. Without warning, the past had risen up, breaking over her in a stark wave that had sent her stumbling to the bathroom, gasping, almost blind with tears, her empty stomach heaving.

She'd cried when Gramps had slipped quietly away after months of illness. She'd cried at the funeral. This was different, a keening sense of loss, a raw upwelling of grief and fury and disbelief that she'd let so many years pass her by because a small, stubborn part of her was still waiting for Gray Lombard.

She'd disguised the waiting as fastidiousness, a lack of sexual drive, concentration on her work, anything but the truth. Once a disgruntled would-be lover had told her she was cold, and Sam had readily agreed. After Gray, and in the painful aftermath of the baby she'd lost, she'd been frozen inside.

The result was that she was alone now, so completely alone it hurt. She had none of the things that many women took for granted: a husband she could love and who loved her. A home. Her child.

She was twenty-nine. Almost thirty. Maybe that had

had something to do with the sudden suffocating realisation that life was quickly passing her by.

While Gramps had been alive, he'd formed a comfortable buffer of weekly telephone calls, infrequent letters and regular holidays. His wry common sense, his steady love, had been a lodestone, especially when her career had demanded constant changes of location. She hadn't realised how much she'd come to rely on that uncomplicated love.

It had been easier than reaching out for the complicated kind. That would have taken courage, and a willingness to once more expose herself to hurt.

When her stomach had finally settled down, she'd forced herself to pick the paper up off the floor, to read the advertisement, and to consider it. Her head might have been buried in sand so deep she could barely breathe, but no more. Gray Lombard was ancient history, and Sam had decided she couldn't allow him to affect her life any longer.

Her resources had been severely depleted. For the last few months of Gramps' illness, she had lived with him and nursed him full time. The sale of the house had covered the final medical bills and funeral costs, but she'd needed another job and a place to live. She had applied for the manager's position and got it.

She had wanted closure from a relationship that had somehow dragged on way past its use-by date, and now she was getting it with a vengeance.

Oh God. The instinct to run, to simply pack up and leave, was so strong that for long moments she stood, paralysed, her pulse racing. Nothing in her plan had allowed for an actual physical confrontation with Gray.

"Get a grip," she muttered to herself. Her reaction was ridiculous. Women met ex-boyfriends, even became friends with them, all the time. She was an adult. She could do this.

Except that she couldn't imagine ever being friends with Gray. Their relationship had been...extreme, like a wild, out of control roller-coaster ride—dizzying, at times terrifying in its intensity. Friendship had never been included.

Sam stared blankly around her cosy, private quarters. While she'd been standing, lost in the grip of the past, it had started raining. Large droplets splattered loudly against the windows, then cascaded down the French doors, blurring her view of the tiny, drenched courtyard garden outside and the glossy profusion of potted plants that shimmered beneath the steady onslaught. It was late afternoon, and the slow, extended twilight had begun, helped along by full-bellied clouds that blocked out the heat of the sun. The temperature, which had been hot for December, had taken an abrupt tumble.

Although it wasn't cold inside. *She* wasn't cold. Beneath the layers of her light summer-weight suit and blouse, she was furnace-hot, her skin clammy with moisture.

With fingers that weren't entirely steady, Sam removed the jacket and carried it through to her bedroom, automatically hanging it in the wardrobe alongside ranks of similar suits and dresses.

In just her blouse and skirt, she felt freer and cooler, although the small flat was still uncomfortably hot and airless. The reason for the stuffiness added to her tension as she pulled pins from her hair, releasing it from its neat chignon.

She'd taken to locking her flat up tight, forgoing all ventilation, after she'd discovered that someone had broken in several days ago. The break-in had been very subtle, and it appeared that nothing had been taken. Most people probably wouldn't have noticed the signs, but Sam had. She was used to living alone, and, while she wasn't neurotic about neatness, her possessions didn't usually move on their own or change the way they were folded.

The sense of violation, of invasion of privacy, had been so intense that she'd actually contemplated shifting to new rooms, until she'd realised what she was allowing. Despite the Royal's constant maintenance problems, she was settled here. She was happy for the first time in months, and she liked her flat. It was situated at the back of the hotel, on the ground floor, and the mellow paint tones, the slightly battered antique furnishings, somehow gave the illusion of home, if not the reality. Since she'd been forced to sell Gramps' house, the only home Sam could remember, that illusion had become all-important.

A spurt of mingled anger and disbelief froze her in the act of finger-combing her hair free of the confining knot. If Gray was part of the Lombards delegation, here to decide the future of *her* hotel, she would have to work with him, make polite conversation with him. Pretend that nothing of importance had ever happened between them.

Sam stared at her pale reflection, too distraught to shy away from the blunt truth that, for Gray, that was exactly how it had been.

Her fury deepened. How dare he stroll nonchalantly back into her life like this? He had all the sensitivity of a slab of granite. She didn't know if she could even be civil to him.

One of her grandfather's favourite sayings rose irresistibly into her mind, as clear and briskly humourous as if the words had been spoken aloud in his shaky, whisky-deep voice.

"Be careful what you wish for, girl, you just might get it."

Well, she thought grimly, as she opened the French doors with more force than was warranted, too wound up to appreciate the rain-scented air flowing in, she hadn't wished for Gray, but it looked like she was finally going to get him.

Anger still simmering, Sam changed into light cotton pants and a shirt, pulled thick-soled boots and a raincoat on, and stepped outside. When she had locked up, she lifted her face to the rain, which had slackened off to a light drizzle. Just the thought of staying in the hotel, knowing that Gray was staying there, too, made her stomach knot. She would go for a walk, take in a movie, maybe check out the bookshops for women's magazines. She needed advice, and there was no one she could ask about such an embarrassing problem.

Not that she was in any way confused, she allowed. Just inexperienced. Thanks to her disastrous relationship with Gray, she had never had another, and she was quite frankly at a loss as to how to proceed.

Somewhere there would be an article outlining strategies for getting rid of ex-lovers.

Hours later Sam walked out of the double feature she'd just seen. It had started drizzling again, and the sidewalk was jammed with people diving for taxis, or pulling on raincoats and flipping up umbrellas. Wisps of steam rose from the pavement and the road that, despite the rain, still retained the heat of the day.

A car cruised by, the horn blared, and a young man hung out the window, swearing his undying love to a group of teenage girls. Sam slipped her raincoat on and belted it, her gaze drawn to a man standing near the teenage girls, who had now become the object of their wide-eyed scrutiny.

He was turned away from Sam, studying the people climbing into taxis, a black leather jacket held negligently in one big hand. Most people were wrapped up against the weather, although it was far from cold. He was distinctly underdressed, and wet, as if he'd been caught in a violent rain shower and hadn't cared enough to seek shelter. The white fabric of his wet T-shirt clung to the broad width of his shoulders and the heavy muscles of his back, revealing the dark glow of his skin where it touched. The taut swell of one biceps gleamed copper as he thrust impatient fingers through his wet mane of black hair, sending a narrow rivulet snaking down the deep indentation of his spine.

But, even motionless as he was, there was no sense of passivity to the rigid line of that back, the tense stance of those long powerful legs. His soaked clothing moulded muscles that were coiled, ready to spring. Most of the people on the sidewalk recognised that dangerous quality, giving him a wide berth, so that he stood like a solitary rock amidst swirling, fickle currents.

Something about the tilt of his head, the wide set of his shoulders, his very stillness in the jostling crowd, made Sam's mouth go dry in startled recognition. She couldn't see his face, but for a heart-pounding moment she was certain it was Gray.

A family strolled past, momentarily obscuring her line of sight. When she saw him again, he'd shifted deeper into the ebb and flow of the crowd, and she caught little more than a fleeting glimpse of that fierce dark head and one broad shoulder as he turned his attention on another section of the rapidly dispersing crowd, systematically scanning, *looking* for someone.

A breeze stirred, flipping dark strands of hair across her cheeks, and she shivered under the lash of memory. The last image she'd had of Gray had been completely, wholly sensual. He'd been naked. They had *both* been naked. He'd been shuddering in her arms, his big shoulders damp with sweat, glistening bronze in the lamplight as she'd wrapped herself around him in an attempt to ease the fierceness of his desire, the raw intensity of his release.

She had closed her eyes, unable to bear the shattering pleasure, the primitive beauty of what he was doing to her. Unable to bear the certain knowledge that he hadn't wanted *her*.

For long seconds Sam remained frozen on the sidewalk, barely noticing the people brushing by. She was caught and held by the image, appalled that it still had the power to shake her.

The breeze swirled against her suddenly hot cheeks, carrying the dampness of the rain. Sam lifted her hand in automatic reflex, smoothing tangled hair from her face. Angry with herself, she turned on her heel and threaded her way toward the taxi rank. Despite the striking resemblance, the man wasn't Gray. Even from the back, he'd looked too wild, too untamed, and there had been an edgy quality to him, an urgency to his search that shouted involvement with someone. Probably a woman.

Gray had never worn his hair long, and he'd only arrived this evening. Besides, any reasons he'd ever had to seek her out were seven years cold and no longer of interest to her.

The last taxi pulled out as Sam reached the kerb, and she was left standing in a queue, waiting for others to pull in.

She glanced back. People were still exiting the big multiplex cinema in a steady stream, but even in the middle of the mass of people, she caught the turn of that distinctive head. He was still searching, his purpose a living thing. She wondered bleakly what it would feel like to be the focus of such purpose, and her hands clenched against a surge of vulnerability so acute that for long moments she felt stripped bare of all defences, her emotions naked and exposed, as tender as a babe's.

No, she couldn't imagine such a thing, and she was crazy even dwelling on it. Abruptly she spun on her heel and walked blindly away, uncaring which direction she was headed.

And she didn't want to see the man's face, no matter how tempted she was to keep watching him. She'd played this game one too many times, although not for years now, and the anguish she'd gone through hadn't been pretty. When she had first left Gray, she'd lost count of the number of times she'd seen his face in a stranger's.

Calling herself every name under the sun for letting the stranger get to her, Sam pulled herself together enough to take some bearings, and fell in behind a laughing group of young people who were amiably arguing about which café they were going to hit next. The teenagers peeled off into a café that brimmed with laughter and light. The mouthwatering scents of espresso and spicy food wafted from the open door.

Sam debated whether she should go for safety and get a taxi or continue to walk. Her jaw squared. She wasn't going back to the taxi rank.

The Royal wasn't far—about five minutes—and how dangerous could it be? Despite the wet weather the tourist season was in full swing. The streets and cafés were alive with activity.

Turning the collar of her coat up, she started across the road; she had to get a grip on herself, and the sooner the better. Her nerves were strung too tight, had been ever since the break-in. Now she was seeing danger in every shadow.

Sam was close enough to the hotel to see a corner of the distinctive Victorian roofline where it loomed, cheek-by-jowl with a squat parking building, when a soft scrape sounded to the side of her. Her heart speeded up. Someone was there. A quick glance showed her nothing but brightly lit shop windows and intermittent shadows that were all the deeper because of the light.

"Heyyy…lady."

Sam's head whipped in the direction of the slurred voice. A youth was slouched in a shop doorway, clutching a bottle and grinning inanely. When she'd looked before, she'd missed him, because the recess was so deep. Sam averted her gaze and walked briskly on. She wasn't alone on the street. There were people ahead of her and people behind. If she needed to, she could call out for assistance. Or run. The boy, because that was all he was, was probably so drunk he wouldn't be able to do more than stumble.

"Heyyy, come back!" she heard the same slurred voice call, then footsteps as he came after her.

She heard a muffled grunt and looked back to see the youth being hauled up and pressed back into the shadowed recess, pinned there by a tall, dark man in a leather jacket.

Another two men materialised out of the shadows, one blond, the other dark. Both were dressed in dark clothing.

Where had they come from? Last time she'd checked behind her there had been two couples meandering arm-in-arm, presumably toward the parking building next to the Royal. There was no sign of them now; they must have turned down another street.

Sam lengthened her stride, spooked to see that now there was no one ahead of her, either. This particular street was empty except for herself, the drunken youth and the three men behind her. She heard footsteps, the low timbre of voices, and lengthened her stride, calculating how far she had to go, the safest options. There was plenty of traffic cruising past, she could always try to stop someone and ask for assistance.

Maybe she wasn't in any danger, but the tight prickling at the base of her nape said that just maybe she was.

Self-defence tactics she'd learned in a class just months before replayed themselves through her mind. She was small, no more than five-four. Her first and best option was to flat-out run. If she had to defend herself...

Adrenaline flooded her system. Make a tight fist. Don't fold her fingers over her thumb or she would break it. Elbows were good, kicking even better, because she didn't have to be in so close and her boots had solid soles.

She glanced back, saw the three men closing on her. The dark, leather-jacketed man was in front. He had a white T-shirt on beneath the jacket. Sam swallowed, her breathing shallowing out. The white T-shirt, something about the fluid, ground-eating prowl of the man's stride, was more than familiar.

She was almost sure it was the man who had been outside the cinema.

He was how far away? Twenty metres? Thirty?

She risked another look, not breaking her stride. The man's head lifted sharply, as if he'd finally sensed her panic, but she still couldn't make him out clearly. He was walking through pooling darkness, the white T-shirt shining like a beacon.

Light flashed across the man, searing his image in her mind. He was big, six foot three or four at least, and grimly, fiercely male.

It couldn't be, she thought numbly. Sam faltered, slowed, then turned to face him, almost completely disoriented now. It *was* the man she'd watched outside the cinema. The man she'd thought was Gray.

He kept coming, his features half in light, half out of it. The drizzle and the street-lighting weren't helping. His features seemed at once both unbearably familiar and alien.

"Sam."

His voice shivered through her, the gravelled tone too deep, too raspy. The rougher cadence sent a shuddering little frisson down her spine.

He *was* a stranger.

Adrenaline jolted her system again. Warily she backed up a step, saw the entrance to a narrow service lane, then plunged into darkness, frantically hoping her eyes would adjust soon, before she went head over tail. At least she knew where she was—the lane twisted and turned between tall buildings, then came out near a service station. From there the rear entrance of the Royal was just a short lope across the road. It wasn't a route she would normally choose, but right now alley demons and derelicts didn't seem nearly so dangerous as the stranger who had said her name.

A harsh command sliced through the shrouded darkness, and Sam found the strength to ignore the wet drag of her raincoat and lift her knees higher as she ran, pushing for more speed. She rounded a corner, skidded in a puddle that was rank with refuse. Her hand shot out, palm scraping against the rough side of a building. She steadied herself, heart pumping furiously, mouth dry as she careened on.

Her name echoed, rasping eerily; then she heard him behind her, felt the ripple of irrational terror exploding up her spine as she caught the dim glow at the end of the alley, like the light at the end of a tunnel. Just as she burst free of the darkness, his hand fastened heavily on her arm and spun her to a stumbling halt.

"Damn," he said tautly. "What in hell do you mean by running?"

His gaze locked on hers. The impact of it almost drove her back a step. Grim purpose radiated from eyes as black as sin, as cold as hell iced over. The yellow glow of the street lamp illuminated the strong, rain-slick contours of a face she knew...and didn't.

He was furious, she realised blankly. Furious enough to wrap one of those big, dangerous hands around her throat and shake her.

It would be one way to die.

"Gray?" Sam sucked in a breath, still not sure that it was, and shocked at the husky alarm threading her voice.

"Yeah, it's me. Gray," he added, as if he thought she needed the reassurance.

She did. Both his hands were on her now, clasped around her upper arms, as if he was afraid he would spook her again. The heat from his palms penetrated even through the layers of raincoat and clothing.

"I didn't mean to scare you, babe," he said, low and soothing, his hold firm. "I thought you'd recognised me. I forgot about this damn voice."

Abruptly he released her and pulled the neck of his T-shirt and the collar of his leather jacket aside, baring the supple, coppery skin of his throat and the ridged line of scar tissue that was now clearly visible. "A knife," he said, soft as rough velvet.

The timbre of his voice quivered through her, and for a split second Sam forgot everything but the evidence of pain and violence. She wanted to reach up, touch the old wound, demand to know why he'd been attacked and who had done such a violent, senseless thing. The impulse died a quick death. He wouldn't want her concern, he never had, and the alarming dichotomy of facing a stranger she knew, *intimately,* struck her anew.

He was bigger than she remembered, broader across the shoulders, deeper through the chest, and looking into his eyes was like gazing into the heart of midnight. They were dark, depthless, and so remote she ached inside. There was no sign of the direct, ruthless male charm she remembered, or the sleepy indulgent humour that had wrapped her in a dazed enchantment for weeks on end. The man she'd fallen in love with had been like a large, sated cat— lazily sensual and playful, sometimes moodily intense, and so absorbed with her that she'd disregarded his warnings, his refusal to make promises.

There was an air of condensed power about this Gray, a seasoned maturity that sent shivers of alarm and unease down her spine. The iron control that tightened the tanned skin across his cheekbones and firmed the sensual line of his mouth only made him look harder, even more bleakly ruthless.

And then another thought drove everything else from her mind. "You were looking for me."

"Damn straight," he said grimly. "When you didn't answer your phone or your door, I made some enquiries. One of the hotel staff said they'd seen you go out walking. Walking!" His voice was rough with disbelief.

Her fingers curled into her palms. One palm stung, and

she absently noted she must have scraped the skin off when she'd nearly skidded over, but right now a little lost skin was the least of her concerns. "You make it sound like walking is a crime. This is Auckland, Gray, not a war zone. Maybe it wasn't the brightest decision I've ever made, but I don't owe you any explanations."

His expression was hooded, watchful. "I'm sorry we frightened you, but that young thug wasn't after conversation."

The graphic image of Gray gripping the thug's collar while he hauled him up to eye level sparked off an involuntary shiver. "Okay," she said quietly. "Thanks for…dealing with him. I think."

Gray released a breath, and she felt a startled awareness of the tension that was gripping him. Tension and relief. Incredible as it seemed, he'd been worried about her. The notion was jolting. The depth of his concern was as alien as his voice, and she didn't know how to respond to it.

"I'll take you home," he stated.

Sam eyed him warily, struck now by the inescapable fact that the man who had been scouring the crowd so urgently outside the cinema *had* been Gray, and *she* had been the focus of his search. Gray looking for her at all was hard to take in; the level of urgency in his search was even more baffling. All she wanted now was to get away from his disturbing presence, to be alone so she could think all this through. "You don't have to bother. It's just across the road."

His brows lifted in what could have been amusement. "I know, I'm staying there, too."

He cupped her elbow before she could answer, his firm grip upsetting her hard-won equilibrium all over again as he urged her across the deserted street. The gesture was old-fashioned and possessive, almost ludicrous under the circumstances, and the heat from his palm, his solid, muscular presence so close beside her, made an awareness she wanted no part of blossom in the pit of her stomach, confusing her even further.

Sam toyed with the idea of simply shaking free of his hold, but to do so would signal how uncomfortable she felt in his presence. She sensed he wouldn't willingly let her go, anyway, not after all the effort he'd gone to to find her.

Footfalls sounded behind them. Sam craned around to see the two dark-clothed men following behind like shadows. She'd forgotten about them.

"They're with me," Gray said in a tone that was probably supposed to reassure her.

Sam almost choked. "Do you mean to tell me there were *three* of you out combing the streets for me?"

Gray's narrow gaze glittered over her. "Sorry, darlin'," he murmured, humour and something very like satisfaction threading his rough voice. "That was all I could spare at the time."

Sam's own gaze narrowed. He made her sound like a renegade mare at round-up time and he the reluctant cowboy who had had been stuck with the job of reeling her in. "It's a shame then, isn't it, that I wasn't lost?"

His gaze lingered on her, and she could almost have sworn he was amused, but he didn't smile.

If he had smiled, she decided bleakly, she would have done what she had planned when he had chased her down in the alley. Plan B wasn't foolproof by anyone's standards, but it had its merits. It involved her knee and a certain part of her attacker's anatomy, and was guaranteed to render any male speechless for a satisfying length of time.

Chapter 3

He had her safe.

That was Gray's first rational thought as he guided Sam toward the badly lit back entrance of the hotel. The return of rationality was damn welcome.

When he had found out Sam had gone out alone at night, on foot, he had almost gone crazy. When that young hood had started after her, adrenaline had slammed through him. He was still tense and edgy from its effects.

Then she had run from *him*.

He could kick himself. He had forgotten about his voice, forgotten just how many years had passed, and if those years had scored their indelible mark on him, they had also tempered Sam. The changes were in her face, and they rocked him. The rounded softness of youth had been replaced by a fine-boned symmetry that added an exotic elegance to her features, a feminine strength to the firmly moulded sweep of her jaw, and made her mouth look even more tantalisingly stubborn.

She was neither stunningly beautiful nor model perfect, but those two qualities had never turned Gray on. It had been the dark-blue purity of her eyes, her remote, untouched quality, that had first attracted him. She'd been like a pristine, tightly budded rose, and once he'd noticed her, it had taken him about ten seconds to respond to the unintentional challenge of that closed, delicately sensual face and get so hard he knew he had to have her.

Some things, he thought with bleak humour, didn't change.

It had always surprised him that he'd got her into his bed so easily and so fast, but after a while he'd realised that, despite the fact that she'd given herself to him, he didn't have her at all. The stubborn, bone-deep reserve that had at first so intrigued him had soon made him furious. He'd never been certain of her, even when he'd had her beneath him with both legs wrapped firmly around his waist.

Although there had been nothing reserved about her reaction tonight. She had run the gamut of panic and fear, relief and anger, and mastered it all with cool courage. When she'd found out who he was, her expression had turned about as warm and welcoming as pack-ice. She had looked at him as if *she* would have liked to kick his ass.

Gray swept the shadows, his gaze intent, his senses acute. Ben and Carter stepped quietly behind him.

When this was all over, he decided, Sam could kick his ass for as long as she liked, and he would take it. He would chuck the active operations and concentrate on the organisational aspects. Gray felt a certain relief at the decision. Yeah, he was ready to settle down. Past ready. He wanted Sam, and he wanted kids. He would do what his mother had been wanting him to do for years: get a haircut and a real job. But he couldn't allow himself the luxury of a future yet. Not when his own brother was dead and the man who had killed him was still free and hunting.

"Is there a back entrance to your rooms?" Gray asked, as they neared the private parking bay at the rear of the hotel.

"Near the store-room, but I don't need—"

"I'll see you safe."

Sam bit back a cool answer. Gray was set on seeing her to her door. Okay, she could live with that. At night, this part of the hotel was poorly lit and decidedly sinister, and after her flat had been broken into, she hadn't been able to wipe the image of the offender waiting out here, lurking in the shadows, maybe watching her until she'd finally left for work.

At a nod from Gray, one of the two men glided past, the dark one. His eyes were faintly amused, speculative. He didn't look like any accountant or hotel executive Sam had ever seen. Neither did the blond guy. The two of them were like a couple of sleek, hungry Dobermans trailing their master.

She heard the metallic scrape of the latch being lifted on the gate that guarded the back entrance to her flat. The security light she'd had installed over her door sprang to life, starkly illuminating the tiny courtyard.

Sam dug her keys out of her pocket as she walked through the gate.

Gray held his hand out. "Let me."

It wasn't a question. With a lift of her brows, she dropped the keys into his palm.

Gray unlocked the French doors and disappeared inside. Sam followed, flicking a light on. Seconds later Gray reappeared, the leather jacket once more held in his hand, his damp T-shirt clinging to his chest. The image of him grimly searching outside the cinema replayed itself in her mind, and a shiver of reaction went through her, compounded by an unnerving sense of being shoved along with no control.

Easing out of her coat, she shook most of the drips off outside on the pavers. The courtyard was now deserted; the other two men had gone, melting away into the night so quickly and silently that she hadn't heard them leave.

''You're bleeding.''

She spun, startled. Gray was bare inches from her, which startled her even more; she hadn't heard him approach. Up this close he was even more intimidating; the chiselled planes of his face were leaner, more darkly tanned, than she remembered, the force of his black gaze mesmerizing. His very presence made her feel absurdly vulnerable. She'd gone out tonight because she needed time to come to grips with the fact that Gray was here at all. She'd planned to be completely composed with the armour of her job, her professionalism, fully in place when she finally met him. Having him in her flat, larger than life, bigger, more *male* than she remembered, definitely wasn't part of the plan.

Shockingly his fingers grazed her temple, the pads warm, rough against her skin, sending another hot tingle of sensation shimmering through her. His fingertips came away smeared with blood.

''Why didn't you tell me you were hurt?''

His expression was accusing. Sam reached up to feel the place he'd touched, but he forestalled her.

''Let me,'' he rasped softly.

His fingers brushed her temples as he parted her hair, searching for the source of the bleeding. Sam froze at the sheer unexpectedness of his actions. The blood in her hair could only have come from her palm, and she was standing here, letting him search for a nonexistent wound while the shatteringly familiar scent of him surrounded her, yanking her into a past she had spent the last few months trying to bury.

Panic grabbed her stomach. She jerked free of his touch. Dear God, Gray might look and sound different, but he still smelled the same: clean, hot, utterly male. "It's my hand," she said huskily.

"Let me see."

"It's nothing." Reluctantly Sam extended her hand. "Just a scrape."

She uncurled her fingers, letting him see her palm. It wasn't bad, but the abraded area was raw and dirty.

"I'll dress it for you."

Sam stiffened, but he cut her off before she could speak.

"You're still shaky. I'm not leaving until I've dressed your hand." Gray's jaw was set, unyielding. "If I step out of line, you can slap me."

Sam knew that expression, the iron force of the will behind it. Gray was used to getting his way. She could argue until she ran out of breath, order him out, but he wouldn't leave until he'd bandaged her hand. Once again she was faced with a choice she had never imagined she would have to make—a choice between an undignified tussle to get rid of him or taking the line of least resistance and letting him have his way.

The notion that he would even want to step out of line was so ludicrous that she dismissed it. "The first-aid box is in the bathroom. It's a red container in the cupboard under the basin."

Sam drew a relieved breath when he left the room, hung up her coat, then sank down in one of two single chairs in the lounge. The couch was out. No way was she having him sitting next to her.

When Gray prowled back into the room, he had a bowl of water and a washcloth, as well as the first-aid box. Instead of drawing the other single chair over next to hers, he pushed the coffee table aside, snagged a footstool and sat down, bracketing her legs with his in order to get close.

Even sitting down, he was big, and Sam was abruptly aware of just how physically intimidating Gray was. The sense of being cornered was acute, and her body was responding to his proximity in a way that was frankly alarming; she was flushed with heat, and her skin had become ultrasensitive, her breasts tight and tender.

Reluctantly she placed her hand in his. He was gentle, but even so, she flinched when he began cleaning her palm.

When he was finished, Gray smeared on antiseptic cream, then applied a dressing. "Does your grandfather still live here?"

"He died a few months ago."

His gaze connected with hers. "I'm sorry. I wish I'd known."

"There was no reason for you to know."

His eyes flared at her curt reply; then his mouth quirked at one corner. "Damn, but you've grown some claws. It must have been rough, losing him. Is that why you've lost weight?"

"I'm not thin," she automatically denied, standing up and, in so doing, getting way too close to Gray. Awkwardly she shuffled the chair back to get around him. "And the way I look is none of your business."

Gray came to his feet. "Don't get in a snit," he said mildly. "I wasn't saying I don't find you attractive."

Sam stared at him in utter disbelief. "I don't want you to find me attractive!"

He crossed his arms over his chest, his head cocked slightly to one side, and a slow smile slid across his mouth. "Then, baby, your luck just ran out. I'm male, and I'm not blind. The plain fact is, you can't disguise the way you walk. I recognised you from behind, even in that tent of a raincoat."

Sam's pulse jumped, not so much at his words, but at the blatant male interest gleaming in his dark eyes. She shook her head, more a reaction to her own disorientation than a denial. She must be more tired than she'd thought; he *couldn't* be flirting with her. "What do you mean, the way I walk?"

As far as she knew, she walked the same way she did everything else. Normally. Joe average. One hundred percent ordinary.

Gray gave her a considering look. "Like warm honey flowing. Hot and sweet and slow."

The rough sensuality in his voice hit her like a hammer blow. Sam retreated instinctively, forgetting he'd moved the coffee table from its usual place. Gray caught her before she tumbled back, moving so fast that she was jerked against his chest before she could even cry out in surprise.

Heat radiated from him, warming her instantly, and the clasp of his hands burned, even through the heavy weave of her shirt. She was caught, held in his grasp, and a sense of déjà vu rose strongly in her, merging the past with the present in a confusing kaleidoscope of emotion. She wanted to move, to escape, but the hot shivery feel of his hands on her was too powerful. It had been so long since she'd been held by anyone, let alone Gray. She felt weak inside, unbearably pleasured by that simple touch, seduced by the mere thought of surrendering to more than just the possessive clasp of his hands.

Her lapse in control brought Sam up sharply, and she couldn't control a keening wave of grief and despair. *No*. Not now. And not with this man. She didn't want Gray.

She couldn't want him.

His hand spread more firmly against the small of her back, as if to reassure her and control her instinctive retreat. She could feel the hard muscles of his chest, stomach and thighs, the heat blasting off his big body. The firmness of his arousal pressing against her stomach.

"Damn," he growled softly. "*Now* you can slap me."

Sam knew she should push free, but the plain fact was, she didn't want to move. Despite her protests, his touch filled her with a heady delight. With those few soft words he'd spun back the years, established an intimacy that had once been piercingly sweet and which she'd never been able to forget.

She had been closer to Gray than she'd ever been to any other human being—including her grandfather—and the loss of that closeness had immobilised her with a grief that was still achingly familiar. Wrapped in the warm strength of Gray's embrace, she wasn't sure what she was waiting for—an apology, an explanation…something. A reason for betrayal and loss.

Of course it didn't come. The sudden letdown left her feeling sick and dizzy.

"Sam?" His hand cupped her jaw, anchoring her against the whirling sensation.

Another low, masculine voice made an enquiry. One of the men she'd thought had left.

Gray answered with an indecipherable rumble; then he urged her down onto the couch and pressed her head gently but inexorably down between her knees. All the while that deep, gravelly voice encouraged and cajoled, calling her babe, and darlin', and making her wonder if she'd finally stepped across some invisible line and gone stark, staring crazy.

This couldn't be happening.

Only hours ago her life had been predictable and very firmly under control. Now the last man in the world she wanted to see was sitting beside her, holding her head down between her legs, and she was as close to fainting as she'd ever been in her life.

The dizziness cleared. Gray's arm was still around her, both arms now, she realised dimly as he pulled her against his chest. The heat and comfort he emanated went through her in waves. She shuddered, for the moment beyond anything but simply accepting his hold.

His chin came to rest on the top of her head. "Does this happen often?"

The intimate rasp of his voice penetrated her curiously disconnected daze. She wondered why he was holding her when he could have simply let her lie on the couch, why he seemed to be taking every opportunity to touch her when she would have thought he would be just as wary, just as distant, as she wanted to be. "Only when I forget to eat."

With relief, Sam realised that low blood sugar was the problem. She'd worked through lunch, and she hadn't wanted dinner. She'd let herself come close to sheer exhaustion through lack of sleep and skipping meals. That, along with the realisation of just how much Gray still affected her after all her efforts to exorcise the past, had floored her, literally.

His hand curved around her nape. The burning warmth made her want to lean back and rub against his rough-textured palm, soak in the pleasure of his touch. Like a hungry cat starving for more than just a saucer of milk, she thought numbly, and knew that, dizzyness and stupidity aside, it was way past time to move. The embrace had started out as comfort, but it wasn't purely comfort any longer. She was all but sprawled across Gray's lap, and he didn't seem inclined to let her go. She could feel the rapid slam of his heart, feel *him* against her hip, firmly, inescapably male.

His arousal jolted her anew, although she immediately rationalised *why* Gray was aroused. It wasn't because of her specifically. Gray was a highly sexed, healthy male animal. He would probably be aroused by the close proximity of any reasonably attractive female.

Even so, she wanted to stay wrapped in his arms.

The admission was difficult, but she couldn't hide from it, not when her whole body was quivering with an almost painful delight. Gray had been her lover, her only lover. He'd been fierce, and so strong he had taken her breath, but at the same time he'd cherished her with such an intense sweetness that their lovemaking had haunted her ever since. She had *loved* him, and it was ironic now that the man she least wanted to see, to touch, to even remember, was the only person left on this earth she'd been close to, who'd shared a piece of her past with her.

He'd asked about Gramps, and the significance of that shook her. No one knew about Gramps. Not any of the employees or residents of the hotel with whom she had struck up tentative friendships—not even her secretary, Milly.

Sam planted her palms on his chest and shoved. Nothing much happened.

"Easy," Gray rumbled. "You still don't look too steady."

Sam pushed again. "It's late. I want to go to bed."

He made a sound that was suspiciously like a groan and let her push free of his hold. Immediately she got to her feet, ignoring the residual swimming in her head. Gray rose to his feet, too. There was nothing cold about his eyes now; they were heavy-lidded, intent, and his mouth was fuller, with a definite sensual curve. Her heart slammed once, hard. She half expected him to say, "Come to bed, baby," in a lazy rumble, the way he had years ago, but he didn't.

His expression shuttered and he said bluntly, "Why did you leave me?"

For a moment the world spun before righting itself. In all the scenarios Sam had ever imagined, Gray had never just come right out and asked that question. Seven years had passed. Years in which he had never contacted her, never to her knowledge made any attempt to find her. She had always assumed that he had happily continued on with the military career he had been taking leave from when she'd first met him. It had never occurred to Sam that a man who had been interested only in a physical relationship would want to know why she'd taken the initiative and left, saving them both a painful scene.

Anger surfaced in a rush. She hadn't realised the anger was still there, she'd buried it so deep. Now it welled up, as painful, as immediate, as the day she had finally realised that Gray hadn't made her any promises because he knew he wouldn't be able to keep them—that the small signals she'd been so sure had indicated genuine caring hadn't meant anything of the sort. She'd wilfully fooled herself, casting aside her natural wariness of any and all relationships, allowing herself to trust.

Something in her had died that day—more than one thing, in fact—but it was the loss of that fragile trust that still cut so deep. Few people penetrated her reserve. She had friends, acquaintances, but the people she allowed past barriers forged in childhood by too much loss, too young, were scant. If Gray wanted to pin her down about a past he'd been only too happy to leave behind, that was just fine with her. She could take his injured male pride. She could take his fury. These days, she could take just about anything.

"There wasn't any reason to stay," she answered with equal bluntness.

His eyes narrowed, and for the barest moment he was the Gray she remembered: moody, intensely physical and demanding of her attention. "I wanted you more than I'd ever wanted any woman."

Something very like hysteria bubbled in her throat. She was tempted to laugh, but mostly she wanted to cry. She was terribly afraid that she might do both at the same time, and then he would know just how badly he had hurt her. "And that was supposed to be enough to keep me hanging around until you decided it was time to spare me a little of your precious time? I was the woman you had sex with for a few weeks—I don't even think the term 'lovers' applied to us. And don't flatter yourself that you have any relevance in my life now. The fact that I took a job with the Royal knowing your firm owns it underlines my indifference. It was a mistake having an affair with you seven years ago."

His sheer lack of expression had Sam's eyes widening in horrified comprehension. He probably thought he could sleep with her while he was here—that she would fall into bed with him as quickly and as easily as she had done before. "You're living in the wrong century if you think you can take up where you left off!"

"I don't want an affair."

And he didn't, Gray thought savagely. He wanted

much, much more. He wanted to snatch Sam up and take her someplace safe, to pull her close and simply hold her, to explain…*everything,* when these days he didn't explain himself to anyone. He wanted to find out what had put those bleak shadows in her eyes and made her mouth look even softer, more vulnerable, than it had years ago.

He knew he shouldn't touch her, but his hand lifted to her cheek anyway. "I missed you." The words grated out, hard and slow.

She felt warm and soft and fragile beneath his fingers. He shuddered at the brief contact, a burst of heat tightening his muscles, making a mockery of his control. The sensation was beyond exquisite—*half*way between pleasure and pain. And all the way toward insanity.

Instead of jerking away, as he'd expected, she stood utterly motionless, her gaze fixed on his while she allowed his fingers to glide over her skin, making him aware all over again of how much he wanted to keep touching her. Then she seemed to realise what she was allowing. They were standing bare inches apart, and he was so close to kissing her that he could almost taste her mouth.

Her breath came in sharply. "No."

She backed up a step, spun and strode to the French doors, standing taut and still while she waited for him to leave.

Her eyes were dark with challenge, unwavering, her mouth a stubborn line. And she still wanted him the same way he wanted her.

Like hell burning.

The knowledge settled inside him. He no longer needed to examine the link that had held him fast to Sam over the years. She fitted him. She could have been made for him, and he was determined to have her.

Gray was uneasily aware that stating his objective was

the easy part of the equation. The hard part would be gaining her trust. She was holding back on him, as he had expected her to do, hoarding herself behind that maddening wall of reserve. He could understand her wariness, even if he didn't like it.

He would give her time. By his calculations, they had a week, max, to sort out their problems. It would be enough. It would have to be enough.

Gray stepped out into the night, every cell in his body alive with a desire so raw, so hot, that all he could do was stand in the rain and wait for the savage ache to ease. He heard the door close behind him, the snick of the lock.

Sweet hell, he'd made a mess of that. He had been too blunt, too rough.

The plain fact was that he'd been out in the cold too long, hunting a killer who was little more than a whisper and a shadow, moving between jungles and slums and bars and living for the piece of information that would give him the edge to end this circular hunt. He knew the disorientation was just that—he would adjust as he always did—but it disturbed him all the same. It made him see how different he'd become. He'd lost touch with normal people, with women; their softness and fragility. With the way he used to be.

The light drizzle intensified as he opened the courtyard gate, whipping across his face, soaking his shoulders anew.

"That's one hell of a seduction technique," a dark voice said from the shadows.

"Reels 'em in every time." Ben had been with them all along—Gray would have been surprised if he hadn't been. "Maybe I should ask you for pointers. I'm a little rusty."

Seven years rusty, to be exact.

The glare of the security light caught the silvery slash of the scar on Ben's cheekbone. An unaccustomed smile slid across the younger man's face. "My track record isn't anything to crow about, but you've definitely lost your touch on this one."

"I didn't know I had a touch." Gray stared at the French doors, at Sam pulling curtains, blocking out the night—and him. Even angry and kicking him out, she hadn't been able to disguise the honeyed languor of her walk, the completely feminine swing of her hips.

Instead of discussing safety precautions and body-guards, he'd taken one look at Sam and lost the plot completely. Not for the first time, he felt a ripple of unease. Taming Sam wasn't going to be easy, and he wouldn't kid himself that it would be anything less than taming. Beneath that polite, ladylike facade she was still mad as hell at him. And unexpectedly vulnerable.

When Sam found out why he was really here, she was going to be even more unhappy. Gray was going to protect her, but the protection would disrupt her life. He sucked in an impatient breath. Who was he trying to kid? The protection would *dismantle* her life.

Damn it all to hell, he wished he didn't have to fire her.

Carter eased out from behind a Dumpster, shoulders hunched against the drizzle. "Smooth moves, boss," he said in his slow, country drawl. "She was eating out of your hand. I could tell by the way she walked."

Gray pulled his gaze from the warmth and light of the courtyard. "Carter," he growled softly, "do me a favour. From now on, don't notice the way Sam walks. Has West checked in?"

A shape glided from pooling shadows so dense that the swirling darkness seemed to cling to his outline. "I

thought you were gonna get us a job someplace dry,''
West groused.

A reluctant smile tugged at Gray's mouth. West had
been staking out the hotel, just in case Sam had returned
before they did. Sheer, black-hearted danger aside, West
looked like an offended cat. He hated getting wet unless
he was supposed to get wet.

Carter peered at West's still, shadowy form. "Damn,
West,'' he muttered irritably, ''do you have to keep sneaking around like that?''

"Like what?'' West asked mildly, but his teeth
gleamed.

Carter led the way to the back service entrance, pro-
duced a master key and unlocked the door. He looked
irritatingly cheerful. "Did you tell her?''

"Not yet.''

"I didn't think so. She was way too calm.''

Calm? Sam had been ready to take his head off. And
he hadn't given her all the best reasons yet.

Another wave of heat slammed into Gray as he took
the back stairs to his suite. He was glad of the gloomy
lighting, glad of the hours of prep work ahead of them.
His lack of control quite frankly amazed him, but then
Sam had always had the ability to disturb him, to *distract*
him. No one else had ever wielded that kind of power
over Gray. Not any member of his family. Not any other
woman he had ever been involved with—and, regardless
of popular opinion there'd been damned few.

Not for the first time it occurred to Gray that, if ever
there was a woman who could get him killed, it was Sam.

Chapter 4

A slim, well-dressed man of indeterminate race—neither dark nor light—of medium height, and with no distinguishing features, set down his drink and walked from the dimly lit bar of the Royal, seemingly intent on keeping an appointment. He didn't hurry, didn't allow his urgency or satisfaction to alter his stride, even though his pulse beat like thunder and a light sweat sheened his skin.

He took pride in his ability to blend in with his surroundings and move in almost any milieu without attracting notice. He would be extremely disappointed in himself if he violated his own strict code. It was an art, of course, that didn't gather much applause, but it had kept him alive when others close to him had been cut down.

The circles in which he moved and plied his trade were as volatile and as vicious as the deep swirling currents that ate at the northern coast of his adopted country, Colombia. He had learned early in his chosen trade that only the most ruthless survived.

A small, grey-haired woman arrived at the doors at the same time he did. He nodded courteously and held the door for her, despite her brisk, dismissive demeanour. He had spent his lifetime studying the subtle and fascinating nuances of respect. The lady was a senior citizen and therefore deserving of a certain cursory respect. He was careful not to use his damaged left arm, not because he couldn't use the arm and the hand, but his incapacity would then become obvious, and the lady might remember or comment on his injury. That was something he couldn't allow.

He smiled blandly as the woman strode past him—incredibly, at her age and in the centre of a bustling city, wearing jeans and hiking boots, and with a knapsack slung over one shoulder. His heart beat a savage tattoo as the door swung closed behind him. The high sent his mood soaring, until he felt as light and buoyant as an iridescent bubble bouncing on the scintillating curve of a fountain, but he managed to hold his glee in check.

Lombard was here. Ahead of schedule.

The shock and delight of that knowledge pooled in his stomach, sent delicious tendrils snaking to his groin, almost closing out the grinding fury. Never in his wildest fantasies had he imagined that Lombard would make this so easy.

He acknowledged that he was perhaps even a tad disappointed. He had expected more from Lombard; after all, the man had come close to destroying him once and was trying to destroy him still.

He allowed himself a moment of disbelief and pure, distilled rage. It was almost inconceivable that a wealthy businessman playing soldier had once not only decimated his network but had dismantled his family and made him look like a fool. In the months after the debacle of that disastrous operation, he had lost his wife and son. Jacinta had run back to her rich Peruvian family and their pure Portuguese bloodline, taking Manuel with her. Not that he was now even remotely interested in that bovine creature or his weak, cowering son, but the desertion had stung at the time, because it had been the final humiliation.

It had taken years to regain the power and respect that should have been his by right. A power originally denied him by his wealthy English family for the inconsequential fact of his bastardy. That power was what he craved. To rewrite an old cliché, it was dog-eat-dog in his adopted world, and he had a truly terrible hunger.

Now that Lombard was in the open, the outcome was in no doubt. It had taken seven years to reach this point—years of sweat and poverty and bowing to the demands of that cultured pig, Delgado. Years in which Lombard had been cloistered in his beloved seclusion, sitting in rich comfort behind a desk, surrounded by bodyguards and administrators and the unearned fruits of his legitimacy—growing richer, growing soft, while *he,* Egan Harper, grew ever more powerful.

This time there would be no mistakes, no distractions.

Soon he would have access to technology he could sell to a stable of wealthy bidders.

Soon there would be no more Gray Lombard.

He smiled at his own punch line, once more reaching for that effervescent high, but this time the power didn't flow, the warmth didn't enfold him, and the faint tremor in his hands transferred itself to his belly. It was as if that glorious burst of feeling had burned him out, like a firework exploding in a shower of flaming sparks, then plummeting to earth in darkness.

He strode quickly across the road. The demeanour of a gentleman dropped from him like the cloak sliding off an illusionist as he became what he was: a cold predator on the prowl.

A Polynesian with tattoos and a gang insignia emblazoned on his black leather jacket made fleeting eye contact, then walked on by, granting a gratifying width of pavement.

Harper barely noticed. The subtleties of predator and prey were second nature to him. The young thug had acted on instinct, and it had been the correct one: Harper would have killed him in the blink of an eye, and barely broken his stride into the bargain.

The shaking in his belly was deep-seated now, insistent. Sweat trickled down the side of his face as he turned a corner and found his car. He shoved his key into the lock.

An alarm screamed. Harper sprang back, spun into a crouch. A knife appeared in his right hand as if it had grown from his very flesh.

He moved in a rapid, crouching circle, his blade a silvery arc slicing shadows. His pulse hammered; fresh sweat broke out on his skin.

He stumbled backward, ran a hand over his face, pinching his burning nostrils. His stomach dipped nauseously. His left arm was throbbing where the knotted flesh pulled at tortured nerve-endings; the badly healed wound on his thigh twinged, protesting the sudden violent grace of his movements. His head swivelled, and for a dizzying second he thought he might go spinning into the night.

He whirled, almost falling on the fender of another car. His gaze fastened on the briefcase that sat at an angle on the rear seat, the coat draped next to it.

This was his car.

He glanced back at the almost identical model that was still wailing into the night and forced himself to be calm as he unlocked the door, folded himself behind the wheel and pulled away from the kerb.

He had made a mistake. An understandable mistake. The sedan he had rented was very common, as was its dark blue colour. That was why he had chosen it. He had been the victim of his own caution. There was no danger; he'd simply tried to unlock the wrong car.

Minutes later, he pulled into the parking space beside his motel room. With tense, jerky movements he locked the car and entered the perfectly average motel room, heading directly for the bathroom, drawn by its only remarkable feature, the shiny, deep green surface of the vanity unit.

The two white lines of powder he carefully constructed looked pristine, almost innocent, against the pseudojade, and he paused for a moment to admire his handywork before bending down and applying the straw.

The power surge, when it came, wasn't impressive, certainly not enough to blot out that momentary loss of control, *the mistake he had made,* but Harper wouldn't allow himself any more. He was meticulous with his dosage of the drug, had been ever since he'd had to resort to using it in the months he'd been on the run, tending his wounds, trying to save the wreck Lombard had made of his arm and the bullet wound that had festered in his thigh.

The mistake with the cars had occurred because he had hung on too long, drunk with the glory of strolling through enemy territory and discovering that Lombard was already here. Awaiting his pleasure. He had let himself get too needy.

His cocaine habit was measured, just as he measured everything, and he wouldn't allow it to rule him. Cocaine was as beautiful as it was deadly, a drug that only the rich could afford, and Harper was now very rich indeed.

But it was also something else, his own sweet guardian angel. It had literally saved his life by helping stop the bleeding from his wounds and staving off the pain while he healed.

He would make certain he adhered to his schedule in future.

He strolled out into the lounge, carefully stripping his jacket from his still aching arm, and idly contemplated his next move. He had made a useful contact in the bar of the Royal Pacific Hotel. A pretty, talkative young man—a hairdresser with the rather unlikely name of Leroy Deville.

Gray stepped from the shower when he heard the first knock. Methodically he blotted moisture from his face and hair and wrapped the towel around his hips. Before he answered the door, he picked up a hand-gun, a Glock 9mm, which he had placed on the bathroom vanity.

He knew who was knocking, but caution was so ingrained that it would have been an unnatural act for him to answer a door unarmed.

Ben replied to his terse enquiry. Gray opened up and stood back while the guys filed in.

Carter set a stack of pizzas down on the small dining table that occupied one corner of the lounge, then pulled off his soaked black T-shirt and draped it over the back of a chair. He shot Gray a rueful glance. "I thought you were gonna get us a job *out* of the rain. I'm starting to get webbed feet."

Ben grinned. "That's just your big farm-boy toes."

"It's his socks," Gray murmured. "He forgot to take 'em off about two months back in the jungle."

West shoved a hand through his hair, grimacing when a wet stream tracked down his spine. He dumped a couple of six-packs of beer by the pizza. "Great," he muttered. "No wonder Harper got away clean. He could probably smell us coming."

Carter folded his arms across his bare chest. "It wasn't my socks he could smell, it was Ben's soap. The little pink heart-shaped number he packs with his toothbrush."

Gray paused in the doorway to his bedroom. "Holding out on us, McCabe? Which lady friend sent that?"

Ben grinned as he dispensed pizza and beer. "Who else but the love of my life?"

Gray pulled on fresh jeans and padded back out into the main room, where West and Ben had also removed their wet shirts. He placed the Glock on the table, sprawled back in his chair and snagged a slice of the rapidly disappearing pizza. "And how is my sweet little darlin'?"

"Waiting for her uncle Gray to make good on his promise about the tea party."

Gray tore the tab off his can of beer and felt the tension begin to drain from him. It was hard to do anything but smile when Ben started talking about his daughter. "Beats me how a sweet little girl like that ended up with a big, bad daddy like you, McCabe."

Ben took a swallow of his beer and grinned as he wandered over to the long black gear bags that were lined up against the wall. He began unzipping them, briefly checking that the surveillance equipment they needed had arrived. "The usual way, mate," he said lazily. "The usual way."

An ache started somewhere in Gray's chest when he thought about having a daughter of his own, of what it would be like to set violence and cold necessity aside and hold an armful of sweet smelling little girl like Bunny

McCabe. Of what it would be like to get Sam pregnant, to see her grow big with his child.

The thought was like a kick in the solar plexus. Sam pregnant.

He was glad he was sitting down, because right now he didn't think his legs would hold him. A wave of longing rolled over him, so deep, so complete, his head spun with it.

He wanted to make love with Sam. He wanted her wrapped around him while he sank deep inside her, and he didn't want to use protection. He wanted to watch her face while she came apart in his arms, and he wanted to stay locked inside her while they made a baby.

He'd been in a state of constant semi-arousal for days. The heavy ache of desire had been riding him hard, making him as edgy and irritable as a frustrated stallion. He couldn't ignore the fact that she had run from him all those years ago.

He wasn't good at seduction. He knew how to touch a woman, to give her pleasure before he took his, but he had no background of techniques and strategies, no easy lines that would coax a reluctant woman to his bed. Having to coax a woman at all was an alien concept; women had always come easily to him.

Maybe too easily, he decided. The only thing he possessed was the raw, sexual instinct of a healthy male. He knew when he wanted a woman, and he knew when she wanted him. Now he needed more. He needed to know how to reach past Sam's reserve, needed the words, the gentle touches, that would allow her to trust him before he took her to bed.

He needed a strategy.

He would have to plan this as carefully as he planned

a military operation. Nothing could be left to chance; there was too much at stake. "I need a strategy."

"Thought we had one," Ben mumbled around a mouthful of pizza.

Gray cast him a brooding look. "I need a strategy for getting Sam back."

Ben choked. Carter whacked him on the back.

West abandoned his perusal of the bags of equipment and opened another box of pizza. "Ever try having a conversation with the lady?"

Amusement took the edge off Gray's grim mood. "Yeah. She didn't like it."

"Did you ever try *asking* her stuff instead of telling it to her?"

Three pairs of eyes turned on West like curious spotlights.

Gray's eyes narrowed. "What kind of stuff?"

West shrugged, looking momentarily perplexed. "Ah, like what she's been doing since she, ah—"

"Walked out on me seven years ago," Gray supplied.

West's brows jerked together. "If you don't want me to go on, just say so."

Gray's fingers tightened around his beer can, his grip threatening to crumple the light metal. "Go on," he muttered, shoving his chair back and going to stand at the window.

"Women are different."

There was a moment of profound silence while they all pondered the differences.

Carter ripped the tab off another beer and settled back in his chair. "Keep talking dirty, West. We're all ears."

West glared at Carter. "I'm not talking about physical differences, I'm talking about the way they think. Their minds are different. There's a lot going on in their heads that we have no idea about. I mean, have you ever wondered why women always carry handbags with them? Or what's in them? A guy? He'll just stroll on down the street with his wallet in his pocket, but a woman has to get a lot of stuff together before she'll even consider stepping out the door. How can you expect someone with a mentality like that to just jump into a relationship? She's going to need to know more about you. She's going to need to know a lot.''

There was a rumble of assent. Every one of them had noticed the handbag phenomenon.

West kicked back in his chair, warming to his subject. ''You have to be aware of the way women think. They don't take their orders from what's locked beneath their zipper, they're a lot more…emotional. If you want a *relationship* with a woman you have to approach things differently. It's not like a pick-up in a bar, followed by a little healthy wrestling. They need to know you're interested in them. You should probably do some talking, too.'' He nodded his head in emphasis. ''You've got to open up to her.''

Ben gave West a brooding look. ''Open up to her? Did you try this stuff out on your wife, West?''

West went blank. He hadn't seen his wife for a couple of years, ever since they had separated.

''Thought not.'' Ben fixed Gray with a direct look. ''You *have* got something to offer her.''

Carter grinned. ''Yeah. Women are generally agreed on one thing you're good at.''

Three sets of eyes locked on a part of Gray's anatomy that had not been discussed, yet was crucial to the process of male/female bonding.

West came to a decision. ''The hell with conversation,'' he growled. ''You've got to play to your strengths. Take her to bed. Let's face it, sex is probably the best interactive skill you've got.''

There was a knock on the door. Silence descended except for the sounds of weapons being palmed and clips shoved into magazine housings.

West picked up the case of his current favourite all-purpose sniper rifle, a bolt-action Remington, and carried it through to the second bedroom of the suite, where it would be out of sight, before taking up a position in the doorway.

Carter automatically took up a position on one side of the front door to the suite.

Ben flattened himself on the other side, his hand on the ornate brass knob. ''We expecting company?''

Gray hefted one of the bags of miniaturised communications equipment that he had helped design and that his company manufactured strictly for special forces use. He set it down on the table, using its bulk to conceal the Glock. ''Yep.'' He picked up a street map of the area surrounding the hotel and opened it.

Ben raised his voice, ''Who is it?''

The reply was high and thin and wavered slightly. ''Leroy from Hair Trends.''

West and Carter snickered.

Ben's gaze narrowed on Gray. ''Are we expecting 'Lee-roy' from…'' He raised his voice. ''Where did you say you were from, Leroy?''

''Hair Trends.''

Ben grinned. ''Looks like your makeover's here, boss.''

Gray allowed himself the pleasure of a slow smile as his gaze touched on each one of the tanned, broad-shouldered, lean-hipped warriors lounging in various states of battle readiness against walls and doors. There was no disguising the fluid grace of bodies used to constant hard physical exercise, the big callused hands more at home holding weapons than calculators, or the dangerous go-to-hell glitter in their eyes, but there were superficial things that could be done to make his dangerous bunch of renegades fit in on a city street.

Carter shifted uneasily. "I don't like the look of this."

West fingered his hair, which was so shaggy it brushed his collar. "Don't tell me, it's bath day?"

Ben gloomily removed the clip from his gun and shoved both items into one of the gear bags. "This is all Carter's fault. He should have changed those damn socks."

"Line up, boys," Gray drawled. "It's your lucky day. Lee-roy is gonna do each and every one of you."

Ben groaned. West looked resigned.

Carter's voice was a low, flat rumble that didn't require actual words to convey his discontent. "Just as long as the *hair* is all he does."

When the door was finally opened, Leroy stepped briskly into the crumbling grandeur of the Governor's suite and faltered. The room was filled with men. Big, rough, half-naked men with hair on their chests. Clothes were tossed over the backs of chairs, and several large black bags, the kind in which sporting equipment might conceivably be transported, littered the room. It resembled nothing so much as what he imagined the locker room of a football team might look like after the big game, except for the electronic gadgetry that was visible in the opened bags.

The big man at the table lifted his black wolf's head, and the messy details of the room faded as midnight dark eyes settled on him. Leroy had never thought of black as a cold colour. He did now. His spine jerked straight, and he came as close to standing to attention as he was capable of doing. There was a cold bite of command about this man that left him in no doubt as to who controlled the other men in the room. He also had no doubt that the other men required controlling; there was something wild and untamed about the lot of them. The word "mercenaries" flashed into his mind, and a chill skittered down his already stiffened spine as if the temperature in the room had just taken an abrupt plunge.

He swallowed the melodramatic notion and lifted his chin, fingers automatically tightening their damp grip on his bag of hairdressing equipment.

That was it, he decided a little wildly. He'd had it with the Pacific Royal and all its eccentric clients. Last week he had been attacked by old Jeremiah Holden's moth-eaten cockatiel. The evil creature had taken exception to his new Gucci loafers and dropped a load of loathsome guano on the expensive, supple leather. To top off what had already been a trying week, the Carson sisters had almost killed him with one of their potted ficuses when the heavy container had tumbled from a spindly Victorian plant stand and missed him by inches.

The cold-eyed barbarian at the table rose to his feet. Leroy controlled a nervous quiver. The man was even bigger than he had looked sitting down, his shoulders massively broad, his arms roped with muscle. He was darkly tanned, as if he'd spent too long in some misbegotten clime, and scars crisscrossed his torso. Leroy wouldn't have been surprised to see a broadsword grasped in one big hand.

He'd had it with moonlighting, too, he decided. It was just too dangerous. He didn't care how much money he was offered, or who did the asking, from now on he would stick with his day job and be perfectly content with nice, safe blue rinses.

Gray eased up on the pressure on the Glock behind the cover of the black bag, which was still sitting on the table, and nodded at West, who checked the corridor, closed the door, then quickly and casually concealed his own gun in one of the gear bags.

Gray studied Leroy. The hairdresser had a cascade of blond ringlets that any woman would kill for, a perfect sun-bed tan, and a small fortune in designer clothes hanging off his lean frame. He also looked like he was about to bolt. "Thanks for coming at such short notice, Leroy," he said as smoothly as his rough voice would allow. "We appreciate it."

Leroy started. Gray's mouth twitched. He was pretty sure he had just made things worse.

"Uh, no problem." Leroy's Adam's apple bobbed. His gaze darted around the room, fastened on the bags of surveillance gear. "You boys with the, uh, telephone company?"

This time Gray didn't try to hold back on his smile, and apparently that didn't help their case with Leroy, either. "Not exactly," he drawled, "but close enough. We are in the communications business."

Chapter 5

Sam slept badly and woke before dawn to the sharp certainty that someone was watching her.

She lay rigid, barely breathing, her ears straining to hear beyond the accelerated thud of her heart. Her bedside clock glowed luminescent green, telling her it was after 5:00 a.m., but only just. Faint street-light filtered through her curtains. She could discern the outline of her dressing table, the open door.

The room was stuffy. She had kicked her bedclothes off, yet her skin was still damp, the cotton singlet she wore stuck to her skin. The heat seemed to press down on her, pinning her to the bed. Long minutes ticked by where nothing moved and there was no sound beyond the ones she couldn't muffle.

"There's no one," she said aloud. Her voice quivered huskily, breaking on the last word, and with a stifled gasp she jack-knifed, hand fumbling for the lamp. Golden light flooded the room. Sam blinked at the hurtful brightness, let go of the breath that had been dammed up in her throat and folded in on herself, hugging her legs.

Her room was the same as when she had gone to sleep, except for the mess she'd made of the bed. The shirt she'd taken off was still draped over the back of a chair; the historical romance she'd tried to read was still sitting on her bedside table, a bookmark neatly inserted at the point where she'd given up trying to concentrate.

Shoving a hand through her damp hair, she forced herself to walk through the flat, switching on lights as she went, checking windows and doors. Everything was still locked, still secure. If nothing else, the stuffiness should have told her that, she thought in an attempt at wryness; if someone had broken in, she would be breathing fresh air.

It had probably been a noise that had awoken her—a cat rummaging through the Dumpster to the side of the parking lot, or a drunk wandering off course. Most probably it had been her own overactive imagination kicking back at her in the form of another bad dream.

Sighing, she grabbed a glass of water, drank thirstily, then headed for the shower. This had happened often enough the past few nights that she knew she wouldn't go back to sleep, so she might as well get an early start on work. God knew there was enough for her to do. The Lombards team had arrived a day late, but she guessed the planning meeting that had originally been scheduled for today would proceed. There would be counsellors and planning people crawling all over the building. And she would have to meet with Gray in an official capacity.

As she walked out of the kitchenette, she saw a black leather jacket lying over the back of a chair, and her stomach lurched. Gray's jacket. He'd left it behind last night. She picked it up, automatically lifting it to her nose. The strong smell of damp leather assaulted her nostrils, along with another faint scent that was subtler and Gray's alone.

Sam dropped the jacket, backing off fast, only stopping when the smooth, cool fabric of the floor-length drapes brushed between her shoulder blades and slid against her calves. Tears leaked from her eyes. She was so tired still, her head throbbed, and she was so hot she felt like she was being slow-roasted and suffocated at the same time.

The simple act of handling the jacket had released Gray's scent into the air so that it filled her nostrils with every breath.

Abruptly she spun and wrenched the curtains apart, unlocked the French doors and pushed them open. A ribbon of light shafted across the courtyard, breaking open the night. She pulled in gulps of fresh air as she stared out into the heavy pre-dawn darkness, eyes straining. Nothing moved; it was eerily still, except for the faint drift of an errant breeze through the shrubbery.

With a shudder comprised of relief and self-mockery, and the chill of perspiration drying on her skin, Sam locked up again, leaving the curtain open in defiance of her fears, and strode toward the shower.

Gray bolted upright in bed, heart pounding, breath held tight in his lungs, muscles taut and sheened with sweat. An anguished tremor coursed through him, and he swore, a short, succinct curse.

Damn. Now that he had finally gotten himself a soft bed, he remembered how much he hated beds, hated sleep. Hated the vulnerability sleep forced on him.

Not that actual sleep was the problem; he didn't fear that, or dreams.

Sometimes he wished he would dream about Jake's death. Although those dreams would be better described as nightmares. He didn't dream about that bloody day. Ever.

He guessed he knew why that was. The stark scene, the hot anguish of guilt, were with him—*part* of him—as fresh, as deeply painful, as if the killings had just happened.

The phrase "time heals" had no reality for Gray. Time hadn't healed; it had just changed the way the grief and guilt rode him. The searing horror of the scene no longer dominated his thoughts, his days; instead it bided quietly, sliding into his consciousness like a shark cruising calm waters, striking in the quiet lull just before sleep or waking, sending a hot river of adrenaline roaring through his veins, making his muscles cord and all his old wounds throb, making his jaw clench against his grief and failure, making him hate and fear that moment of utter vulnerability.

Gray shoved himself out of bed and paced, naked, to the window. Something had woken him, catapulted him out of sleep, and he knew better than to ignore his instincts. Maybe it had simply been city sounds; he'd spent a lot of time in small villages and jungles lately, and his senses hadn't yet become attuned to the change of environment. But maybe not.

The night was inky-black and still, weighted with the dense rain-rich canopy of cloud that didn't so much hover over the city as sink and smother it. Another hot, sweaty bitch of a night.

Gray opened the window, relieved when a faint breeze sifted across his damp skin, cooling him. He ran a hand over his hair, accustoming himself to the sleek shortness of it, the nakedness of his nape. As he stared out at the cityscape, his nostrils flared, catching the aroma of bread baking, mingled with the tang of the sea and the underlying mustiness of the Royal's old timbers, which evidently soaked up the humidity like a sponge.

He wondered where Harper was at that moment, although the thought was only fleeting. Once they dangled the bait in front of him, it would take Harper several days to obtain the people and equipment he needed—even so, when he arrived, he would be at a disadvantage. He would be cut off from his usual area of operations. This time he would be on Gray's territory, playing Gray's game.

He didn't question that Harper would take the bait. Gray knew him as intimately as if they were brothers. Harper wouldn't be able to stand the blow they had just struck to his network or his ego. Even though he couldn't know that Gray was directly behind the assault, he knew Gray was involved with the operation to hunt him down.

Grabbing a glass of water, Gray prowled the confines of the suite, not bothering with lights, not needing them. Inevitably his footsteps carried him to the bathroom, which looked out over the back of the hotel. With a resigned oath he pushed the tiny window open and peered out and down. His heart slammed hard against his chest. A small ribbon of light flowed across the courtyard two storeys below. Sam was awake.

A fierce satisfaction filled him. It looked like he wasn't the only one having trouble sleeping.

An hour later, Sam was at her desk, a cup of coffee steaming at her elbow as she began planning her day.

The main problem, of course, was that after this morning's meeting, she might not have a hotel to run, and nothing more to do with her day than look for another job, but that didn't change the fact that there was paperwork that needed completing, plumbing repairs to arrange and oversee, a leak in the roof that needed urgent attention.

Edith had left a note detailing a complaint by Jeremiah Holden, a wealthy eccentric who occupied a small suite on the second floor. Jeremiah had seen another ghost, and he wanted something done about the problem.

Grinning, Sam scribbled a note to Milly, instructing her to call in a team of ghost busters, ASAP.

Her smile faded. Not that they would need that kind of service. Gray would probably pull the Royal down; then the ghosts would have to leave along with everyone else. There would be nothing left to haunt.

Sam sipped coffee as she worked and periodically massaged her temples. Her concentration kept fragmenting, and finally she threw her pen down and leaned back in her chair.

She still felt a sense of unreality that Gray was actually here; that he had gone out into the streets last night, looking for her; that he had been in her flat and she had somehow ended up in his arms, pressed so close against him that she could feel his arousal pushing into her belly.

Her cheeks heated at the memory, and, on cue, an older memory superimposed itself over that one.

Gray's entry into her life, when she'd been twenty-two and working at Lombards of Sydney, had been just as explosive. She had been new and inexperienced, and trying to control her first bar fight. Gray had waded in and dealt with the sudden eruption of violence, pulling the men apart, then ejecting them from the hotel.

That was the first time she had spoken to him, although she had been aware of his presence all evening. He had been sitting in the shadows, shoulders propped against the wall, while he slowly sipped a beer. He had been dressed all in black: black T-shirt, black pants, black boots. Even his wristwatch had been matte black, with a cover that hid the face. His hair had been military-short, his eyes as dark as his clothes, but definitely not sombre.

He had helped her right the last of the chairs, and when she had caught his gaze on her, a slow smile had curled his mouth, almost stopping her heart.

There had been something more than just simple dark-and-dangerous about him. He had had too-hot-to-handle written all over him, from the cool speculation in his eyes to the blatantly carnal promise of that mouth. If she had had a mother to object, Sam had no doubts she would have been yanked back home and cloistered until the big bad wolf found other older, more experienced game to hunt. But she hadn't had parents, and her grandfather was already old and an ocean away.

It hadn't seemed to matter that Gray Lombard was every mother's nightmare; from where she had been standing, he was every woman's fantasy.

He had asked what time she got off and then sat back down and waited for her. When the bar had finally emptied, he had taken her dancing, bluntly telling her, "It was the quickest way I could think of to get my hands on you."

And he *had* put his hands on her, not in an overtly sexual way, but he had touched her constantly, small possessive touches—his hand at the small of her back, on her arm, or simply holding her hand as they walked. He had staked his claim with a directness she had found impossible to counter, even if she had wanted to.

She hadn't gone to bed with him that night; she'd turned him down at her door. She had been, and still was, too reserved to allow that degree of intimacy so quickly.

He'd grinned, dipped his head and kissed her. He hadn't used his tongue; he hadn't needed to. Just the brush of that incredible mouth against hers had made her go weak inside. She had leaned against the wall, grateful for the support as she watched him walk away.

Seven years ago she had known that it would be only a matter of time before she gave in. Two days, to be exact.

He still wanted her now.

Sam sat up jerkily. Her elbow caught a file, knocking it to the floor and scattering papers. Automatically she reassembled the file, restoring everything to its usual neat order.

"Get real," she muttered to herself. She had already figured this one out. Gray wanted sex. That was all he had ever wanted. The fact that her proximity had aroused him was no particular distinction.

Gray Lombard strode into the planning meeting with all the sombre, brooding grace of a hungry tiger.

Sam paused in the act of transferring files from her briefcase to the polished, antique kauri table that had been set up in one of the small reception rooms for the occasion.

"Here we go," Milly, Sam's secretary, said, echoing the thought of every one of the thirty-odd employees, residents and city planning people assembled to meet the Lombards delegation.

"Lord," Milly muttered, as they watched the aged members of the now defunct Royal Pacific board cluster around the mysterious, reclusive head of the Lombard Group. "That man even manages to look dangerous in a suit."

Sam couldn't help thinking that seven years ago he'd looked dangerous naked.

She blinked, suppressing the urge to rub her eyes. Gray

looked nothing like the cool-eyed warrior who had chased her down in the service lane last night.

He'd cut that black stallion's mane of hair and put on a suit, although that didn't fully explain what he had done. Somehow he had managed to tone down, to mask, all that raw male power with what she could only describe as corporate camouflage.

Perhaps she would have been fooled if she hadn't seen him dripping wet, his T-shirt clinging to his chest and shoulders, hadn't seen the cold glitter in his eyes when he'd caught her. But she had, and she was acutely aware that, beneath the wealth and sophistication that clung like a sleek mantle about his big shoulders, he was as broodingly dangerous as any barbarian warrior had ever been.

Milly let out a low, almost silent whistle. "That man is built for trouble. A woman could go blind just looking."

"Then don't look," Sam warned, her gaze captured by Gray's hard, clean profile. "Because trouble is exactly what he is."

"Not *him*." Milly directed Sam's attention away from Gray. "I'm not interested in any of those hit men. I want the little cute one."

Sam was more than happy to be diverted by Milly's intent expression, her wild red hair and off-the-wall luau dress. Milly was forty-five going on eighteen, and she'd decided it was way past time she dropped her widow status and found herself a man. "The little cute one *is* the hit man," Sam said dryly, recognising Jack McKenna. "He's McKenna, Gray Lombard's right hand man. He can do more damage with his calculator than all the rest combined can do with their muscle."

"He's got real power, huh?"

"Right where it matters—in the bank account."

"Okaaay," Milly said, subjecting McKenna to the kind of relentless scrutiny she normally reserved solely for the chocolate doughnuts in the bakery window just down the road. "I'm ready to be turned on by power. You can work on those big guys, I'll subvert the little bad one."

Sam studied Jack McKenna with a definite feeling of foreboding. She had met him once, when she had been interviewed for this job, and he hadn't changed. He was mid-forties, lean, immaculate, and he looked every bit the coldly brilliant corporate raider she knew him to be—and he was staring at the cracks in the plaster ceiling as if he expected the building to start disintegrating all over his perfectly creased suit.

"Forget McKenna," Sam said, noticing the small, oddly vulnerable frown pleating her secretary's brow, and suddenly afraid that for once Milly wasn't joking. "He's no push-over. He's here to do a job that he is very, very good at, and if he's got a sense of humour, no one's ever found out about it."

Milly didn't answer, and Sam suppressed a pang of alarm. Like many of the other employees, Milly flatly refused to believe that the grand old hotel, with its glorious wood floors, antique furniture and faded oriental carpets, could soon be nothing more than a pile of dust and rubble. Sam knew that was all too likely. When she'd taken this job, she hadn't expected it to last for more than a few months, just long enough, she had thought, to conclusively prove to herself that she was finally free of her old infatuation with Gray.

Gray's gaze fastened on her. He was surrounded by people, but his impatience was plain in the taut set of his jaw, the restless shift of his shoulders.

Milly, almost forgotten beside her, let out another low whistle. "Looks like the Warrior Prince just lost his favourite concubine. If I didn't have three children who all want to be doctors, I'd probably throw myself in his path. Purely for research purposes, of course.''

Sam muttered something indistinct in reply, her attention all for Gray, who was now cutting a path directly toward her.

She was as prepared to meet him as she would ever be after last night. Her suit was plain but elegant, her hair neat, her make-up understated. What she wasn't prepared for was the burn of sensual awareness that clenched delicately at inner muscles and sent heat sliding across her skin.

''On second thought,'' Milly murmured, ''since I don't get paid danger money, I think I'll go drink a double espresso for both of us while you find out if the Warrior Prince is gonna save both our jobs.''

''Thanks a bundle.'' Sam got out from between stiff lips. ''Don't forget to put cream in my half. I really hate straight coffee.''

Damn him, she thought a little desperately. Why hadn't he gotten fat? Or ugly? A beer belly would have taken his edge off nicely. But nothing so convenient had happened. Gray was six foot four inches of raw male power that looked more like Delta Force than Office Desk.

He came to a halt in front of her, his shoulders successfully blocking half the room. His gaze swept her, as alarming as the gleam of light caressing a blade. ''Nice suit.''

''It's my executive stress outfit,'' she said shortly. ''When I put it on, all the black makes me feel really ruthless.''

''What did you have for breakfast?'' he murmured. ''Nails?''

Sam lifted her brows, disdaining to reply.

He didn't wait for one. "I need to talk to you," he demanded bluntly. "In private."

Sam's heart jackhammered in her chest. She didn't have any problem identifying the cause; it was fear, pure and simple. Only yesterday she had been sure she was over Gray, that she had successfully cut him from her life, and now she knew that wasn't so. All he had to do was walk into a room and she instantly became more vulnerable than she ever wanted to be. Deliberately, Sam transferred her attention back to her briefcase, unloaded the last file and clicked the case closed. She frowned when she discovered her fingers were trembling. "The meeting's about to start."

"Jack's running the meeting."

Her eyes widened. Jack McKenna and his team were the only ones who were supposed to come in the first place. "So why are you here?"

"The usual reason. Looking after the interests of Lombards."

"No. Why are *you* here? As you so aptly pointed out, Jack McKenna is running the meeting. He does the hotel takeovers and makeovers."

Gray's gaze moved around the room. She realised he was constantly doing that, and unlike McKenna, he wasn't looking at the cracks in the plaster, he was studying people. "Maybe I came to see you."

Sam didn't bother to hide her incredulity. "After seven years? I don't think so."

"I do have a reason, but I'm not going to discuss it here."

Sam suppressed a shiver at the bleakness of his tone and wondered again just what had happened to change Gray so radically. Then she registered what he had actually said. He had a special reason for coming, and it could only be to do with the hotel. Suddenly the possibility that the Royal would be completely demolished and they would all be out on the street without jobs was a chilling reality. "If you're here to give us bad news, then I'd appreciate knowing as soon as possible. My staff, and some of the long-term residents, are…naturally concerned."

"But you're not."

She stiffened. "I don't have as much to lose."

He shoved his hands into his pockets, parting the lapels of his jacket. The gesture was restless, oddly uncertain, the small silence that followed more eloquent than words, and suddenly Sam knew. *He was going to fire her.*

The blow was unexpectedly stunning. She thought she had been prepared for dismissal. When she'd taken the job she had planned for it.

Now the thought of leaving filled her with dismay. She didn't want another job, even though she knew she could get one. At the Royal she had found friendship and loyalty, a fragile sense of family when she'd been more alone, more adrift, than she had ever been in her life.

Her chin came up. If she was going to be fired, so be it. She wouldn't whine, but she wasn't about to take it lying down, either. "I want this job, but I do have other prospects. If you're going to fire me, then just say so."

"You'd like that, wouldn't you?" There was a hint of a snap in that rough voice. "Why, Sam? When you went to the trouble of getting this job?"

For a moment Sam couldn't breathe. Gray had shifted uncomfortably close to a truth she had only just realised. Taking this job had been more than a simple purging of the past. She had thrown down a gauntlet. She had wanted Gray to acknowledge her existence, if nothing else. If he fired her, so much the better; then all links really would be severed.

"I'm supposed to be at this meeting," she said, ignoring his question. "If you're going to fire me you can do it here and now. I don't need to be alone with you to hear bad news."

"The hell with the meeting," he said impatiently, the low register of his voice carrying.

Conversation in the room faltered, then stopped. If this was Gray's version of low-key and private, Sam decided, he was about as subtle as a hand grenade. The only compensation was that McKenna now had something else to occupy his mind besides the rotting plaster.

Sam stepped pointedly away from Gray. She was generally quiet and well-behaved, which fooled quite a lot of people, but beneath the manners instilled in her by years of private boarding schools and a guardian who would have been more at home in the last century than this one, she could be as stubborn as rock when she chose. She chose now. "I don't take orders well, and I don't want to be close to you."

"But then, we don't always get what we want, do we?"

Sam controlled her almost panicked need to escape, but Gray didn't attempt to touch her; he simply waited. Along with everyone else in the room.

Sam drew an impeded breath and stalked to the door. Gray strolled along beside her as if nothing untoward had happened.

A kitchen hand pushing a tea trolley cast them a curious glance as Gray opened her office door and stood aside for her to enter. Sam didn't see that she had any choice in the matter, even if his manners were a little late in showing up.

"I'm not usually such a Neanderthal," he murmured as she swept past.

Sam dropped her briefcase beside her desk. "Only

when you want your way. I bet you gave your mother a hard time.''

''I gave her holy hell, but then, so did Blade and Jake—''

The abrupt cutting off of his sentence drew her attention. His tone had been close to warm, almost teasing; now his expression was back to grim.

He closed the door and crossed to the window to stare out at the odd, brassy light of another summer storm rolling in from the coast. The sun was still shining, but it had already started to rain.

''Damn, it's hot in here.'' He took off his jacket, tossed it over the back of a chair, then unfastened the top buttons of his shirt, as if he disliked the constriction of a collar. ''So, are you going to tell me why you took this job?''

''I needed to work. I saw the position advertised and applied.''

''There were other positions available. Better ones.''

She tore her gaze from his broad back. In the heavy humidity, the thin weave of his shirt was already clinging to his shoulders, the deep indentation of his spine. ''I wanted this one.''

''Why?''

''What difference could it possibly make to you?''

He turned to face her, and her gaze was instantly drawn to the open V of his shirt and the crisp dark hair that grew there.

His expression was brooding. ''You've never married.''

She stiffened at the abrupt change of topic. ''I thought we were talking about my employment with Lombards.''

''When you walked out on me,'' he said softly, ''I came after you.''

Sam's head jerked up. If he had wanted to shock her, then he had just achieved his purpose.

"I found where you were living. I watched you walking in the park with your grandfather."

Sam's mind shifted, telescoped. She remembered the day. It was not long after she had come out of hospital after losing the baby. Gramps had dragged her out for a walk, insisting she needed fresh air. They had spent a quiet hour in the park, soaking in the sunshine, smelling the damp earth and the flowers, listening to the birds. She remembered seeing the back of a man's head, experiencing another one of those stark, transfixed moments of almost-recognition, followed by her decision in that moment to stop looking, to stop expecting Gray to simply walk back into her life. "I think I saw you," she said blankly. "Why didn't you…?" She stopped, shaken by what she'd been about to ask.

His eyes narrowed, and he took a step toward her. "You wanted me to come after you."

The flat certainty in his voice burned through the hazy recollection like hot sun striking through mist. In that moment she couldn't mask her shock that she had hidden something so basic, so intrinsic to her character, from herself. When she had left Gray, she had run—like every woman since Eve—in the hope that he would give chase. She had been confident that he would come after her, if only to see how she was. The fact that he hadn't had altered her perception of him completely. Now she had to readjust. He *had* checked on her, even if he had chosen not to approach her.

"I couldn't come after you straight away." He touched the scar at his throat. "I was in hospital for this and a couple of other…complications. When I came around after surgery, they had me strapped down." His mouth twisted. "It was hardly necessary. I was as weak as a baby. Even so, if I could have managed it, I would have walked out of hospital then and hunted until I found you. How's that for primitive?''

Sam wondered briefly what the other ''complications'' had been. ''Obviously not too primitive for you to overcome. Correct me if I'm wrong, but it *has* been seven years.''

The instant the words were out of her mouth, she knew she should have ignored the temptation to goad him.

Gray closed the distance between them so fast she barely had time to catch her breath. His hands curled around her upper arms, his face was so close to hers that her stomach tightened in anticipation of that sinful mouth gliding against hers.

The kiss didn't happen. She could feel his breath, warm and damp on her lips, almost taste the coffee he'd had for breakfast and the toothpaste he'd used afterward. Her hands were spread against the unyielding warmth of his rib cage, and she could feel the slam of his heart against her palm. The desk was a solid barrier behind her, Gray a solid wall of muscle in front of her, his thighs easily corralling hers.

Sam knew that if ever there was a time to cut and run, this was it. Her conviction that Gray's interest in her was fleeting and based only on physical desire had just crashed and burned. There was nothing fleeting about the sombre intensity of his gaze. His eyes were hot and dark, pulling her in so deep that she felt as if she had been summarily jerked off balance and, if she wasn't careful, would fall right into him.

Abruptly he lifted his head, but instead of backing off entirely, he caught her hands in his and raised her fingers to his lips. The hot stroke of his mouth was subtly shocking. The force of his sensuality boiled up, engulfing her like a wave of heat spilling from a furnace.

"I'm late, and I apologise," he muttered in a low, dark purr. "But I'm here now. And you're right, I didn't come on behalf of Lombards. And I'm sure as hell not here for this old wreck of a hotel."

His gaze shifted to her mouth, and her lips tingled and burned as if he *had* kissed her long and hard. "I came for you, Sam. I want you back."

Chapter 6

Lightning flashed. Sam flinched, both at Gray's words and the hot, bright flare of light. Thunder reverberated drowning out the sudden heavy downpour of rain. On cue, the hotel's lights flickered, then dimmed, before returning to normal.

The door was flung open. Milly strode in. ''Now that weasely McKenna is gonna can us for sure! Why, oh why did we have to have a storm now?'' She stopped, her eyes enormous in her thin face.

Sam blushed as she became instantly aware of how the situation must look. She was backed up against the edge of her desk, and Gray was all but on top of her. He still had hold of her hands, and even though he had shifted his attention to Milly, the taut, heady sensuality that had pinned her in place still hung in the air, as tangible as the frustration that burned briefly in his gaze.

Sam tugged to free her hands. Gray let her go immediately, making it look like she'd *wanted* to hold hands with him. He backed off a step, but his expression had "later" stamped all over it.

She slipped sideways along the desk, breathing a sigh of relief when she was at what she judged a safe distance.

Milly's gaze was fixed on Gray's chest. There were crease marks on his shirt where Sam had clutched at it, and an extra button had come unfastened, revealing some major male real estate and an intriguing expanse of dark hair. He looked rumpled and dangerous and sexy, like he had just had a woman crawling all over him.

Sam stared fixedly at an invisible point over Gray's right shoulder. "Are you going to put your jacket on?"

"Yes, ma'am," he drawled, managing to make it sound as if he'd taken his jacket off at her order in the first place.

Sam glared at him. His lashes drooped, and, as unexpectedly as the sun bursting from behind a big, black storm cloud, he smiled back, a heavy-lidded, sleepy smile that took her breath and made her chest tighten.

Sam decided that one had "later" written all over it, as well. Gray had said that she was the reason he was here, that he wanted her back. Her mind reeled from the concept, rejecting it. She was almost certain she hadn't heard right. Somewhere along the way she had missed a vital piece of conversation that would put that statement in a more acceptable context.

None of this was in the internal script she had prepared.

He wasn't supposed to want her.

And, Lord help her, she wasn't supposed to want him.

Milly cleared her throat. "The power's out in the kitchen, and the chef's threatening to put a meat cleaver through the fuse-box. Sadie Carson says the roof is leaking all over her dragon plants."

"Sadie lives on the second floor."

Milly cleared her throat again, her eyes wide and meaningful, as if she didn't want to say the real problem out loud.

Gray had no such difficulty. "If Sadie's getting wet on the second floor, then that means the two floors above will be getting it, too."

"Unless it's a burst pipe," Sam interjected, struggling to concentrate on the hotel instead of her own internal dilemma, and feeling faintly ill at Milly's bombshell. A burst pipe was trouble, but not as major as the roof.

Gray shrugged into his jacket. He shot Milly a sharp look. "Get an electrician in to look over the wiring. It's probably just a blown fuse, but in a building this age, we can't take the risk that that's all it is. Sam and I will check out the roof."

Sam lifted her brows at the arrogant way he had assumed control of a situation she was well equipped to handle. Gray returned a bland stare that managed to convey the sheer, immovable granite backing his will.

Not that he had to do any reminding, Sam decided grimly. She and Milly would both do as they were told. After all, Gray owned this building and pretty much everyone in it. "I'll get the keys."

She collected her set of keys for the top floor, which was presently unoccupied because of maintenance problems. Thunder continued to reverberate as they strode toward the lift. The rain was a steady rumble of noise.

Gray didn't try to take her arm or touch her in any way, but she couldn't shake the feeling that she was being hurried along, herded in a direction she didn't want to go, and the cowboy with the cattle prod was prowling right alongside her.

Gray opened the elevator doors. "After you."

Sam entered, supremely conscious of Gray's sheer size when he joined her in the elegant but small confines of the elevator. The door grumbled closed. He punched in the fourth floor. The lift began its upward motion with an arthritic jolt.

Gray made no comment, but Sam winced. She could feel his cool, analytical judgement, the disapproval pouring off him in waves. "It may be old, but it's reliable."

Sam watched number two light up and mentally calculated how many more seconds there were left until she could escape the lift and the enforced proximity with Gray.

He regarded her levelly, but Sam couldn't decide what he was thinking. That poker face he pulled could hide anything from utter distaste to indifference. The lights flickered, the motion of the lift stuttered, then stopped altogether, as they were plunged into darkness.

Sam closed her eyes, then opened them wide, in an effort to ward off a sharp jab of panic. The panic lasted for all of a second before she managed to bring herself under control. She'd been afraid of the dark when she was a child. Although she had largely overcome that fear, every now and then it crept up on her and took her by surprise. Logically she knew that the fear had grown out of her immature concept of death she'd had as a child, and her fear that her parents were locked in perpetual darkness.

Her teeth sank into her bottom lip. The similarity of this small space to a coffin was overwhelming.

"Are you okay?" The sound of Gray's voice was a welcome distraction. "The thunderstorm must have knocked the power out."

Sam sucked in a measured breath, a breath that didn't nearly fill her lungs.

"Sam?" he prompted in a low murmur.

The warm velvet quality of his voice seemed to reach

out and surround her, as tangible as a touch in the disorienting blackness, making her want to shuffle closer, to burrow her head against his chest and be surrounded by his arms as well as his voice. The darkness, when she closed her eyes, would then be comforting.

"I'm okay." Her pulse was still racing, her fingers locked into tight fists, the ring of keys biting into her palm, but the rumble of Gray's voice had somehow diffused her momentary fear.

A dim glow lit the interior of the lift. A torch, Sam thought in disbelief. Gray had a battery-operated torch.

She sank against the support of the wall. The relief of that small beam of light was enormous. "You've got a torch," she said, shakily stating the obvious.

"I'm a regular Boy Scout," he murmured. "Here. I need you to hold it for me."

Sam's fingers closed gratefully around the penlight, and instantly her fear of the dark seemed ridiculous. She marvelled at the sudden sense of control, when seconds before her heart had been pounding. She decided then and there that she was going to buy one of these little babies and keep it in her handbag. You just never knew when you were going to be caught in a black-out.

Gray motioned her to step closer and direct the beam on the control panel. He studied the panel, then opened it and checked inside. With a grunt of satisfaction, he straightened, then simply opened the first set of doors, reached up and depressed a lever, then opened the outer set of doors.

The darkened fourth floor was about three feet above the floor of the lift.

Gray turned to her. "Hand me the keys and I'll give you a boost."

He dropped the keys in his pocket. She noticed he

hadn't asked for the torch, for which she was grateful. Even though they were almost out of the of the lift, it was still very dark, and she was loathe to give it up. A small amount of light filtered from beneath the room doors into the corridor, but only enough to make her aware it wasn't the pitch-blackness she had experienced before.

Gray's big hands settled at her waist.

"Put your hands on my shoulders," he murmured next to her ear.

Sam gripped his shoulder with her free hand and settled for simply bracing herself with the other, which was wrapped around the torch. She was intensely aware of the pliant strength shifting beneath her fingers as she was lifted and set down on the floor, her legs dangling. One of her shoes slipped off. Gray picked it up and fitted it to her foot, not lingering over the task, then waited for her to get to her feet before flowing up and out of the stalled elevator in one smooth, muscular movement.

Immediately his hand cupped her elbow. Sam knew she should shake off his hold, but after those moments in the elevator, she was grateful for the warmth of his touch.

She knew from experience that Gray was naturally courteous with women. He automatically did things that a lot of men neglected, small gestures like opening doors and holding chairs, offering a woman his full attention when he was with her. That attention to her needs, combined with the sheer battering force of his masculinity, had held a seductive allure. Seven years ago she hadn't been able to resist him; she had been dazzled by all those small attentions. This time would be different. She *knew* Gray, knew just how little those courtesies meant. She wouldn't allow herself to tumble under his spell again.

Reluctantly, Gray released his hold on Sam's elbow and handed her the keys. She unlocked the door to the first suite, pushed it open and absently handed him back his torch. Gray clicked the beam off, slipped the torch back into his pocket, then propped a shoulder against the door-jamb and watched as she surveyed the damage.

Water had already soaked the carpets and continued to drip steadily. The entire roof needed replacing, an expense that any company would balk at for such an old building.

Something very like relief lightened his mood. It wasn't that he wanted the Royal to go under, he simply wanted Sam, and her attachment to the Royal was standing in his way. There were enough barriers between them; he didn't need to be cast in the role of villain over this leaky old mausoleum. Sam was a businesswoman; she could do the figures.

This happening on top of that damn elevator breaking down should clinch it.

His jaw tightened as he watched her wander from drip to drip, staring up at the widening patches of damp on the ceiling, the ominous bulges in a couple of places.

"This is it, isn't it?" she demanded.

Gray should have guessed Sam wouldn't tiptoe around the issue. What he hadn't known was how much the Royal would mean to her. Hurt shimmered in her eyes before she spun on her heel and paced to the window, and conversely he wanted to tell her that he would fix the roof, he would fix any damn thing she wanted if it made her happy. "The specs on the roof indicated it needed replacing."

"But you won't be replacing it."

"No." Gray let go of a breath, cursing inwardly. "You have to leave anyway," he said gently.

"I lose my job."

It wasn't a question. "Yeah."

She wandered restlessly around the room, examined the

king-size bed, which was turning into a king-size sponge—like the rest of the building—then surveyed the area of greatest damage, which was smack in the middle of the room. She held out her hands, catching drops, her demeanour so grave he had to fight the urge to pull her into his arms and wrap her in tight against him. The urge was male and protective, rawly sexual and possessive, and something more, something he only associated with Sam—a deep, wrenching tenderness he'd never forgotten, an alien, disturbing emotion that had haunted him all the years they had been apart and which he had come half-way around the world to find.

Sam let the water dribble from her palms. "Did you know that the Royal used to be one of the most expensive, grandest establishments in the South Pacific? A lady calling herself Baroness Belle occupied these apartments for several years. She wasn't royalty, but she had style and money to burn. She was the highest priced hooker in town, and she entertained only the finest clients. Apparently she adored ships' captains, and if she was taken with a man, she would offer her services for free. This entire floor used to be called Belle's Palace."

Gray eyed the bulge above Sam's head and decided it was time to get her out of there. He stepped around a growing puddle and coaxed her from the danger zone. "I don't think Belle would be doing much trade in here now."

She gave him a fierce look. "There's no hope? What about the people who work here? The residents?"

Her expression almost broke his heart, and Gray had to steel himself against his frustration with this whole charade. He was no diplomat; he never had been. The Pacific Royal deal was Jack's baby. Gray had little to do with it beyond business planning and policy decisions made at the executive level. He wanted nothing more than to wrap his fingers around Sam's arm and demand she leave with him. Now. Aside from being a surveillance nightmare, this whole building was unsafe, and he didn't want Sam here. What would have happened if she had been in that elevator alone?

She had been frightened, even though she'd tried to hide it. Gray had felt the tension in her silence, confirmed it in the uneven tenor of her breathing.

He'd wanted to reach out to her then, but he had refrained from doing anything more than murmuring reassurance, because he hadn't wanted to risk disturbing the hold she had on herself. It didn't take a genius to know that Sam was balanced on some precarious edge, that there were things he didn't know and that she wasn't about to tell him about in a hurry.

The knowledge that she was holding out on him was infuriating. The fact that he wasn't being entirely honest with her didn't come into it. Illogical or not, he still wanted to take her in his arms and soothe her, to use the moment to try to break through that cool reserve and gain her trust. "We're lucky the council hasn't condemned the building out of hand and ordered an evacuation. It's dangerous, Sam. Everyone will be well-compensated. They'll find other jobs, other places to stay. We'll give them all the assistance we can."

Sam stared fixedly at him, as if she had just come to a conclusion that astonished her. "You really did come to see me," she said huskily. "Why else would you be here? Your mind was made up before you came."

She backed off a step, the astonishment fading, as if she had just given herself a mental shake. "If you'll excuse me, I need to get some tradesmen up here to do some damage control before that ceiling caves in and someone really does get hurt.''

Gray watched her go. He didn't like the fact that she was walking out on him—practically running from him—but he had just enough sense not to push her any further.

She needed time to get used to having him back in her life. Seven years ago he had been young and brash and hadn't taken the care of her that he should have. He would make up for that lack soon. After Harper was dealt with, he would spend every moment he could with Sam—make love to her, cuddle and hold her, cement their relationship with all the rituals of courtship he had disregarded before. He would be free to woo her, and he wouldn't rest until he had banished every last shadow from her eyes. But for now his methods would, out of sheer necessity, have to be blunter, cruder.

He didn't have time for anything else. He would have to bind her to him in the most primal way he knew. And soon.

Chapter 7

Sam walked numbly down the stairwell. The power was still off, but the stairwell had adequate window lighting.

Of all the shocks she had had since she had answered Edith's phone call last evening, the one she had just received stood out above the rest: Gray had come after her—seven years too late.

She walked into her office, barely noticing Milly's curious stare or the fact that for once her secretary didn't rush after her demanding to know what had happened.

A ripple of unease slid down her spine as she began to comprehend her situation; the unease extended to an actual chill, roughening her skin and lifting fine hairs all over her body in primitive warning of danger. Gray wanted her back, and she...

She was in trouble.

She had thought she had dealt with her hopes, torn them out like the stubborn weeds they were. But she knew now that she hadn't; the roots of that hope had sunk too deep, wound themselves around the very fibre of her being, and no matter how hard she tried, she doubted she could ever kill them completely.

She couldn't afford to be attracted to Gray, let alone care about him. She had been hurt too often and too deeply by the people she loved.

He had hurt her.

All she had to do was stay away from him. That shouldn't be hard, she thought grimly. He had just fired her. If she left, she would be safe.

But even while she laid it all out in her mind, Sam couldn't dismiss the one central fact that nagged at her and undermined all her fledgling plans. If she hadn't been able to forget Gray after seven years of concerted effort, what made her think she could do it now?

Milly appeared in her doorway. "How bad is it?"

"The roof is leaking. The fourth floor is uninhabitable."

Milly pressed a cup of coffee into her hands. "You want me to ring that roofing firm? They're supposed to be here doing the repairs now."

"We need a whole new roof, not repairs." Sam sniffed the coffee. There was something alcoholic in it. Brandy.

"Drink it," Milly declared gruffly. "You look like you're ready to collapse."

Sam sipped, then gasped. The potent mixture bypassed the usual channels and burned a hole straight through to her stomach.

"You gonna tell me what's going on with you and Lombard?"

Sam sipped again and shuddered. "Is it that obvious?"

Milly snorted, pulled up a chair and sat down. "Maybe I shouldn't have put that brandy in there," she muttered. "Drink enough of that fire-water and next time you won't back down from whatever it was you were leading up to when I walked in on you earlier. Honey, I didn't know whether you were going to black his eye or trip him and beat him to the floor. I thought you said you barely knew the man."

"Oh, I know him. Or, at least, several years ago I thought I did."

"So it's no use trying to seduce the boss to save our jobs, huh?"

Sam forced a smile at a joke that was now well past its use-by date. Seduce the boss? *She* was the one in danger of being seduced. Besides, she doubted she could make Gray do anything he hadn't already made up his mind to do. "Hand to hand combat's more likely. But if you want to have a shot, Milly, go for it—although I wouldn't recommend the aftermath. If Gray Lombard lies down with a woman, it's for one reason and one reason only, and, believe me, what you want won't come into it."

"Yeah," Milly muttered morosely. "I know exactly what you mean. McKenna's the same. Rich, powerful, too cute for his own good. A real pain in the ass."

Milly took over the job of organising emergency repairs, with Jack McKenna in close attendance. It seemed McKenna wasn't satisfied with Sam's appraisal of what work needed to be done. He had to see for himself, and he had to have Milly with him.

Sam checked on the kitchens. Power had been restored, but the chef was still irritable and sharpening his cleavers—always a bad sign. Gray and two of his men were fiddling with the elevator, and the Carson sisters were busily fussing around their plants. By lunch-time, every-thing that could be done had been, and the sun was shining brilliantly, in blatant mockery of the disastrous morning.

The familiar heat hit Sam as she walked into her rooms. After making herself a sandwich and drinking a glass of milk, she checked in with Edith at reception to tell her she was taking an extended lunch to deal with personal business. Slinging the strap of her purse over her shoulder, she headed for the rear of the hotel, where her car was parked.

Minutes later, she was merging smoothly with traffic on the motorway, her attention taken up with avoiding the huge freight trucks that channelled through the tight bottle-neck that was Auckland and the mirage-like heat shimmering off the road.

A quarter of an hour later, she brought the car to a stop outside the gates of a cemetery in a suburb not far from where her grandfather used to live. After locking up, she walked through, grimacing as grass whipped around her ankles and water from the earlier downpour trickled into her shoes, wetting them for the second time that day.

A gust of wind flattened her blouse and skirt against her, and made her jacket flap open, but the wind was warm, with a soft, melancholy quality, as if it shared in the lonely beauty of the grounds, the sleepy, peaceful rows of graves—many dating back to the last century.

The sound of another car pulling into the car park had her glancing back. She didn't recognise the man who got out of the car, and for a moment she tensed. He didn't look at her but headed toward another part of the cemetery. Reassured, Sam turned her attention to the quiet mossy corner that was as familiar to her as her grandfather's house had been.

Automatically her breathing slowed, quieted. She always had the absurd notion that if she was quiet enough, she would hear or feel something—a trace of her family lingering like some vital essence in the air.

Of course she never did. Time passed, but the peace she was looking for didn't materialise.

Coming here was a habit, a ritual she had played out as a child and which her grandfather had encouraged, because he hadn't wanted her to forget her parents and how much they had loved her. She tried to picture their faces, the timbre of voices long gone, but there was no instant replay in sharp Technicolor. The memories were distant, faded, and the harder she tried to pull them into focus, the more indistinct they became.

Instead her mind was filled with Gray. Tension gripped her. How could he dominate her thoughts *here?*

The answer was in the elevated rhythm of her pulse, the excitement that simmered through her veins, even now. She was alive, and she wanted Gray with a gathering momentum she felt powerless to stop, despite the past, despite the fact that she knew she couldn't trust him.

Maybe Gray was capable of loving her in the way she needed to be loved, but he had never delivered. He had always pulled back, leaving her achingly aware of just how vulnerable and exposed to hurt she was.

She stared at the tiny grave in front of her and confronted the guilt she had never been able to vanquish entirely, despite logic and medical fact. She had wanted her baby so much but was haunted by the possibility that her unhappiness had somehow contributed to the miscarriage. Maybe if she'd been stronger inside, more sure of herself as a woman, she would have carried the baby full term?

The sun beat down with a heavy heat that had her shrugging out of her jacket, folding it over her arm and loosening the collar of her blouse. Perspiration sheened her skin, trickled between her breasts.

Gray had said he wanted her back. Her stomach clenched at the instant sharp image of Gray, naked and aroused and reaching for her. Could she stand it? she wondered. Was she brave enough to throw herself into that particular fire again?

She shivered, despite the heat, and knew the answer. The lonely years had forged one thing in her, at least, a hunger to taste life, and—she closed her eyes against the almost painful upwelling of need—finally, the willingness to take the risks that went along with it.

Sam strolled back to her car, a measure of calm restored despite the momentous decision she had made—a decision she shied away from examining in any close detail yet.

Her heart slammed once, hard, when she saw Gray leaning against a black four-by-four truck, arms crossed casually over his chest, a pair of sunglasses shading his eyes.

"You followed me."

His gaze was watchful behind the dark lenses. "Yeah. We got interrupted this morning, and since then you've been hard to pin down. I figured the only way to finish our conversation was to talk to you away from the hotel."

"How did you know I was here?"

He jerked his head in the direction of a tall, dark man climbing into a nondescript sedan, the same man Sam had seen follow her into the cemetery.

"You had me followed?" Last night he and two others had been out searching for her; she still didn't know why he had gone to so much trouble. None of it made sense.

"I have my reasons, and I'll explain. You should get out of the sun first. There's a bottle of water in the truck."

As soon as Gray suggested it, she felt thirsty. Almost before she could make a conscious decision to accept the shelter of his truck or a drink, he had the door open and was helping her up into the passenger seat. Gray swung into the driver's seat and handed her a bottle of mineral water. She noted that half the water was gone. As she unscrewed the lid and put the bottle to her lips, a shiver of awareness coursed through her at the intimacy of placing her mouth where Gray's had been.

"It's habit to carry water with me," he said, half turned in his seat, his gaze on her mouth as she drank. "I've spent the last few years in places where it would be safer to tangle with some of the local wildlife than drink the water. I spent time in those places for a reason. About the same time you walked out on me, my family was facing a kidnap threat. I was overseeing security in Sydney. My brother, Jake, and his fiancée were taken hostage by a man called Egan Harper. I went after them, but I was too late to stop the executions."

He glanced away, his hand curled around the steering wheel, tightening into a fist.

"My God," she whispered, appalled at the series of statements, the utter lack of inflection in Gray's voice. Sam stared at his profile, the grim set to his jaw. She knew that his older brother had died, but she'd had no idea how—she had avoided reading anything at all about the Lombards. The changes in Gray began to make a horrible kind of sense.

"That day I saw you in the park, I walked away for a good reason. You were safe and with your grandfather. I had just got a lead on where Harper had gone to ground, and I had to go after him."

"You wanted vengeance?"

His expression was almost completely immobile, stark and implacable, the kind of look she imagined a front line soldier might have, or a cop. "What I wanted," he said

softly, ''was my brother back. The next best thing was—
is—justice.''

''And did you find…justice?''

''Harper is still free.'' Gray's voice was cold, his sunglasses a frustrating barrier that served to emphasise his
almost inhuman control. ''Last week we tracked him to
his lair. He got away, but amongst the documentation we
recovered we found your photo. I'm still hunting him,
Sam, but now he's involved you. What I told you in your
office this morning is true. I want you back, but I'm also
here to protect you.''

To protect her? For the second time that day she wondered if she had heard right. She couldn't conceive of why
anyone, let alone a murderer, would be after her. She had
never done anything wrong. She'd never even had a parking ticket!

''Aren't you going to ask me why?''

A chill struck deep inside her as she realised that Gray
was deadly serious, that the man who had murdered his
brother had her photograph. The thought of a stranger
having a photograph of her was disturbing enough to
make her stomach clench with alarm, but a killer?
''Why?''

''Because Harper knows you're mine.''

The flat statement was as stark as Gray's expression,
and it shook her as nothing else could. Sam stared straight
ahead, at the timeless, unchanging familiarity of the cemetery while she grappled with a situation that was beyond
anything she had ever experienced. She was floundering
helplessly, out of her depth, and at the same time shaking
with a slow burning rage at what this man, this *Harper,*
had done to Gray and his family. To Sam, life was un-
utterably sacrosanct and fragile; that anyone should want
to *take* a life was almost inconceivable.

Clumsily she screwed the cap back on the bottle of water and placed it on the floor of the cab. She reached into her bag and felt around for her car keys. The keys were cold and sharp against her skin, and the illusion of control they gave her was just that, an illusion. Her tidy life had careened sideways and gone wildly out of control. She was being followed. She needed protection from a murderer—a shadowy man who had her photo, but who *she* wouldn't recognise if she passed him in the street. She could get in her car and drive, but even then, she would be followed and marshalled in the direction Gray wanted her to go. On top of the helplessness and rage, she now felt pursued, herded.

Gray made no move to touch her. "If you want to go anywhere, one of us will have to go with you."

"And if I want to be alone?"

"It won't be for long. A week. Maybe two."

"You're going to catch him." It wasn't a question, it was a demand, and the answer was in Gray's eyes—a ruthless determination to bring his brother's killer to justice.

Sam climbed from the truck. She heard the slam of Gray's door as he followed her.

"You forgot your jacket."

She fumbled with the keys, almost dropping them. Finally she got the door unlocked, tossed her jacket and handbag on the back seat, and opened the door wide enough to help dissipate some of the heat that had built up inside. When she turned around, she almost slammed into Gray's chest. His hands settled on her arms, glided up to her shoulders.

He had taken off the sunglasses and slipped them into his shirt pocket. Without the lenses, there was nothing to shield his essential nature from her. A raw shudder swept her. She'd thought that looking into his eyes was like looking into the heart of midnight; now she knew just how deep that darkness went.

He cupped her neck, his thumbs stroking along her jaw. "I shocked you," he said roughly. "I should have found a better way to tell you."

"I doubt there is one." And if she had any sense, she would pull away from Gray's touch now. His expression was bluntly possessive and male, completely centred on her, and she knew he wasn't going to let her go easily this time. He had staked a claim on her; in primitive terms, he had marked her as his territory, pledged to protect her. But despite her fear and confusion, the helpless rage, she wasn't capable of walking away from him.

What she had just learned had shaken her, but in a strange way it had pushed her closer to Gray. She had never thought *she* would feel protective of *him,* but she did. His brother had lost his life, but Gray had been hurt, too—brutalised by the very manner and senselessness of his brother's death.

He tilted her chin, as if he had somehow divined her moment of capitulation. Her lids drooped against the glare of the sun. His head lowered, and the delicious coolness of his shadow replaced the glare; then his mouth angled over hers, stifling a sound that was suspiciously like a whimper as she clutched at his waist and opened for him. His tongue was hot and muscular, slightly rough; it curled around hers then plunged deep, and seven years shimmered into oblivion.

The kiss was raw and sensual, and so needy that her whole body clenched around a shaft of desire that actually made her go weak at the knees. A low, drawn-out moan rose from the pit of her belly, almost smothered by the pressure of his lips.

He withdrew his mouth with reluctance, still nipping at her lips, as if he couldn't get enough, either. Dazed, she made no move to pull back, to think through just what she wanted from Gray and whether or not she should be setting limits. With that one kiss she had tacitly surrendered, and he knew it. Setting limits now would be like tying up a tiger with a piece of string and expecting it to stay.

He cupped her face with his palms. His expression was hard, intent, his beautiful mouth damp and blatantly carnal.

"Sam," he said on a guttural note.

Her hands shifted to his chest. He was still wearing the same shirt he'd had on that morning, and her breath caught in her throat as she tried to comprehend the passage of time since then. It felt like several days had passed—more, a year, a lifetime. The woman who had watched Gray take off his jacket in her office this morning had been naive in a way she now found hard to credit.

In the space of a few hours she had been fundamentally changed; every part of her life had been tipped upside down and rendered unrecognisable. The only constant she had been left with was her inner sense of herself. And Gray.

Gray. Her head still whirled with what he had told her, the implications battered at her like rising waters pummelling at a floodgate. She had wondered how he had spent the last seven years, and now she knew. He had lived them in darkness and isolation, searching for a killer. The thought hurt her. She knew about darkness and isolation, but violence was completely alien. No wonder he had become so grim and cold. He had been out in the cold, literally. "Damn you, Gray, why didn't you tell me?"

His fingers moved through her hair, he pulled her close, hugging her against him. "I couldn't," he said simply. "How could I ask you to share something like that?"

"I would have wanted to know."

He tilted her head, his gaze locked with hers. "You know now."

Because he had been forced to tell her. Because somehow she had got tangled up in the serpentine coils of violence that bound him. It wasn't good enough, but for now she had to accept it. She understood his need for control, to hold the darkness in, to stop it permeating everything, even if she didn't like it.

Her hands moved reflexively on his chest, and she felt the tight, hard points of his nipples through the cloth of his shirt, felt the shudder that wracked his body at her touch. His breath came in sharply. With a rasping sound that was half curse, half supplication, his hand closed on her nape, and he lowered his mouth back to hers.

His mouth was fierce, almost brutal with need. Sam wound her arms around his neck and held on, a part of her glorying in his loss of control, that in this, at least, he was vulnerable. His mouth shifted to her jaw, the tender skin of her throat, starting shivering streamers of fire with each caress, and she forgot about anything but the demanding heat of his mouth on her skin, the rough glide of his hands. Her head lolled back, the sun heavy on her closed lids.

Gray had pushed her up against the car; now his weight pinned her in place. She arched against him, almost mindless with delight, instinctively rubbing against the muscular planes of his chest to ease the unbearable tightness in her breasts. The heated metal of the passenger door burned through the lightweight material of her skirt as his thigh nudged between hers, forcing her skirt to ride up.

The weave of his pants rasped against the sensitive flesh of her inner thighs, the hard ridge of his sex pressed into her belly. He moved his hips once, twice. A hoarse groan rumbled from deep in his chest, and he swore with a soft violence that barely penetrated the haze.

"Damn," he muttered, as he eased himself away, his hands lingering on her waist as he steadied her. His gaze was hot, still fierce, but his voice was unexpectedly gentle. "We can't do this here."

Sam blinked, still swamped by the battering sensuality of the kiss.

"If you keep looking at me like that," he said in little more than a guttural purr, "I'm going to forget about being sensible, and we're both going to get arrested. Are you all right to drive? I need to get you back to the hotel."

Sam straightened, jerked away from his touch. She still felt dazed and disoriented, while Gray now looked as cool as ice. "Of course I can drive."

"I'll follow you."

Sam ignored his helping hand. The seat burned the backs of her thighs when she sat in it, and she began to perspire from the smothering heat. She started the car, wondering if she was fated to be slow-roasted at every turn. She met Gray's gaze with as much ice as she could manage at such short notice, but it wasn't much, considering that she had been bare inches away from being seduced against the side of her own car in a public place. Outside the cemetery where her family were buried, for heaven's sake. "Do you always get your way?"

She glanced at the tell-tale bulge in his pants. She saw with satisfaction that he was still fiercely aroused, despite that aura of control.

Gray caught her glance. He planted both hands on her car door and leaned down to the window. His mouth curled in a slow, wicked grin that one hundred years ago would have had dowagers calling for their smelling salts and debutantes reaching for their fans.

"Darlin'," he drawled, low and husky, "couldn't you tell? I haven't had my way in a long time."

Chapter 8

Gray slipped his sunglasses on the bridge of his nose as he pulled out of the parking lot and followed Sam. His expression was grim.

He had watched her at the cemetery for only a few minutes, but according to West she had stood staring at what must be her grandfather's grave for close on an hour.

She had given no tangible signs of grief, unless you counted that blank lack of expression he had noted as she had walked toward him. If she had cried, he wouldn't have been able to stand it; he would have wrapped his arms around her and held her, and the hell with her objections.

She had looked so lonely that he had been on the point of walking over to her anyway; then she had started toward him, her face as remote as a porcelain doll's.

He frowned, shifting down and muscling out a low, red Corvette that was trying to swing into the too-small gap between his truck and Sam's car. The passenger, a young

tough with a shaven head, flipped him the finger. Gray
eyed him coolly, and the 'vette dropped back.

Even staring at her grandfather's grave, Sam had managed to keep that cool reserve intact.

Cool reserve be damned. West had said she had stood
there, almost motionless, for *an hour*.

Gray examined everything he knew about Sam and her
family. Her parents and an aunt and uncle had died in a
light plane crash—a crash in which Sam herself had been
a passenger. Sam had been seven years old, and, mirac-
ulously, she had survived virtually unharmed. Her grandfather had been her last living relative. She would have
had to have borne all the final rituals of his burial alone.
He had been an old man, so it was likely she had had to
care for him, maybe even nurse him as his condition
slowly deteriorated. Gray hadn't bothered to find out those
kinds of details, he hadn't had time, but he would damn
sure do so now.

The blankness of Sam's face bothered him, when he
knew how much her grandfather must have meant to her.

Knowledge struck him like a fist between the eyes, and
fury channelled through him at what Sam had hidden from
him, what *he* had been too blind to see.

She was frightened, and the big surprise would be if
she wasn't. He had seen and experienced fear in many
manifestations, watched men he worked and trained with
cope with it. In battle fear could be as healthy as sweat,
and it kept you alive as nothing else could. Then again,
he had seen it work in the opposite way, freezing men in
battle, making them incapable of the smallest action to
save themselves.

He knew what it was like to feel crushing grief, but he
couldn't comprehend what it would feel like to bury his
entire family. What must it feel like to love with depth

and loyalty, then lose not just one family member, but all of them?

Sam shied away from intimacy because she had lost everyone she had ever loved. And that included him.

His jaw tightened. He felt at once relieved that he had isolated the problem...and furious. Damn, he thought bleakly. It didn't take a genius to figure out how Sam would react when she found out that not only was he hunting Harper, but that Harper was doing his level best to kill *him*. That for the past few years he had walked a continual tightrope of danger and risk.

That from whatever angle you chose to look at it—predator or prey—he was a man who could die any day.

Sam parked in her reserved space behind the Royal. Gray's truck nosed in seconds afterward, dwarfing her much smaller hatchback. She pushed her door open, gathered her jacket and handbag, and locked the car. When she straightened, Gray was beside her. It was a measure of just how much she had changed that she calmly accepted his closeness, but something about the watchfulness of his expression made her uneasy. "Have I got something on my face?"

"Yeah." He dipped and fastened his mouth on hers with a casual intimacy that took her breath. "Me."

The world spun, then levelled out. Gray's hand settled possessively at the small of her back, and she found herself moving toward the rear entrance of the hotel, her mouth still tingling from the contact.

Gray opened the back door, and they strolled into the cool shade of the hallway. When they reached the lobby, a surprising number of people were milling near the elevator. A man peeled off from the group and lifted a camera. The flash momentarily blinded her.

"Mr. Lombard," a svelte brunette declared, materialising from behind a large palm, "is it true that you're intending to take up residence in New Zealand?"

A confusing barrage of questions followed. Gray stepped past the young woman, his arm around Sam's waist, keeping her close to his side. Taken by surprise, Sam lost her balance, half falling against him. His arms closed around her, hugging her in close and restoring her balance. Several cameras clicked at that point. Ben and Carter appeared, and the noise escalated as they began hustling the reporters out of the hotel.

"Who's the mystery lady, Mr. Lombard?" one of the men yelled over Carter's brawny shoulder. "Is she the reason you're here?"

"Rumour has it you're engaged," someone else called. "Have you set the date?"

Gray kept his arm around Sam, shielding her from the reporters as he urged her toward her office, closing the door.

"Sit down," he ordered, but when she did so without argument, he wished she'd bit back at him as she usually did.

She was too pale, too quiescent, and she had dark shadows under her eyes. She looked like she hadn't slept, and he was frankly worried. Sam had sustained more than one shock in the last twenty-four hours, and there were more to come. "Did you eat breakfast?"

"I had a sandwich for lunch."

He went down on his haunches beside her, even so, they were still eye to eye. It reminded him all over again just how small she was. "Stay here. I'm going to get you a cold drink and some food. If I find you've moved, I'll make you take the rest of the day off. In fact, I might just do that anyway."

"I don't see how. You fired me earlier." Her voice was flat, almost listless.

"I said you lose *this* job. I didn't fire you." Gray picked up her hands and rubbed them between his palms. They felt limp and icy cold, and that worried him even more. It was hot, not as humid as it had been earlier, but hot all the same.

Sam watched Gray stride out the door. Her head was swimming, and she felt sleepy. Not surprising, she guessed, when she had had so little sleep lately, and the day had been both dramatic and stressful. Standing in the sun for all that time at the cemetery hadn't helped.

Gray returned within a few minutes, a brown paper bag in one hand and two enticingly frosted cans of apple juice in the other. He set one of the cans and a salad roll in front of her, then perched on the edge of the desk, watching her with an assessing gleam that told her if she didn't feed herself, he would commandeer the task.

It was disconcerting having Gray so close, having his attention locked on her. She sipped the juice and ate the roll, surprised at how hungry she was and how much she enjoyed the food.

"You said you were here to protect me," she said when she'd finished the roll. "I think you had better tell me just what the protection will entail."

"I want you away from the Royal as soon as possible. The house is ready...you can move in tomorrow." Gray began filling in the basic details of the safe house and the surveillance programme he'd devised.

A knock on the door interrupted him.

A slim, neatly groomed woman with dark, shoulder-length hair strolled in, a handbag slung over one shoulder. She smiled at Sam, then turned to Gray. "Gray Lombard?

I'm Elaine Farrell. I was told by the lady at reception that you were in here.''

Gray rose from his comfortably propped position on the edge of her desk. He shook the woman's hand, then glanced at Sam, his expression enigmatic. ''Sam, I'd like you to meet Detective Farrell. She's going to be taking your place for the next few days.''

Gray watched, narrow-eyed, as Sam shook Farrell's hand. Her composure was unruffled, her manner pleasant, as if she had expected the detective and was quite prepared to step aside while the other woman took her place.

Gray wasn't fooled. He had watched Sam carefully as he had outlined the safe house arrangements. She hadn't so much as blinked, simply listened.

He now knew that her very lack of reaction was a worst case scenario. If she had got upset or angry, *that* would have been a normal response. The calmness meant she was too upset to react naturally, that she was instinctively pulling inside herself, withdrawing from the hurt inherent in this situation—the loss. It meant that she was hiding herself from him.

Concern turned to irritation as he watched her put the detective at ease, even going so far as to offer Farrell her own seat behind her desk.

Sam's eyes met his, her expression so remote he felt like shaking her. ''If you'll excuse me, I need to check the damage on the top floor.''

Detective Farrell rose from her seat. ''And I need to familiarise myself with the building and meet the staff.''

Gray let Sam go because he had no choice; Farrell needed briefing. He stepped out into the corridor and watched Sam walk away, noting the straight line of her back, the rigid set of her shoulders. He knew she was hurting, just as he knew he had to find a way to give her something back out of all of this. Although how he could give her back the Royal, he didn't know. The place was falling down around their ears.

Carter and Ben passed Sam, tool belts slung around their hips. They had ostensibly been helping with repairs. In actuality, they had installed a series of surveillance cameras around the hotel and in more remote locations outside, linking them all to a central control unit in his suite.

Their banter stopped. Two hungry male gazes settled on the gentle sway of Sam's hips. Gray's jaw tightened. He didn't need to be told what they were thinking: he knew. They were thinking the same hot, male thoughts that were crowding his brain.

"Just in case there's any confusion," he said in a low, rasping voice, "she's already taken."

There was a low exhalation of air, a sudden release of tension.

"Are you sure you want her?" Carter asked wistfully.

Gray turned a cold gaze on him. "I'm sure."

Elaine Farrell gave Gray a speculative look, then eyed Ben and Carter with weary amusement. "Don't tell me, you guys are the cavalry?" She angled her head mockingly. "The testosterone levels are about right, you must be."

Carter blinked, the lust instantly disappearing from his expression to be replaced with an entirely healthy wariness.

Gray tried not to let his amusement show as he made formal introductions. Farrell was shaping up to be a martinet.

Minutes later, a trim grey-haired woman button-holed Ben and Carter.

"Sadie Carson's the name," she announced briskly. "Milly said you were helping with the clean-up. Addie and I need some major muscle to move our dragon trees, and we figure you boys are bound to be in good trim."

Sadie then proceeded to eye them both as if they were prime specimens in a beefcake show and she heartily approved.

Carter cleared his throat. "Uh, what makes you think that, ma'am?'

"Oh, you're one of those elite special forces teams. Addie and I recognised that straight off."

Ben went for a blankly surprised look. "What makes you think we're special forces?"

"Well, you've got that big gun down your pants for a start. You working undercover?"

"Uh…"

"Can't say, huh? It's all right, your secret's safe with me, but if you need any help, give us a yell." She whipped a gleaming Smith & Wesson out of her rucksack.

Ben and Carter both ducked.

"It's not loaded," she said, serenely tucking the black-and-silver pistol back amongst her cuttings and plant spray. "Dropped it last week and the darn thing went off. Blew a hole clear through the wall. Addie had to do some real creative plastering to cover it up. Since then, we figured it was probably safer to leave the clip out." Her eyes narrowed shrewdly. "I see you got Leroy to cut your hair." She nodded. "You fit in a lot better than you did."

Carter eyed Sadie Carson even more warily than he had eyed Farrell.

"It really looks very nice, dear," Sadie said reassuringly, patting her own severely cropped hair. "Leroy does my hair, too, you know. But be careful what you let slip around that boy, he's a real blabbermouth. Told on that old coot Jeremiah Holden for keeping a bird in his room. Now Jeremiah has to hide Cocky in his bathroom, which, owing to Cocky's uncertain temper, isn't the safest of arrangements for a man, if you get my meaning. Follow me and I'll show you where I want these plants moved to.''

Carter watched Sadie walk briskly up the stairs in her faded jeans and hiking boots. "Did you see that, Ben? I've got the same haircut as Sadie Carson.''

"And it looks very nice, too, dear," Ben mimicked as they obediently trailed Sadie up the stairs.

Carter turned a considering gaze on Ben. "Laugh all you want, big guy, but next time you look in the mirror you might notice that, colouring aside, thanks to Lee-roy, we could be twins.''

Chapter 9

Sam moved through the fourth floor, surveying the wreck of Belle's Palace. She had showered and changed into jeans and a white tank top that was already damp and clinging. The heat that gathered in these upper storey rooms had dewed her skin with perspiration within a matter of seconds.

In two rooms the ceiling had been taken down completely, the mess piled on tarpaulins spread on the floor. Roofers had made temporary repairs to the roof itself, but it was clear that the deterioration was widespread and that the entire roof did indeed need replacing.

She stopped at a window, enjoying the golden glow of the setting sun and the way the light brought a richness and warmth to rooms that had seen a lot of living and, according to legend, even more loving. It was hard to accept that soon these suites, with their echoes of the past and the people who had occupied them, would simply cease to exist. She wondered if Belle really did still haunt these rooms, or if any of her clients hung around on the off chance of a little afterlife hanky-panky. The Royal looked like it could house any number of ghosts.

The last of the warm light slid from her skin. Abruptly the room was plunged into deep shadow, presaging the night to come. Sam stared out at the anonymous office block across the road, which was responsible for blocking out the setting sun, and an odd tension gripped her, raising the fine hairs at the base of her neck. She shook her head in an attempt to dislodge the spooky sensation, caused no doubt by the sudden darkening, but the chill persisted, rippling down her spine and roughening her skin.

She backed away from the window purely on reflex, almost stumbling over a footstool with a tapestried cushion. Faint but deliberate footsteps echoed down the corridor, the sound eerie in the thickening gloom. Sam's heart began to pound. She had been thinking about ghosts, and, silly as it seemed, she had to wonder if she hadn't just conjured one up.

Tiptoeing to the door, Sam checked the corridor, feeling ridiculous as she did so. The footsteps probably belonged to one of the hotel residents who had sneaked up to look around, even though this floor had been declared off limits, or an employee who wanted to do what she was doing, survey the damage and say goodbye to a gracious old lady and the bawdy legend that was Baroness Belle.

The corridor was empty. Sam strained to hear, but the silence had an odd muffled quality, as if these rooms were somehow cut off and shrouded from the rest of the world. The suite she was in was at the far end of the corridor; she would have to pass several rooms before she reached the stairwell. Treading lightly, glad she had had the sense to wear sneakers, she passed first one door, then another. It was getting darker by the second, but the rooms closest

to the stairs still contained the residual golden light that
hung in the sky long after the sun had finally set. She was
level with the fourth door when shadowy movement
caught her eye.

Sam faltered and froze. The shadow moved again, re-
solving itself into a man dressed entirely in black and seen
from behind—one hand braced on the wide architrave of
the window, his head bowed, broad shoulders taut. His
head came up as if he had caught the whisper of her step.
He glanced over his shoulder, and his gaze collided with
hers across the width of the room.

The naked torment of Gray's expression hit her like a
blow, and Sam recoiled a step. A strong sense of déjà vu
gripped her, although why it should be déjà vu, she
couldn't fathom. The last time she had looked into Gray's
eyes and seen a stranger had been barely twenty-four
hours ago.

His expression grew shuttered, closing out the bleakness so swiftly that she wondered if that moment of despair had simply been a trick of the fading light.

"Sam." His voice was low and beguiling, edged with
a need that altered the very quality of the air, so that it
closed around her, velvety warm and so heavily laced with
sensuality that in that moment she could almost believe
in the possibility of a ghostly Belle lingering long after
her death. This had been her suite; maybe not everything
in it had belonged to her—the bed was too modern, for
one thing—but the escritoire, the chaise longue and the
large ornate oval mirror on a stand in one corner were
vintage Belle.

Gray abandoned his leaning posture against the window
frame and turned to face her. The dying light outlined the
powerful width of his shoulders, throwing his face into
shadow.

Her stomach knotted at the blatant sexuality glittering from his dark eyes. An aching heat flooded her lower belly, and her nipples grew almost painfully hard. Gray's gaze lowered to her breasts, then fastened on her mouth. Her chin lifted. She knew it had been futile to think he wouldn't notice what was happening to her.

His shoulders moved, as if he had just taken a deep breath, then, incredibly, he turned back to his contemplation of the view. The movement was stark and lonely, his dismissal of her so complete that for long moments Sam stood transfixed, watching the brooding width of his back.

She was half-way across the room, with its intricate mouldings of vines and flowers, its air of secrecy and liaisons, before she questioned the impulse.

For the past twenty-four hours she had been running, backtracking, looking for a way out of a situation that had spun far beyond her control. She was bone-tired of simply reacting.

And she was through with running.

She wasn't quite ready to be caught yet, either. That was a whole different situation, and she would face that, too, in her own time.

Her step faltered as the reality of what she was about to do crashed in on her, but she forced herself to follow through on the impulse that had carried her this far into the room.

She could understand Gray's need for isolation, but that didn't mean she had to accept his terse dismissal. He had laid claim to her this afternoon, but she wanted and needed, too, and right now she needed to comfort Gray, to reach out and be the one who touched, who offered.

She came to a halt behind him. He didn't move, but she felt his concentrated awareness of her in his very stillness. Her hand settled on his back. She felt his shudder and flinched at the jolt of savage awareness that just touching him caused. He was hot, so hot. A wave of longing and incredulity swept her. How could she ever have imagined she could forget…?

"What do you think you're doing?"

Sam swallowed at the cold roughness of his voice and concentrated on that one pulsing point of contact, the simmering tension in his tautly held muscles.

Taking a breath, she slipped both arms around his waist. If he rejected her now, she didn't know what she would do.

He was stiff, unyielding, as if he couldn't quite believe what she had just done. She could barely believe it, herself.

"What's the matter, Lombard?" she said, her voice husky. "Hasn't anyone ever hugged you before?"

His reply was low, measured. "I was giving you a chance to leave."

He turned in her hold, his hands curving around her waist. There was something bittersweet in his expression, an unexpected melancholy that tugged at her, made her lift her head and search for signs of emotion in those cool black warrior's eyes.

It was like staring at herself in a dark mirror, the terrible strength of needs and uncertainties that twisted and pulled deep inside, producing…vulnerability. It was as if he had ripped off a mask and was finally letting her see who he really was, and in that moment she *knew* him with an inner knowledge that startled her. He had said she belonged to him; for the first time she considered that he belonged to her.

Tears banked up behind her eyes, and grief closed in on her throat—grief for all they had lost, the years that had passed, and the certainty she hadn't been able to shake that the future held more of the same, despite the deep link she shared with Gray. Would he still look at her with such burning need if he knew she had carried his child and lost her without ever telling him?

His kiss when it came burned her with its sweetness. He whispered her name and she opened her mouth for him, taking his tongue inside her with a familiarity that pulled at the very centre of her being. Then, just as suddenly, the wispy melancholia tightened into something much fiercer, much more intense. She needed him with a power that shook her. She wanted the scent and taste and touch of him; she wanted to fit herself tightly to him, be wrapped in his strength and absorbed by him.

Grief shuddered through her again. This close to Gray, she could almost forget that he was a master at shutting her out when he chose, and that there was no guarantee that he would be any different this time. His physical passion was real; he wanted her so badly, and, God help her, she still wanted to believe in him.

His mouth slanted with increasing force over hers, demanding, giving. His hands curled around her bottom, lifting her so that his arousal pressed bluntly into the soft apex between her thighs and her breasts were flattened against his chest. The intimacy of his touch made her cry out.

The small, hot noise almost shattered the last vestiges of Gray's control. He hugged Sam to him for long minutes while he fought back his unruly hunger.

Only seconds before he had resolved to back off.

His retreat made sense on more than one level. Sam was hell on his concentration. Getting her in his bed wouldn't be enough, just as it hadn't been enough seven years ago. He wanted her until he ached, but he wasn't about to repeat the same dumb-ass mistake he had made before.

He couldn't lose her again.

It had been hard to admit his own vulnerability, that Sam was *necessary* to him. He had spent the last few years shedding vulnerabilities, isolating himself in order to protect those he loved.

He couldn't afford to reach for his own happiness, yet, and he didn't want to hurt Sam by taking when he wasn't in a position to give. The deeper he went with Sam, the more fractured his concentration would become. Tomorrow their pictures would be splashed over the newspapers. His past, and that of his family, would be picked over and examined.

Harper would take the bait.

Reluctantly he loosened his hold, but not entirely; the feel of her in his arms was too sweet, too damn rare. The fact that she had reached out, of her own accord, and touched him was…more than rare. That small touch had shaken and elated him. He caught the flash of movement in the mirror just off to the side of the window and was instantly transfixed by the vision of Sam wrapped in his arms.

He had resolved not to take, but desire rolled through him anyway. His jaw locked against the sweet, hot throb of arousal, and something even stronger, deeper: a need to cherish the woman in his arms, to let her know just how much he needed her, even if they couldn't be together just yet.

Sam's head lifted. "What is it?" she asked huskily.

"I don't want to hurt you."

"You should have thought about that before you came back."

He didn't miss her unspoken admission. If he could hurt

her, she still cared for him. His chest expanded on a sharp intake of air. "You want me."

He turned Sam in his embrace until she was facing the mirror. The contrast of her feminine delicacy against his much bigger, male frame had his jaw tensing again, and for a taut moment he was caught on the edge, uncertain that he could hold back long enough to give Sam pleasure without taking his.

Sam stared at her reflection, at Gray's shoulders encased in a black T-shirt, his bronzed arms caging her. She could feel his heat all down her back, feel the hard, male shape of him pressed against her, smell the clean scent of his skin as if he, too, had just stepped from the shower.

With a groan he pushed her hair aside and laid his mouth on the tender joint of neck and shoulder. His teeth fastened gently, and Sam sagged against him as sensation scythed through her like dark lightning. She felt her tank top being pulled from the waistband of her jeans and watched as his long fingers pushed up the flimsy white fabric, revealing the pale glow of her skin, the lacy cups of her bra, the swell of her breasts.

He pushed the bra up, and his hands cupped her. She gasped, arching at the shocking intimacy of his hold, the almost barbaric picture they made, with his big hands cradling her much cooler, paler flesh, making her seem fragile, utterly feminine, in comparison. Her skin burned at the contact, the callused roughness of his long fingers. She felt almost unbearably swollen and tender, her nipples stabbing into the heated centres of his palms.

His gaze locked on hers in the mirror, and when he spoke, his voice was strained. "Say that you want me."

Too much, and that scared her more than anything. If she let herself need, Murphy's law dictated that she would lose what she needed. "Yes."

His hands tightened. Sam closed her eyes.

"Don't do that," he said hoarsely.

"What?" She gasped as she watched his fingers flex again, felt the hot sensuality of his slightest touch. If she had any sense, she would push his hands away, at least until she could figure out how she could be with Gray and not break inside when he left.

"Don't look like you want me to make love to you. You're not ready, and I'm trying to keep us both out of trouble."

The mirror threw their reflection back, softened by twilight and so erotic it took her breath. "This…is keeping out of trouble?"

"This," he whispered, nuzzling her nape and nipping at her lobe, "is driving me crazy."

The restless glide of Gray's mouth, his hands, trailed fire everywhere he touched. She watched him unfasten her jeans and push them down on her hips, revealing cream lace panties that matched her bra. She felt wanton and decadent, almost as if she belonged to another century and was being seduced by a ruthless buccaneer. Gray's hand slipped between her legs, and she cried out at the exquisite sensation.

Gray inhaled sharply at Sam's soft, needy noises, and he cursed inwardly. He could feel how hot and damp she was, even through the barrier of lace. He bent his head, burying his face in her neck while he held on to the ragged edges of his control. She moved against him, a restless arching that stroked him to within bare centimetres of insanity. Her breasts were so full and pretty, he longed to taste them, the dark shadow beneath the ivory lace of her panties so enticing his entire body was clenched with need.

Framed by the ornate gilt border of the mirror, Sam

looked sensual and elegant and exotic. Gray decided that if Belle had looked anything like Sam, the port must have been crammed with ships and captains unwilling to leave. The entire South Pacific must have ground to a halt.

He forced himself to cradle her gently, to not move when she rubbed up against him. Taking in a tight, hard breath, he eased his fingers beneath her panties. A raw shudder rocked him at her intense heat, the sweet moisture he found.

She wasn't sure she wanted him yet, but her body was.

Sam gasped, moving against the glide of his fingers, and with a groan he slipped into her—one finger and then two, his thumb brushing the delicate bud just above.

Her head fell back on his shoulder, her neck as fragile and delicate as the stem of a flower. Gray turned her head and dipped, taking her mouth as she trembled and shook in his hands, plunging his tongue deep in compensation for all he was denying himself.

He wouldn't take, no matter how much it hurt him. If he had to repeat all the reasons like a damn mantra, he would do so—anything to stop him laying her out on that bed. Sam had said she wanted him, but he'd had to wring the admission from her. He shouldn't be touching her now, because somehow he had to find the strength to walk away from her until the situation with Harper was resolved.

Sam trembled and burned in Gray's grasp. His arm was wrapped around her waist, anchoring her against him as wave upon wave of pleasure rippled through her, as she shivered around the beguiling stroke of his fingers, the demanding rhythm of his mouth on hers.

He withdrew his hand after a taut few moments. His breath moved across her cheek, and then abruptly she was standing alone, staring at the reflection of his back in the mirror.

Sam's legs were wobbly, and her fingers shook as she adjusted her clothing. Unexpected tears wet her cheeks. She wasn't sure why she was crying, because he had made her feel more desirable, more vibrantly alive, than she would ever have believed possible—or was it because that was all he had done? She hadn't felt ready to make love with him, and he had honoured her wishes. Disappointment should be the last thing she was feeling.

"Are you all right?" He met her gaze, and the dark hunger in his expression stopped the breath in her throat.

"Why didn't you—" Her cheeks warmed. "Why didn't you make love to me when you know I would have let you?"

Something dangerous glinted in his eyes. "I want you, Sam, make no mistake. But this time I'm not going to seduce you. If you want me, you're going to have to ask."

Chapter 10

Later that evening, a dark shadow coalesced in the corner of Gray's sitting room.

Gray glanced up from the reports he had been attempting to read, when in reality he had been staring at the print and brooding about Sam. He consulted his watch. "You took your time."

Blade emerged from behind the smothering length of a gently rotting velvet drape. "I nearly got spotted. A woman came out on her balcony to water her plants. I had to wait until she'd gone."

"Is everything in place?"

"We're ready. You need to get Sam out, though. This building is like a damn rabbit warren. I don't think I've ever seen so many entry points. It's giving me an uneasy feeling."

Gray's own unease crystallised. He'd had an itch down his spine ever since he'd arrived, which was unusual. He had thought it was simply the situation with Sam, the odd

sense of the past merging with the present and the diffi-
culties of juggling two goals when he needed to be con-
centrating only on one: Harper.

There was no way Harper could be here yet, but Gray
didn't discount the margin for error.

He had reason to doubt his own judgement. Seven years
ago, that judgement had cost lives. "I'm shifting Sam into
a safe house tomorrow. Farrell, the police officer taking
her place, arrived today. Everyone has been briefed. The
whole place is as wired for surveillance as we can get it
and not advertise the fact. There's no way Harper can
enter this building without being spotted."

"Did you spot me?"

Gray jerked a thumb at the adjoining bedroom, where
Ben was seated in front of a monitor. The screen was
presently split into four quarters, each showing a different
view of the outside of the hotel. "Saw Sadie Carson douse
you with the watering can. That drainpipe must have got
real slick, but you hung on good. Glad to see you haven't
lost your edge."

Blade grunted and ran a hand over his wet hair. Water
trickled down his neck. "Maybe you should put Ms.
Carson on the payroll. With any luck, she'll do the same
for that bastard Harper."

Sam came awake, her heart pounding, senses straining.
Her bedroom was flooded with an almost preternatural
light despite the closed drapes, courtesy of an almost full
moon. But it had been something else that had roused her,
a sound that her sleep-fogged brain couldn't quite identify.

It came again. A small cry, a shuffling sound.

She strained to hear. If there was someone outside, she
should do something about it, instead of cowering inside,

imagining any number of reasons for that sound. She should at least try to see if someone was attempting to break in.

Slipping from bed, she pulled on her jeans, felt around for her sneakers and slipped them on. On impulse she inched a drawer open and pulled out a dark T-shirt, pulling that on over her thin cotton singlet.

Leaving the flat in darkness, she walked from window to window, opening the curtains just enough that she could see outside. The liquid silver light of the moon threw the back of the hotel into stark relief, so that parts were almost as bright as day, and shadows appeared so black they were utterly impenetrable. Nothing moved. Sam watched until her eyes ached. When she was just about to give up, she detected movement at the periphery of her vision, over by the Dumpster.

The movement came again, followed by a thin, reedy cry.

The cry was so like a baby's that for a wild moment she thought someone must have abandoned a baby in the Dumpster. Then she saw the outline of a cat. Kittens! The answer made her weak with relief. The cat must have crawled into the Dumpster to give birth, and now she was leaving her babies so she could hunt for food.

The only problem was, the Dumpsters were picked up and emptied regularly, and if that happened, the kittens would be crushed. Sam wasn't sure when the next pickup was. The kitchen staff generally notified the firm when the bin was nearly full, and the bin was emptied early the next morning.

Sam didn't hesitate a moment longer. The kittens would be tiny and fragile, and she couldn't let them die. She located a cardboard box, lined it with newspaper and slipped outside, turning her security light off so it wouldn't alarm the cat, and leaving the French doors ajar. She would transfer the kittens into the box and place them in a sheltered place nearby, where the mother would be able to locate them. It wasn't much, but it was all she could think of to do. Gray was moving her into a safe house tomorrow, and she wouldn't be able to look out for the kittens. She would have to get someone else to do that.

Tension tightened the sensitive skin all down her spine as she walked toward the Dumpster. Aside from the faint mewling noises, it was unnervingly quiet. It was as if the city had been caught in a freeze frame and everything had simply stopped. There were no cars careening late at night with stereos pounding, no music drifting from all-night clubs, no breeze blowing to lift the weighty mantle of humid heat and disturb the lush tropical growth fringing the car park.

Now that she had left the comparative security of her flat, she felt exposed and…vulnerable. It was probably an over-reaction, but she figured she was due one, and she gave herself leave to move surreptitiously, keeping to the shadows as much as possible, her head swivelling continuously, her tread as silent as she could make it.

When she reached the Dumpster, she flattened herself against the side, listening in order to locate exactly where the kittens were. A tiny mewling pinpointed their location. She edged around to the kittens, tossed the box in and planted her hands on the metal edge, tensing her muscles preparatory to hoisting herself over the side.

A hand landed heavily at the back of her neck, grabbing a handful of her T-shirt and a hank of hair with it. She was hauled back, spun around, pinned against the Dumpster, all the breath knocked from her lungs. For a heart-pounding moment she couldn't inhale and wondered dazedly if something vital had been crushed. When the air finally rushed in it was impeded by cold, hard metal pressed up into the soft arch of her throat.

Sam gasped as her assailant tightened his grip on her hair, holding it wound in his fist, pulling her head back so that bright moonlight washed over her face. She didn't notice pain; the shock of the assault had numbed her senses to everything but two salient facts: she was caught and held by a large man who towered over her, and the cold metal pushing into her throat was probably the barrel of a gun.

His breathing altered. He swore and loosened his hold on her hair.

"Sam," a low voice rasped. "What in sweet hell are *you* doing out here?"

Gray. She gulped down a breath, then another, and all the aches and pains began to register. She tried to speak, but her throat was still tight with shock. An odd gasping noise came out instead.

Gray released her completely and stepped back. The moonlight caught him as he smoothly holstered his gun somewhere beneath his left armpit, then his hands settled on her shoulders, and he hauled her out of the shadows.

His gaze swept furiously over her. "I thought you were a prowler. You could have got yourself badly hurt or killed."

Her eyes narrowed. She jerked loose from his grip. "Badly hurt?" she muttered, not bothering to hide her disbelief. "My scalp is stinging where you pulled my hair. My throat is going to have a bruise on it where you tried to feed that gun to me intravenously. By my calculations, the scare you just gave me lost me at least ten years of my life. When I'm an old lady I'm going to *need* those ten years!"

There was a moment of silence. "Uh, I didn't mean to hurt you, if only I'd...known."

His voice was odd, strangled, and his shoulders were moving as if he was...

Sam sucked in an incredulous breath. "I don't happen to think this is funny."

"Not funny," he agreed, and this time he laughed out loud. The sound was rough and warm, and it surprised her, sending a delicious thrill shooting through her body, but mostly it incensed her.

She pushed him. He gave a step, his shoulders still shaking. "Sam—"

She hit him and winced. "Ouch," she muttered. "Now I've skinned my knuckles." His stomach had felt about as yielding as a wall.

"Sorry," he murmured, still backing up as she stalked him. "I'll try to be softer in future."

"What future? We have no future."

He backed up another step and bumped into the weatherboard side of the hotel, and Sam found herself confronted with a situation she wasn't prepared for. She had literally shoved Gray into a corner, and now she didn't know what to do with him.

"Don't stop now," he invited silkily, neatly outlining her dilemma. "You've got one more step to take."

"I've done enough walking for tonight."

"Amen to that." He caught hold of her hands and pulled her against him, taking her by surprise. "I'm sorry about pulling your hair." His fingers slid into her scalp, massaging the sore area and effectively holding her captive. He dipped and his warm breath shivered across her cheek just before his lips caressed her mouth. "And I'm sorry I hurt your throat."

Using his hands, he tilted her head back and transferred

his mouth to her throat. His breath once more warm and damp against her skin, his tongue startlingly hot as he stroked the sore area.

He lifted his head and stared down into her eyes; the moonlight struck him full on, but evidently he didn't think he had to make any effort to hide the wicked grin that curved his mouth. "But most of all I'm sorry about those ten years. I was looking forward to spending them with you."

Sam gritted her teeth and shoved. He controlled the movement with ease. Her knee came up purely on reflex. He countered that move too quickly for her to make the satisfying contact she wanted, but his initial grunt as her knee jabbed his thigh was better than nothing. At least he let her go.

Their eyes locked. His were darkly contained, assessing.

"Now that you've had your fun, it's my turn." She stabbed her finger at the shoulder rig and gun. "What are you doing prowling around out here with *that?* And I think it's about time you told me more than the half-truths you've been doling out. Who are you working for? Is it still the military?"

"You've been watching too many movies. Aren't you scared that if I tell you, I might have to kill you?"

"I'll take my chances."

He shrugged. "I don't work full-time for the military, I haven't for years, but I am still...affiliated. I maintain a certain level of training and weapon skills."

"Affiliated?" She didn't bother to hide her disbelief.

He hesitated, and then seemed to come to a decision. "I was with the Special Air Service for a time. I'm still attached in an unofficial capacity."

"The SAS." Several jagged pieces of the puzzle that

was Gray had just slotted neatly into place. Special forces. She should have known. "Still attached in an 'unofficial capacity.' I should have known that, too." With a last baleful glance at Gray, she turned on her heel and strode away.

Gray caught her before she'd gone two steps. "What in hell are you talking about?"

"The secret agent role fits you perfectly. No explanations, no complications, just action and more action—a little sex on the side—then you just…" She threw his hands off. "…disappear!"

"I wasn't the one who disappeared."

"Don't split hairs!" Sam hauled in a breath.

"You're not going to hit me again, are you?"

"You should be so lucky."

His hand lifted as if he were going to reach for her again; then he thought better of it. "So…now that you've calmed down," he murmured in a soothing, cajoling voice, as if she was a mental patient who needed pacifying, Sam thought furiously, "are you going to tell me what you're doing out here?"

"Rescuing kittens." She spun on her heel and started toward the Dumpster. "What's your excuse?"

"I heard glass breaking and went to have a look. A couple of street lamps got knocked out. It was probably random vandalism."

She hauled herself over the side of the Dumpster, landing in amongst the rubbish as lightly as she could. Even so, her foot squelched in something gross, and the squalid smell made her wish she could cancel breathing for the next few minutes. Although the smell wasn't nearly as bad as it could be. The bin was filled with a large quantity of flattened cardboard boxes and newspapers, which was probably why the mother cat had decided it would be such a good place to have her kittens. Retrieving the box she'd chucked in earlier, she handed it to Gray. "I'll pass you the kittens. Your job is to put them in the box. No gun required. Definitely no licence to kill needed."

She handed him the first squirming bundle. The kitten was absurdly tiny in his big hands. He awkwardly but tenderly placed the kitten in the box.

"Maybe you've got potential," she allowed as she picked up another kitten.

He cradled it with the same care. "I'm also nice to old ladies and young children. My mother likes me."

Sam located another kitten.

"I do have a mother, you know." His voice was deceptively meek as he accepted the kitten. "I wasn't hatched."

"I'll bet your mom's relieved to hear it."

There was a small silence while Gray transferred the wiggling bundle into the box. "Know what, Munro? You've got a smart mouth, but you're in luck because—" He took the fourth and final kitten from her. Before she could draw back, he leaned forward and boldly stole a kiss, reminding her just what a pirate he really was. "—I like that in a woman."

Sam blinked at the swift, warm pressure of his mouth on hers, unwillingly charmed by Gray's whimsical behaviour and angry with herself for letting him run such circles around her. Just when she thought she was getting the advantage, he neatly turned the situation around, leaving her with more questions than answers.

She vaulted over the side of the Dumpster, determinedly banishing the giddy delight of his mouth on hers, glad that Gray's hands were fully occupied with the box of kittens. She had the feeling that if he hadn't had the box to hold on to, he would be holding her, and she doubted her ability to handle him in his present mood. Somehow, in the last few minutes, their relationship—such as it was—had just undergone a major shift. She had been sparring with him. Cancel that, she had been *flirting* with him. And Gray had given as good as he'd got.

"Where do you want these?"

The mother cat slunk from the shadows. The kittens were snuffling and mewling, and she looked anxious.

Sam pointed to a loading bay, where goods were usually dropped off. The structure was little more than a wooden overhang, but it was sturdy, and usually dry underneath. Gray disappeared into the inky shadows and emerged seconds later. The cat slipped by like a wraith, homing in on her babies.

Sam sighed with relief. "Thanks," she said softly. "I'll see if the Carson sisters will look out for them while I'm gone."

Gray insisted on seeing her to her door. He frowned when he saw that she'd left her French doors open and the security light off, and insisted on checking the rooms. Before he slipped through the doors, he palmed the big gun with the smooth ease of long familiarity.

He reappeared seconds later and switched on a lamp. Sam stepped inside, and Gray immediately closed the doors and pulled the curtains.

The gun was back in its holster. He was dressed completely in black, as he had been the evening before, but in the mellow glow of her lamp she could see the black webbing that held the shoulder holster in place.

She had listened to his terse recital of the facts, but the gun shoved the reality of the violent situation they were both apparently caught up in into her face.

He reached out and caught her chin, lifting her head so he could examine the dark shadows beneath her eyes, mute testament to too many disturbed nights. "You're shaking. Damn, I *did* scare you."

She moved away from his hold. "I guess I'm not used to guns."

"Just like you're not used to terrorists and safe houses." He prowled the small environs of her lounge, his gaze drifting over her belongings, the small horde of photos of her family grouped on top of a bookcase, the ornate Munro family bible her grandfather had kept with its last single entry, her name.

He picked up a small black and white snapshot framed in silver and seemed absorbed by the toddler she had been clutching at her father's much larger hand. He glanced across at her. "I'm staying with you for the rest of the night."

"No." Her denial was instinctive. Gray had moved in on almost every aspect of her life. These small rooms, her possessions, were her world, a world which would be abandoned to who knows what mayhem within a matter of only a few hours. "I thought you said you weren't going to seduce me."

"You've got a spare room, I'll sleep there, but I'm not leaving you alone. If you know someone is within call, you'll probably get some sleep."

Sam eyed Gray warily. She was tempted. Oh, she was tempted. Sleep had become a scarce commodity lately, and she knew she would have trouble achieving more than a state of fitful dozing until it was time to get up. She was so very tired. If Gray was here, there was a slim chance that she might relax enough to actually sleep.

"You need to sleep," he said, pressing his advantage. "Are you going to show me where the linen is kept, or do I have to look for myself?"

Sam stared at him in blank frustration. His gentleness

threw her off balance. She didn't want him being gentle or perceptive, and despite the simple comfort of having another human presence near, she didn't want to have him sleeping so close that she could listen to his breathing, hear every slide of the sheets across his skin, the rustle he made as he turned over in bed and hooked his arm beneath his pillow.

Maybe she was wrong in thinking she might sleep; chances were she wouldn't be able to relax enough to even doze.

Gray lay in the narrow single bed, listened to the gentle rhythm of Sam's breathing in the next room and wondered if he would go crazy before morning.

The broken street lamps niggled at him. Maybe they were just a coincidence? But Gray had never trusted in coincidence. The only thing he trusted in was the possibility that he had missed something vital and that all his plans would disintegrate because *he* had miscalculated. Again.

He couldn't afford mistakes—lives were riding on the success of this operation. Sam's life was at stake.

He shifted, kicking the sheet aside, cursing at the stuffy heat of the little flat. The rasping glide of the sheet against his semi-aroused sex almost made him groan out loud. He was so hot, and his skin was damp with sweat. He had half a mind to simply pick Sam up and carry her up to his rooms—at least it would be cooler there—but he had more sense than to touch her now.

Gray surged to his feet in one lithe, frustrated movement and stalked out into the lounge, naked. He brushed the heavy drapes aside and opened the French doors to stare out into the night, letting the cooler air slide over his skin.

No, he couldn't afford to touch Sam, even if he didn't seem able to keep his damn hands off her.

He had run the logic and made the decision. Tomorrow he would install Sam in the safe house and leave Carter on baby-sitting duty. Gray's place was here, with Farrell. He had worked seven years for the opportunity he had just created. An opportunity his gut instinct told him would work when nothing else had. There was too much at stake for him to risk blowing it all by letting his focus slip.

The unease that lately had become as much a part of him as his pulse tightened the skin at the base of his neck as he studied the moon-drenched landscape beyond the small courtyard. He trusted that unease above anything; it had saved his life more than once.

Sam would have to wait.

Once Harper was in the bag, he would have all the time he needed to repair the mistakes of the past and finish the job of taking down that stubborn reserve one brick at a time.

Gray locked up again and padded back to bed, but instead found himself in Sam's room. She had kicked back the covers and was lying on her back, one arm flung above her head on the pillow. The thin singlet she was wearing clung to her breasts and lifted to expose the delicate hollow of her navel. Her skin was moonlight pale and dewed with a satiny sheen of sweat, her panties thin enough to reveal the darker shadow beneath.

His hands clenched into fists at his sides; his breath drifted from between clenched teeth. Despite the attempt at control, his sex stirred and rose, lifting to full, painful arousal. He swore beneath his breath and returned to his room, the too-small bed and the heated ache of building frustration.

He had trained himself to sleep in catnaps, hell, he had trained himself to sleep under fire, but he knew now that he wasn't going to sleep at all.

Sam was surprised to find she'd slept like a baby.

She woke in the early dawn, faint streamers of light probing the edges of the curtains. Throwing back the quilt, she pulled on her robe, finger-combed her hair and headed for the shower. Sounds in the kitchen drew her there instead.

Gray was standing at her counter squeezing oranges, dressed in the black pants and T-shirt he'd worn the night before. The sleek muscles of his shoulders and arms rippled with every movement of his hands.

He spared her a moody glance. "Breakfast in five," he murmured in a low, raspy rumble.

"I don't usually bother."

"You need to eat."

"I wasn't aware you were monitoring my food intake."

"Baby, I monitor everything about you."

He washed his hands, then dried them on a towel, watching her all the way.

Sam eyed him cautiously. "You look like you got out of bed on the wrong side this morning."

"Put the emphasis on 'wrong bed' and you've got it." He picked up a glass of juice and placed it in her reluctant hand. "I didn't sleep worth a damn. That bed was built for an undersized midget."

Sam pointedly set the juice back on the bench, but he just picked it up and wrapped her fingers around it again, holding her hand against the cool, damp glass with the heat of his palms.

"Drink it," he said, the irritability evaporating as if it

had never been. "You can't operate under stress if you don't give your body what it needs."

What her body needed was standing right in front of her.

The scandalous thought brought a blush to her cheeks that had Gray's eyes narrowing speculatively.

Instead of following up on his advantage, he released her and began poking around her tiny pantry. "Where's the cereal?"

"I don't have any."

He gave her a look of disbelief. "Eggs?"

She shook her head.

"That probably rules out bacon. How about bread? The whole of the western world runs on bread, you've got to have some."

"It's in the freezer. I eat it one slice at a time."

He said something beneath his breath, pulled open the freezer compartment of her fridge and extracted a half-loaf of heavy grain bread. In his big hand the bread looked both puny and unsatisfying.

Sam sucked in an irritated breath and set her juice down on the bench untasted. "I'm going to have a shower."

"Do that," he muttered. "Drive the knife in deeper."

When she didn't move, he tossed the bread and caught it in his palm as if it were a baseball. His mouth curled in a predatory smile that made her pulse hammer. "Go get your shower," he prompted, low and rough, "before I decide to forgo breakfast and join you instead."

Chapter 11

Sam had almost finished packing when someone knocked at her door.

When she opened up, Milly thrust a copy of the morning paper at her chest. "Have you seen the newspaper this morning? According to this, you and the Warrior Prince are the hottest thing since that star went super nova!"

Sam stared at the enlarged black and white photograph splashed all over the front page. She and Gray were locked in what looked like a passionate clinch. The caption, "Lombard To Wed?" was splashed across the page in bold print.

Milly snorted. "You know you were engaged, girl?"

Sam spared Milly a brief glance. "I'm not engaged."

Instead of the snappy one-liner reply Sam expected, Milly fixed her with a level look. "Lombard gave us a version of what's happening. I say 'version' because I know a cover-up when I see one. He said you're in danger from some wacko and that Farrell will be replacing you for a few days, playing at being sick in your flat, while McKenna runs the hotel. McKenna! Beats me how that man manages himself, let alone a—"

"Did Gray tell you anything about the…danger?"

"Only that you were being threatened because of him and it was his job to protect you." Milly looked fierce. Abruptly, she stepped forward and enveloped Sam in a quick hug. "I don't know what exactly is going on around here, but you watch your step, do you hear?"

Sam returned the hug with one of her own. "It's only for a few days, then I'll be back."

At least, she hoped she would be back. She didn't know how long she would have to stay in the safe house, or what would happen to the Royal while she was away. "There's a box of kittens underneath the loading bay. Will you ask Sadie to look out for them while I'm gone."

"More strays?" Milly sniffed. "This place is full of strays."

"But you'll make sure they're all right and leave some food out for the mother?"

"Along with the rest of the cats the kitchen supports. If that humourless man from the health department calls, *he'll* probably have kittens."

Sam latched the chain behind Milly, then forced herself to read every word of the article about her supposed relationship with Gray, both past and present. She'd read stories like it before and dismissed them as distasteful but part of life. Now she felt stripped bare. Very little had been left out; the details were stunningly accurate. She wondered who in the vast Lombard Group they had questioned to find out so much about her past relationship with Gray.

There was a separate, rather sketchy, piece written about the Lombard family and the kidnapping. Gray had said he'd been wounded; the article stated in black and white just how badly he had been hurt. He had nearly died.

Sam sat on the edge of a couch. The paper began to shake in her hands.

She had nearly lost him.

In all the years since she had walked out on Gray, she had never imagined that he might die. The mere thought of death and Gray coupled in the same sentence was obscene.

Gray hadn't told her how or where he'd been wounded, other than to point out the visible scar on his neck. She knew now; he had been shot. While she'd been sitting in her grandfather's house, waiting for Gray to come and claim her, he had been fighting for his life.

She had run from a situation that had escalated out of her control, panicked by the shock of an unplanned pregnancy and frankly terrified by the vulnerability her relationship with Gray had forced upon her.

She had left Gray when she had needed him most—and when he had needed her even more.

The safe house was located in an older suburb with large sections, mature trees and high fences.

The house was large and rambling, with cool, cream plastered walls and bricked courtyards overflowing with a profusion of tropical plants. Inside, the house was airy and welcoming, with well-worn hardwood floors, comfortable furniture and a definite air of being lived in.

"The house belongs to a friend," Gray commented as he carried her cases in. "He's out of the country at the moment."

"Is he in the SAS, too?"

Gray's remote gaze touched on her, and she could almost see him gauging what response he should make. He had been carefully aloof when he'd come to collect her. In a pair of tailored linen pants, a thin shirt of some fine woven stuff that could also have been linen, and leather loafers that were just as expensively casual as his other attire, he had seemed as far distant from the moody, restive creature who had rummaged through her kitchen this morning as it was possible to be.

That distance had suited Sam then. After the stormy scene in the kitchen, followed by the even greater turmoil she'd been thrown into when she'd read the newspaper article, she had needed time to think.

He closed the door, shutting out the warm, humid breeze that carried the threat of yet another rain shower. "As a matter of fact, he is. That's why this house is so useful. Caleb's a security expert. He's installed a sophisticated alarm system, and all the windows and doors have secure bolts and locks."

Sam chose a bedroom and unzipped one of the two cases Gray had placed on the bed, extracted the newspaper she'd slipped on top of her clothes and carried it out to the large sprawling room that combined a state-of-the-art kitchen, dining room and lounge. She set the newspaper on the table, went into the kitchen and made coffee while she waited for Gray to return from his circuit of the grounds. Carter would be here shortly, and she didn't know when she would see Gray again. This might be her only opportunity for a very long time to question him about the past, and she wanted answers.

Gray walked in off the patio, leaving the glass doors open. The cool, moisture-laden air flowed in, bringing the tangy scent of the garden with it. He saw the newspaper on the table and glanced sharply at her. "Who gave you that?"

"Milly."

"I was hoping you wouldn't see it."

Behind Sam, the coffeepot began to fill with dark, fragrant liquid, adding its own rich aroma to the scents of the garden and impending rain. "The article says you nearly died," she said flatly. "I want you to tell me exactly what happened."

Gray glanced at the paper, then back at Sam. She was wearing a camisole and a full, light floral skirt of some drifting, semi-transparent material that was driving him crazy. The swirling lilacs and blues made her seem even more softly feminine and emphasised her delicate, pale skin and the deep, exotic blue of her eyes; eyes that were presently levelled on him and waiting for answers he didn't want to give her.

Milly might be Sam's friend, but she hadn't done Sam any favours today. The details the paper had printed were raw and graphic. He had supplied factual information only, but the press had evidently done some digging of their own. "Maybe you should sit down."

"I'll stand."

Gray's jaw clenched against the tension that gripped him, the loss of control that had put an edge on his already damaged voice. "The story in the paper isn't pretty. My version isn't much better."

"I don't care. I want to know what happened to you."

Gray couldn't conceal his surprise. "To me?"

Somehow he had never thought of what had happened as being in conjunction with himself; for Gray, the story had always been about Jake.

"Yeah, Lombard," she said low and flat, as if she was reining her temper in, but just barely. "I want to know what happened to *you*."

The coffee machine finished dripping. Sam reached for

mugs and began pouring. The mundane movements, the straight line of her back underlining her quiet determination to know the truth, somehow made it easier to start.

Tersely he began outlining the bare facts of the encounter, but the simple act of retelling conjured up stark images he doubted he would ever be able to forget.

Seven years ago in Sydney the day had been humid with the promise of rain, dark with the weight of clouds, when he'd slipped off his Kevlar vest in order to squeeze through a small, high window in an inner city warehouse they had raided on a tip.

It had been gloomy in the warehouse, the air close, thick with the scent of dust and packing materials and machine oil. The place was a warren of rooms and loading bays, with one huge storage area. He ghosted from room to room, his stomach tight with dread, still reeling from the shock of recovering Jake and Rafaella's bodies the day before, and with every room he entered, he feared what he would find, but urgency drove him on. Sam was missing. And he was sure Harper had her.

He didn't find Sam, but he located Harper, radioed for help, then hunkered down to wait. But there was no time. Harper and his men were leaving. Gray had no choice but to act or lose them. He had to get Sam back, and he wanted Harper with an ice-cold fury.

He took out one of the men as he walked past his hiding place. A whisper of noise alerted him, and he spun, drawing his handgun as a second beefy man charged out of nowhere, crashing into his side and propelling him back against a tall bank of heavy packing boxes. The pistol, a Sig Sauer, spun from his hand. Gray rolled, evaded a roundhouse punch, then sprang to his feet in time to deflect the next bull-like charge. The next moments passed in a blur as they grappled, neither man gaining the advantage in the congested storage area, until the thickset brawler bounced off a steel pillar and went down like a fallen ox.

They had made enough noise to raise the dead. Harper was waiting for him.

"Lombard," he said as smoothly as if Gray had just turned up at his club and they were about to share a companionable half hour over a drink. A blade appeared in his hand.

Gray could see the gleam of the Sig where it butted up against what looked like a tractor case. He lifted his gaze to Harper, his fingers closing over the hilt of his fighting knife.

"Where's Sam?" he demanded, sweat trickling down his temples, stinging his eyes as they circled and parried, playing what was evidently Harper's favourite game.

"Lost your girlfriend, Lombard? You should be more careful."

"What have you done with her, you son of a bitch?"

Harper's eyes were cold. "Nothing…yet."

Tension vibrated through Gray, cording his muscles, tying his shoulder up so tight it burned with each tiny flex of his fingers, each flick of his wrist. Harper's knife dived, swivelled, flashed where it caught the light. Gray whirled, and cold fire seared across his stomach. He was cut. He could feel the hot spill of blood, the cool that followed. Fury channelled through him. He feinted, lunged. His knife sank into muscle, and Harper stumbled back, his left arm hanging useless at his side.

With a roar, Harper charged. Gray feinted, avoiding the manoeuvre; then something smashed into his back, throwing him forward. Harper's knife scored his neck, then Harper himself was abruptly jerked back. The snapping report of the two shots, then a third, echoed in the cavernous hollow of the warehouse as the floor rose up to meet him.

When Gray came to, he knew he'd been shot. In the back.

He was aware of movement. Harper staggering to his feet, clutching his thigh with his good hand, then he was gone from Gray's vision. There were more gun shots, the sound of a vehicle, then…silence.

He was having trouble breathing. Something was wrong with his neck. He could feel the heat of his blood on his skin, the coldness seeping into his very core, the deep aches he instinctively knew were bad—like pain just waking up.

He was going to die.

A part of his mind mulled over the concept of the justice in dying while trying to fix his mistake, as if it was an intellectual question and he was part of some impartial jury presiding over his bleeding body. The visual was so real he could almost swear he was hovering over himself, staring down at the entry wound in his back. Then the illusion telescoped into a point of black, the darkness swirling at the edges of his vision as he opened his eyes and was sucked back into the grim, only-too-real present.

The floor was hard and cold, his sense of smell almost painfully acute. He could easily separate the smells of dust and sweat, and his own blood. God, his blood, so rich and sweet, and it was draining away.

The thought shoved his heart into overdrive. Abruptly the life force rose in him like a ball of pure, white-hot energy vibrating at his very core, pulsing, driving upward as if it would burst from his mouth. He clenched his jaw; he didn't want to die.

The hell he would die.

Gray sucked in a breath as the pain flowered, breaking

through the odd, numbing stasis. The enormity, the all-encompassing nature, of the pain forced him into a foetal position, even though the slightest movement made his head spin. His stomach tightened, rolled, and for a moment he thought he was going to be physically sick. An odd rattling groan was torn from his damaged throat. If he threw up now he probably *would* die. Breaking into a sweat at the exquisite agony the movement caused him, Gray felt down his body, located the exit wound the bullet had made, then rolled, trapping his hand over the wound, applying his own pressure to help staunch the bleeding.

He must have blacked out again. When he opened his eyes, he was on his back and Blade was leaning over him, breaking open an ampoule of morphine. There was a faint sting as he injected it directly into the wound. Hazy warmth washed through Gray, swept him like a lazy ocean swell, rocked him gently, each undulation easing him further from the jagged bite of the pain. With every pulse the terrible tension that gripped him eased, and his mind drifted.

Gray tightened his jaw, hanging on fiercely. He didn't like losing control, even to the morphine. He was afraid that if he let go, he *would* die. He had to stay awake. He had to live.

Blade was talking as he ripped open packets, telling Gray what he was doing, cursing him for getting shot, threatening Gray with a long, drawn-out death if he did die on him.

Gray felt pressure on his belly and a fresh wave of nausea rolled through him as the pain broke through the morphine haze.

"Give me another wound dressing. Now!" Blade snapped.

Time became elastic. No matter how hard Gray tried,

he kept losing his hold on the present, slipping off the edge into the blackest midnight he'd ever known; it pulled at him, beckoned, warm and dark, but there was a reason he had to stay awake, a reason he had to keep going.

The reason crystallised. "Sam," he said in a tortured rasp.

Blade leaned over him, so close that Gray could see the moisture in his eyes. It hit him like a hammer blow: Blade was crying. Blade never cried. He was the hardest of the hard men, and he almost never revealed what he was really thinking. Gray knew him, they were close, so alike in many ways—intensely private, single-minded, wary of commitment. Blade ran deep, too deep for most, who chose to see only what he allowed them to see—the cold, utterly professional soldier when he was working, the love-'em-and-leave-'em outlaw when he wasn't.

"Sam's not here," Blade said grimly. "We've searched this whole viper's nest and questioned the scumbag who shot you in the back. She was never here."

He had lost consciousness at that point. Three days later, he'd surfaced from heavy sedation. It had been weeks before he was fit to travel.

Gray turned from the view out of the kitchen window that he had barely registered because the images of his own private hell were so much brighter, so much more intense.

Sam's face was paper-white, her eyes almost black with an inner pain that caught and held his attention. She was still standing by the coffeemaker, her hands gripping her bare upper arms as if she was chilled, the mugs of coffee steamed unnoticed beside her on the counter. "You thought *I* was there? You nearly died because—"

"It was a reasonable assumption to make. You went

missing the same day Jake and Rafaella did. Sometimes coincidence is a real bitch.''

''You were looking for me.''

Gray's gaze narrowed on her face. ''I shouldn't have told you.''

''I already knew most of it.'' Fury replaced the blank shock that he had almost died for her and she hadn't known. ''Take off your shirt.''

''Sam… If I'd been paying any kind of attention to what was and wasn't happening between us, I might have worked out that your disappearance wasn't connected with Harper.''

Sam wasn't in the mood to be placated. ''Take off your shirt,'' she repeated. ''I want to see.''

Gray didn't move. Sam stepped closer, pulled his shirt from his pants, then started on the buttons.

His hands covered hers. ''Sam…''

She threw off his hands and continued. When all the buttons were unfastened, she pushed the shirt from his shoulders, letting it peel down his arms and fall to the floor.

For a long moment she couldn't see beyond the sheer, muscular beauty of his torso. His skin glowed copper in the brassy light of the approaching storm; dark hair shadowed his chest and ran in a line to the waistband of his pants. He was startlingly male and primitive in the civilised confines of the ultra-modern kitchen. Without the concealing mantle of clothing, danger and heat poured from him, animal-strong, intense and vital. He smelled delicious. The clean male scent of his skin, edged with an aroma that was musky, male, filled her nostrils and almost made Sam moan out loud.

She wanted to be closer. She wanted to wrap her arms around his lean waist, burrow her head against that broad chest and breathe her fill of the erotic, intimate scent of him. He would be hot to the touch, the pelt of dark hair on his chest enticingly rough against her cheek, his skin satin-smooth, pulled taut across heavy muscle. That edgy vitality would shiver and throb through her, as if in touching him she'd transferred some of that pulsing, vibrant energy to herself.

And then she saw the scars.

An ugly, sunken welt just up from his hip that she instantly knew was the bullet wound. An arcing slice across his flat, muscled stomach. She could actually envisage the knife slicing through the hard muscles of his belly, the fleshy explosion of the bullet ripping into his back.

Before she could stop herself, before she could think beyond the shock of what had been done to Gray, Sam touched the scars, her fingers running lightly over the devastating injuries as if she could comprehend the violence, as if she could absorb some of the pain he must have felt.

He jerked at her touch, his breath coming roughly, but he didn't move away.

Gray was such a beautiful male animal, and someone had hurt him. Anger rose in her. Not just hurt him—someone had done their very best to kill him. "Damn you. How dare you nearly die for me?" she demanded raspily.

His gaze glittered down into hers, and she knew he would do whatever it took, risk himself again if necessary.

She ran her fingers over the bullet wound again. "You're going to catch this man—this *Harper*."

It wasn't a question, but he answered anyway. "Yes."

She absorbed the flat intent in his voice, and something else, a new tension. She was touching Gray, standing so close that he could encircle her with his arms if he wanted. Her hand jerked back, but she wasn't fast enough. His fingers captured hers, wrapping them tight. She was surprised all over again by the rough tingling heat of his grip and the effect it had on her.

Her breath came in sharply. She was going crazy. No, strike that, she was already there. Gray Lombard was the last man on earth she should be attracted to, the last man she should want to touch. He was too arrogant and too rich for his own good, and he didn't need or want her worry, or her protection. He had nearly died for her.

And she loved him.

More, she was in love with him. She knew it, starkly, without any sense of wonder or elation. She loved him, and she couldn't bear a world without him in it.

"Don't let him hurt you again," she whispered. "Do you hear me?"

Gray touched her face; his thumb rubbed gently across her cheekbone. "I hear you."

"But you won't listen. You're going after him. There's no guarantee you won't be shot again. There's no guarantee you won't—"

"He won't kill me."

Sam drew in a breath, unable to hide her fear or the fury that grew out of that fear. The emotions were too well-known, too closely married to the dark, empty places inside her, because she knew with a stark certainty that if Gray died, she wouldn't want to live.

Not that she was suicidal in any way, simply that she would take no joy in life. She would live, she would continue to breathe and do all the things that normal people do, but she would simply be going through the motions, as she had done for the last seven years. If Gray died, it would be like a part of herself dying, and she knew she had to tell him that. After today, there was every possibility that she might not get another chance. "I love you."

He went still, his expression utterly blank; then his expression hardened, settled more fiercely against the bones of his face. "I have to go."

"I know."

He swore, sharply and succinctly. Keeping her hand in his, he retrieved his cell phone from his pants pocket. He stabbed in numbers and spoke, holding her gaze as he did so. Sam heard the low rumble of Gray's voice but had no idea what he actually said. His intent smouldered in his eyes, as blunt, as straightforward, as the way he was physically keeping her close.

He wanted her, and he was going to have her.

Just admitting what was going to happen next turned her knees to proverbial jelly. She didn't have the strength or the will to stop him, not when this was what she wanted more than common sense, more than logic or safety.

Gray snapped the cell phone closed and slipped it back into his pocket. "Carter's got a job to do before he gets here." One big hand curled around her nape, trapping her in a grip that was both predatory and possessive. "We've got two hours."

Chapter 12

Elation burst through Sam as Gray's mouth settled hungrily over hers. She could feel the blood pounding through her veins, the sweet, heavy throb of desire pulling her muscles taut, making her skin tight and hot, almost unbearably sensitive to his lightest touch.

Her palms came to rest against the intriguing roughness of his chest. He shuddered and groaned and pressed closer, herding her against the counter. His mouth left hers and trailed along her jaw, down her throat; then, as abruptly as he had kissed her, he let her go.

"If you don't want this, you'd better say so now. I need you so much you make me shake."

He grasped her hand and pressed it to the centre of his chest. She could feel the rapid slam of his heart, the almost imperceptible tremors that shook him, but it was the words he'd chosen that moved her the most. He *needed* her. Somehow, that was more than she had expected.

She knew he would more than likely hurt her again,

but suddenly she didn't care; either one of them could be dead tomorrow. "If all we have is two hours, I'll take it."

He let out a breath; his lashes lowered over his eyes. "The first time we do it, I don't want to be standing up. I want to see you. We need a bed."

He swung her into his arms and carried her through the darkened hallway to the bedroom she'd chosen, set her on her feet and began systematically stripping the clothes from her body.

He surveyed her for a tense moment, holding her gaze as he kicked off his shoes and peeled off his pants. His hands settled on her hips, moving up in a rough stroke to cup her breasts, plumping them up into full mounds as he lowered his mouth to first one nipple, then the other. Sam trembled and arched under the onslaught, the exquisite pull of his mouth, the hot, wet heat of his tongue. The backs of her knees connected with the bed; then she was tumbling. Gray's weight pinned her to the mattress, flattening her breasts against the solid wall of his chest, his thighs spreading hers as he settled himself between them. Sam shivered in his grasp, assaulted by an overload of textures that were at once alien and familiar. His body was hot, his textures rich and varied: satin skin and crisp hair on his chest and thighs; hard unyielding muscle and callused hands; the heavy, gliding heat of his sex as he moved over her.

Gray's gaze locked with hers as he probed and found her entrance. Sam shivered at the tantalising pressure, the searing liquid heat that flooded her lower belly. Her hips lifted of their own accord to capture and contain him. The breath hissed from between his teeth. He reared back, surveyed her for a taut moment, then retrieved his pants from the floor and extracted a foil packet. Swiftly he sheathed himself. "I had planned to court you when this situation was over. I still will, but it will be after the fact."

One hand cupped the back of her head, fingers locked in her hair, anchoring her in place as he reached down and positioned himself. "I've dreamed of this," he whispered. "Look at me while I take you." The demand was low, rasping, as relentless as the pressure between her legs.

Sam gasped at the dark, hot intensity of his gaze, the burning pleasure of his touch. She dimly understood that even now, despite Gray's fierce arousal, the need that simmered in the banked heat in his eyes, he was controlling their lovemaking. He'd had the presence of mind to take care of contraception—something she hadn't thought about, and which should have been flashing like a neon sign in her mind. He was still holding back, while he demanded everything from her.

She gasped as he pressed deeper. Her fingers dug into his shoulders. It had been so long, and she'd forgotten how it felt, how smoothly muscular he was, the difficulty she had always had accepting him. He was only part way in, and already she felt unbearably stretched.

"Relax," he crooned, stroking one hand down between her breasts, over her belly, to the exquisitely tender flesh between her legs. His voice was rough and tender, telling her how pretty she was, how much he wanted her, just how hot his dreams had been.

His words washed over her, as velvet-soft as the stroke of his fingers as he soothed the point of penetration where she gloved him so tightly, then slipped up over the exquisitely sensitive bud just above. Sensation broke through her, white-hot, so complete she arched, mindless with the terrifying power of her climax. The intensity of feeling was shattering. There was no turning back. She had made her decision, and there was nothing she could or would do to stop him. She was open and completely vulnerable on every level. If loving Gray was going to hurt her, it was too late to worry about it now; she was committed, for better or worse.

Not that Gray was giving her a chance to change her mind. He was sinking deeper, taking advantage of the shimmering convulsions, her internal moistening, to ease his way.

His hands tightened on her hips as he lifted her to him, adjusting the angle so he could plunge deeper still, and the feel of him buried inside her, the unadorned intimacy of penetration, tore away the last tattered remnants of her defences.

She wanted this.

She had never felt so tinglingly alive, never taken so much joy in living. The discomfort was fading, giving way to a hot excitement. She lifted, accepting him fully, crying out at the sweet, rasping ache. She wanted life, she *chose* life, and in that moment she accepted Gray—his implacable will, his code of honour, his smothering protectiveness—all three things that still threatened to lock her out of his life, just as they had done for the past seven years.

"Touch me." The demand was hoarse and raw, more a groan than actual words.

Her hands slipped along the damp curve of his back, glorying in his strength and slickness, the bunch and slide of his muscles as he began to move. Sam flexed her limbs beneath his solid weight, feeling him impossibly hot and heavy inside her, wanting more than his gentleness and restraint, half wild for more.

Her mouth opened over his skin. The salt taste exploded across her tongue, and she arched, shimmying against him. A rough sound was torn from his throat; he bucked, then shuddered and drove deep. He was like a storm, on her and over her, pounding inside her. She wanted all of him, everything he had to give, everything he could make her feel. She had been lost for seven years, lost and so alone without him.

Gray's weight came down on her fully, crushing her into the bed; his mouth slanted over hers, and the concept of loss and loneliness was smothered by the sleek, hot thrust of his tongue. He tasted like salt and musk and need. He tasted like a passion so extreme her head spun with it. He felt like the sun, hot and heavy as he sank deep within her, burning her away until she was nothing without him.

Leroy was proud of his salon.

True, it was small, and the location was definitely dragged down by the presence of that rat-infested hotel on the corner, but he had learned to count his blessings. The rat-infested hotel had offered him a steady income when his trendier clientele tapered off, and he did meet the occasional wealthy eccentric here.

Take, for example, the man whose hair he was trimming now. He had stumbled across Mr. Soames in the dark, musty confines of the Royal's private bar, evidently enjoying the rather doubtful ambiance. It didn't take a genius to know that the man had money, real money. He was nothing to look at; in fact, Mr. Soames was remarkably nondescript. But he still reeked of quality. His suit was Armani, and not off-the-rack Armani, either, the tailoring was too perfect. Besides, Leroy had discreetly inspected the label. His shoes were handmade, his nails manicured, his linen the finest.

Leroy continued trimming the gentleman's hair, wishing all his clients could be so well-dressed, so well-groomed. Mr. Soames had an air of real class about him. Leroy shuddered delicately as he thought of the Pacific Royal. His clients there were nothing more than peasants and ruffians. If he didn't need the money to supplement his income and his upwardly mobile lifestyle, he wouldn't go near the place.

"I hear you do a lot of business with the Pacific Royal."

Leroy jerked, caught off balance by his client asking a question about the very thing he was thinking of—almost as if Mr. Soames had been reading his mind. "Unfortunately, yes," he muttered.

"Then you must cut Samantha Munro's hair," the man said in his light, bland voice.

Leroy's eyes widened at the obvious search for information; then he smiled in satisfaction. Samantha Munro was a classy lady. She stood out like a diamond amidst dross at the Royal. Perhaps that was what—or should he say *who*—had drawn Mr. Soames to spend time in the Royal's bar. He probably assumed that Leroy was Samantha Munro's stylist. He wasn't, but he didn't see that that little point needed explaining when Mr. Soames was playing such a subtle game. "Sam has gorgeous hair," he murmured resuming trimming.

"I saw her picture on the front page of this morning's paper. Looks like she's engaged to Lombard. A step up from managing the Royal, I imagine."

Leroy's scissors jerked again at the mention of the cold-eyed barbarian who inhabited the Governor's Suite. He was more of the opinion that having any kind of association with Lombard was a step down—especially for a lady like Samantha Munro. It was almost inconceivable that Lombard was one of *the* Lombards and as rich as

Croesus. If Leroy had only known that, he would have charged him more for the haircuts he'd done. He should have had danger money just to step inside that suite. "*If* the engagement's real," he said, not bothering to hide his disdain. If Samantha Munro was engaged to Lombard, he was a horse's ass.

Mr. Soames smiled pleasantly into the mirror, his expression enquiring without being vulgar.

Leroy didn't need further prompting. Something out of the ordinary was going on at the Royal. Samantha Munro had been whisked away and replaced by a lookalike, and those barbarians in the Governor's Suite who claimed to be in the telecommunications business were up to something. He wasn't certain what, but he was only too happy to fill in the gaps with his own inventive guesses.

Gray walked into the kitchen of the safe house. He had showered and dressed and was now ready to leave.

"I'm making arrangements to shift you to Sydney until this is over," he said abruptly. "You can move into my house. The security's better than anything I can rig up here, and my sister, Roma, will keep you company."

Sam put down the coffeepot, which she had just rinsed, leaving it to drain, and eyed him levelly. "I don't want to go to Sydney. If you're in danger, I want to be here."

"If a situation develops, I'll handle it better if I know you're safe. If you're within reach, I won't concentrate worth a damn."

"In other words, I'm a distraction."

A muscle in his jaw worked. "You know you're important to me."

Sam took a deep breath, swallowing her hurt, the emotions that clamoured for release, and simply concentrated on keeping her face blank. She even managed to lift her shoulders in a dismissive shrug. "Then I'll see you...whenever," she said coolly.

He went utterly still, and this time she had trouble breathing at all. There was something tense and dangerous about that complete stillness, like the calm centre of a storm or the waiting moment before a large predator sprang on its chosen prey, and she realised she'd finally managed to goad him beyond that iron control.

He was on her so quickly that she barely had time to blink. The world tilted wildly as she was hoisted over his shoulder. Her belly was uncomfortably squeezed as he strode along, his arm anchored across her legs. Her skirt flipped up so that cool air sifted against her thighs and thinly clad buttocks, leaving her feeling vulnerable and exposed, which was odd when she considered that she had been naked with Gray just minutes before and now she had all her clothes on.

The room cart-wheeled. She was on her back, lying across a bed, her legs dangling over the edge. It was a different bedroom, she realised, a different bed. Gray had simply carried her to the nearest one.

For the second time that day he stripped her panties from her and tossed them aside. He tore open his pants and pushed them down just low enough that he could free himself. He was inside her in one fierce motion. Sam braced herself and arched into his thrust, and the raw force of it lifted her from the bed. The intensity of pleasure that washed through her made her shake. He hadn't bothered with a condom, and the knowledge made her breathless with excitement; a part of her gloried in that loss of control. She closed her eyes and lifted her hips in an attempt to contain him, but he pulled back.

"Open your eyes," he demanded.

Her eyes flickered open and fastened on his. She

moaned, lifting again, but again he evaded her attempt to sheathe him. He caught her hands and held them above her head, and his thighs shifted, spreading hers further apart until she was completely open to him, unable to move beyond that simple arching of her back.

A dark flush moved across his cheekbones; sweat sheened his face as he loomed over her. "Don't do that again," he muttered, low and taut. "Don't close yourself off from me."

"You want too much."

Her words tailed off in a gasp as he penetrated her again with one hard shove. The relief of the penetration quickly gave way to the familiar heavy tension that laced her belly and lower back as he began to move with long, powerful strokes.

There was no seduction, no teasing foreplay or gentle build-up. She didn't want those things right now, she realised as pleasure spiralled fiercely. She'd goaded him, and he had responded, giving her exactly what she needed: his undivided attention. His lovemaking was raw and powerful and primitive, but it *was* lovemaking. He was frustrated that he wasn't getting his way with her—that she had had the temerity to dismiss him—and was fighting back the only way he knew how. But if he didn't care for her, he wouldn't be making love to her now. He had been leaving; their time together had been over for the foreseeable future. She had challenged him on the most basic level, and he had responded like the healthy male animal he was.

His rhythm shallowed out as he pulled her more firmly beneath him, one hand still shackling her wrists while he tilted her hips to take more of him, deeper. His thrusts became shorter, sharper, as he relentlessly drove her toward climax. He wouldn't allow her not to climax, she realised dimly, and it wasn't something she could withhold, anyway. But then, it had always been this way. How could she hold on to her reserve when she was locked beneath him? It was a wonder she could hold on to her sanity.

The storm broke outside, darkening the already sullen day, scattering rain against the windows and increasing the smothering heat rather than relieving it. Fresh moisture sheened her skin, and when Gray released her wrists, she clung to his shoulders, her fingers twining in his shirt to anchor herself against his heavy thrusts.

Her clothing was twisted and uncomfortable and sticking to her skin; her breasts throbbed fiercely against the constriction of her bra. Her breathing was fast and shallow; she couldn't seem to get enough air. It was as if the storm had sucked up all the available oxygen and left her floundering, her world narrowed to the dark, slitted intent in Gray's gaze as he pushed her further, higher, than she'd ever gone before.

His thumb rasped across the small, swollen bud between her legs. Her hips jerked, and she screamed with the stunning force of her climax. A low, grating sound broke from Gray's throat as he rode her hard through it. Heat shimmered, furnace-hot wherever skin met skin. Sweat trickled between her breasts, plastered his shirt to his broad, heaving chest, and still he drove into her, his gaze fixed on hers, demanding an even greater surrender than the one she'd just given him.

Tension coiled with abrupt suddenness, and the wildness boiled up, taking her again with shocking swiftness. He groaned as she tightened around him, but this time he shuddered, arched, his muscles corded as liquid heat exploded deep in her belly, swamping her senses, wiping her mind clean of everything but Gray and utter, bone-melting exhaustion.

The rain continued to fall, heavier now, the dull rhythm a balm as she lay quiescent beneath Gray's heavy weight, floating in a haze.

She was hot, so hot, but she didn't want to move; she wanted to stay here all afternoon and wallow in the afterglow of complete physical exhaustion, to drift in a daze that had no beginning and no end. She didn't want to do anything that might disturb Gray. She could feel him still, lodged deep inside her, and she didn't want to relinquish any part of him. He had made love to her as if he owned her. The act had been darkly erotic, unbelievably carnal, a primitive claiming that had satisfied something deep inside her that she had never acknowledged. He had ripped away her feeble defence, and he had done it ruthlessly and deliberately. She knew she should regret it, but with the scent of their lovemaking filling the room, swamping her senses, she wasn't capable of regretting anything.

He might have forced her surrender, but in the end she had given it gladly. She knew with sudden clarity that she more than loved Gray; he was a part of her, whether he wanted to be or not, enmeshed in her past and, now, in her future. Loving him had forever changed her, and she couldn't change back.

There would never be another man for her. No one else could, or would, ever take Gray's place—he burned too vividly, too strongly, to ever be eclipsed.

She had waited for him for seven years, unknowingly kept herself chaste for him. If this was all she would ever have of Gray, then she would go to her grave, if not content, then at least knowing that she had tasted the dizzying heights.

He stirred and raised himself on one elbow. His fingers

brushed her cheek, pushing hair back from her face. His voice was soft, dark, a bare whisper. "Did I hurt you?"

Sam framed his face with her hands, his stubble deliciously rough against her palms. "What do you think?"

He eased himself from her body, fastened his pants, then pulled her up by her hands until they were both standing beside the bed. "I think I went a little crazy. I didn't use a condom."

He pulled his phone from his pocket and made a call, his voice terse as he told Carter to delay for another hour; then he picked her up and carried her through to her room, then her bathroom, and began removing her clothing. Sam stood quietly, her legs wobbly as he peeled her rumpled skirt from her.

When she was naked, he removed his own clothing and flipped on the shower lever, waiting until the temperature was to his liking before coaxing her into the shower with him.

Lukewarm water cascaded down on Sam's face, washing away the heat and sweat, dousing her in a stream of coolness that made her shiver with delight.

His hands were gentle as he washed her, his voice a low, dark rumble, as raw as the storm outside as he murmured his praise of her body, of how much he loved to touch her, the things he wanted to do to her, the things he wanted her to do to him.

Sam absorbed it, like parched soil soaking in the water streaming down. His concentrated attention, the earthy promise behind every brush of his fingers. The dark delight of his voice.

He made love to her in the shower, lifting her and setting her back against the tiled stall. She braced herself on his slick shoulders as he wrapped her legs around his

waist. Time stood still as his fierce gaze settled on hers.
"You're mine."

She touched his mouth, traced his strong jaw and felt
that same primitive fierceness well up in her. "And you
belong to me."

His eyes flared, his chest expanded, and she felt the rub
of his chest hair against her sensitive breasts, the hot
nudge of his naked sex between her legs, and then he was
pushing inside her, his entry difficult because she was still
swollen and tight from the last time. "You won't leave
me again. I want you living in my house, sleeping in my
bed. And when this is over, we're going to get married."

"Yes." Sam didn't see much point in denying what
she wanted so much. The simple act of declaring her love
had cut the ground from under her feet. She couldn't hide
from Gray anymore. She loved him. She would walk
through fire to be with him. If she had to be separated
from Gray while he was in terrible danger, then she would
do that, too, no matter how much she feared for his safety.

He penetrated her increment by slow increment. She
was sharply aware that he hadn't sheathed himself this
time, either, and that she didn't want him to. Heat flushed
her skin. The sense of fullness was utterly delicious; she
felt poised, on the brink, held firmly in his grasp, yet
holding him inside her. He was so powerful, and yet she
contained him and ultimately eased him in a physical act
that made even the strongest man vulnerable. Maybe she
would never have all of him, never have the certainty of
his love, but at least she had this.

She felt the deep prod of him snug against her womb,
and then gasped as he withdrew, then surged back into
her. The storm was pulsing both inside and out. Gray held
her tightly in his grasp, the powerful flex of his hips and

torso dictating the rhythm as they stood beneath the warm cascade.

When it was over, he dried them both and carried her back to bed, sliding in with her and immediately covering her with his body. She felt his intent, knew what he was doing and couldn't deny him. He was making sure of her, holding her beneath him—physically dominating her in an act as old as time. She didn't protest, but gloried in the fact that he felt he had to be sure of her when she was the one who wasn't certain. In his very domination he gave her the security she needed. As he gently entered her again, she lifted herself willingly to meet the slow, careful invasion, offering him the reassurance of her body in return.

He hadn't said he loved her, simply that he wanted her, and that would have to be enough for now, because she loved him so completely that there was no choice. She knew what it was like to love and lose, to have no one.

All the important relationships in her life had been marked by death: her parents, her aunt and uncle, her grandfather, the baby she had conceived with Gray. Now Gray was entangled in a ritualistic, vicious dance with death, and she didn't think she could bear it.

"Don't you die on me," she said in a voice that was little more than a husky whisper. From somewhere she found the strength to lift her head and press her mouth to his damp shoulder.

"I won't die." He raised himself enough that she could feel the delicious chill of the sweat that had sealed them together evaporating from her skin, see the implacable set of his jaw, the narrow, intent glitter of his eyes. He moved his hips, and her breath hitched in her throat. He dipped, his teeth fastened on the tender join of her neck and shoulder, making her arch helplessly into his next gliding thrust.

"I won't die," he repeated. "I'm coming back for more of this."

Chapter 13

The phone rang. Gray climbed from the bed and strode into the en suite bathroom to retrieve his phone from his pants pocket. When he reappeared, all the lazy warmth had faded from his expression. He was once more the grim, cool warrior, his emotions locked beneath the iron grip of a control she was only now coming to understand, and fear.

He left the room, naked, to complete the conversation. When he came back, Sam knew that this time he was leaving.

There was the sound of a vehicle, followed by a sharp knock at the front door.

"Carter." He swore softly. "Damn his hide. Why couldn't he be late for once?"

He leaned down and kissed her, his black gaze possessive. "We still need to talk, but there isn't time. I've taken too much time as it is."

Sam sat quietly, propped against the pillows, a sheet

draped across her breasts, while Gray pulled on his pants and shirt, then went to let Carter in.

When he was gone, she picked up her sadly crumpled clothes and tossed them in the laundry basket in the corner of the room. She noticed the absence of her panties and quickly freshened up, then dressed in jeans and a shirt from her case, before padding barefoot to the bedroom just off the kitchen, where they'd made love. She couldn't bear the thought of Carter perhaps choosing this bedroom, walking in and finding her discarded underwear on the floor.

She found and stuffed the lacy scrap in her pocket, and was on her way out the door when she heard Gray talking to Carter in low tones, his voice little more than a rumble. Sam paused just short of the kitchen door, pleasure humming through her at the velvety cadences of that deep, hypnotic drawl. Just the sound of his voice made her tighten up inside, the delicious languor of lovemaking giving way to a soft burst of heat that made her breath catch.

Gray was her lover, and he wanted to marry her. She could already be pregnant.

Joy welled, threatening to overflow the bounds of her natural caution. There were hurdles to overcome before they could be together, she couldn't fool herself on that score.

She hadn't yet told him about the baby she had lost.

Gray was possessive, territorial; he wasn't going to like it that she'd kept the pregnancy and miscarriage from him. The fact that *he* had cut her out of his life wouldn't come into it. Crazy as it seemed, as strong as he was, Gray needed her, needed the reassurance of her complete capitulation.

It would have to wait, just as she would have to wait

for an emotional commitment from Gray. She didn't like leaving the situation unresolved, but they had no choice.

Words began to filter through her dazed absorption, then entire sentences. Gray was discussing a change of plan, a plan that had included her. She had served her purpose, and now he wanted her out.

Sam went still inside. She had been set up. Used as bait in a trap to capture Harper, but her usefulness was now over.

She had become a liability. A distraction.

A small sound forced its way from her throat. Her arms banded across her stomach. She wanted to curl around the pain, lock it in tight. She had just spent the day making love with Gray. She had told him that she loved him, and even though he hadn't committed himself in the same way, a part of her had hoped.

Sam stumbled down the hallway. A side door beckoned, and she pushed her way outside, standing in the shelter of a broad patio, gulping in mouthfuls of damp, fresh air. She'd once likened her past relationship with Gray to a roller-coaster ride. That was exactly how she felt now, as if she'd just climbed off a wild ride and was still finding her legs.

The rain had slackened off to a misty drizzle; the sun was breaking through the cloud in places. Already steam was rising from the smooth emerald lawn, wreathing the tiled patio and pool.

The door creaked behind her. She knew it was Gray before she turned her head.

His expression was guarded. "You heard?"

She nodded.

"I can explain," he said quietly.

A small shudder wracked her. She was tempted to say, "I'll bet." She wondered how he would try to manipulate her this time. Sex had been very effective, but even if she wanted to, she didn't know if she could make love again today.

"If you don't mind," she said, stepping down on to the wet lawn, "I don't want to hear it right now."

"Dammit, don't clam up on me!"

Her pulse jumped as she heard him come after her, but she wasn't going to run. There was nowhere to go, anyway.

He caught her hands, shackling her wrists gently but firmly. "Come inside, Sam, it's still raining and you're getting wet." His voice was pitched low, the entrancing roughness a cajoling purr that somehow still managed to seduce her senses.

She jerked against his hold. "Don't you dare try and *soothe* me."

He was barefoot. He hadn't bothered to fasten his shirt, and it hung open, clinging transparently to his broad shoulders where the misty drizzle had dampened the gauzy fabric. Diamond droplets of moisture were forming on the dark hair covering his chest. Not so many minutes ago her breasts had nestled against that rough pelt. She could see small red marks on his skin, marks *she* had made.

Her cheeks heated. Carter had to know what they'd spent the last few hours doing. All of Gray's people probably knew. No doubt it had been in the *plan*.

His hands tightened briefly; then he released her. "I'm sorry you were upset by what you heard. I used you, but I couldn't see any way around it unless I kept away from you, and that wasn't an option. I'd stayed away for seven years, I sure as hell wasn't staying away for another seven."

"You don't have to explain," she said remotely. "I

understand why you did it." Even if it hurts that I'm way, way down on that cold list of priorities you have, she said to herself silently. Even if it demonstrates that I may never be first on that list. "Did you organise the photographers?"

He inclined his head.

"The clinch looked good. It went well with the headline."

"The clinch wasn't planned."

"Just convenient. And the seduction scene? Can you tell me our relationship has nothing to do with setting this trap?"

"No," he said curtly, "because our relationship has everything to do with it. You were already at risk. Harper had a file on you. It was inevitable that the second he knew we were together, you would join me at the top of his hit list. I've done what I've had to do to keep my family safe—to keep you safe." His voice dropped, roughened. "And that was no seduction scene. You wanted what happened as much as I did. I've never needed a woman the way I need you. I meant what I said, Sam. I want you with me. I want to marry you. If you don't want any part of that, you'd better say so."

In that moment Sam wished she could say just that, but she couldn't. The unadorned truth was that she wanted any part of Gray that he was willing to give her.

The singular strength of that notion was like a cold wave slapping her in the face. She loved Gray with a depth and intensity that stunned her. If she could have only a small part of him, then she would take it. She accepted in that moment that he would probably never love her as she wanted him to.

Sam closed her eyes. "You want everything."

"Yes."

The risk, the shattering vulnerability, of her position shook her. If she had been stripped bare and staked beneath the merciless glare of the midday sun, she couldn't have been more defenceless. He was asking too much, but it was already too late. She loved him, and she hurt.

But what did she have to lose? she thought fiercely. She knew the terrible events that drove Gray, the long years he'd isolated himself from the people he cared for most—from the life he should have been living—in order to protect them.

She was one of those people.

That streak of ruthlessness had probably kept him alive in places and situations she could barely imagine; it was an essential part of the man she loved. Even though she was bruising herself against it, she couldn't wish it gone.

She lifted her chin and met his gaze coolly. "I said I loved you. That hasn't changed, nor is it likely to. I'll go to Sydney, move into your house, I'll even marry you if that's what you really want—"

"Sam—" He stepped toward her.

"No! Don't stop me. I haven't finished." She swallowed against the husky rawness of her throat. "There's something I need to tell you, before you go and do whatever it is that you do. Before you go and risk yourself and maybe get killed. You asked me why I left you all those years ago. I only gave you half the truth." She paused, dragged in an aching breath. "I was pregnant. I lost the baby at four months. I miscarried."

Pregnant.

Of all the reasons for Sam to run from him, that one had never occurred to Gray.

Just the thought of Sam pregnant with his child made him weak inside. Then he remembered the day he'd seen her in the park—that had been months later, and there had been no sign of a pregnancy then.

He swore softly, his hands curling into fists to keep from touching her, from demanding to know more than that bare statement. She would fight him if he so much as laid a finger on her; he knew that as surely as he knew he had to reach past this new barrier.

Another wall, another damn mystery. She hadn't told him, not one word, not one hint that they'd made a child together. She'd chosen to shut him out of the most intimate of bonds. His hands clenched into fists. If he'd known...

If he'd known, what then?

Gray sucked in a deep breath, trying to ease the tightness still banding his chest. He was still having trouble grasping the enormity of what she had hidden from him. *A baby!*

The concept shook him. Sam had been pregnant with their child. His child.

Yet, even now, she hadn't wanted to tell him. She had given him her body, agreed to marry him, but still she was blocking him out. Even though he was doing the same to her, through sheer, cold necessity, it made him furious that she could close herself off from him so easily. He felt like a thirsty man in the desert gifted with a handful of water, yet even as he lifted the water to his mouth, it slipped from his fingers, sliding away no matter how hard he tried to hold it, and his thirst, barely slaked, raged on.

"I lost the baby," Sam repeated in a flat voice. "I wanted her so much."

More than she'd wanted him.

Again Gray had to restrain himself from touching her, demanding more than the distant grief in her eyes. It made him crazy to know that she had needed him, but instead of reaching out, she had run from him. Sam's grief was like a punch in the place that used to house his heart. She had buried their child with only her aging, sick grandfather to buffer her against the loss.

"Dammit, Sam you should have told me," he said flatly. "I should have been with you. You should have let me help you. *Me*. Not anyone else. If I'd known, I would have married you then."

"And what?" she challenged. "Stashed me in your house and left me alone for seven years while you went off and hunted your brother's killer?"

Gray's jaw tightened on a pulse of fury and despair. For the first time he allowed himself to wonder if the hunt for Harper had been worth it, if he hadn't simply created more damage by trying to bring his brother's killer to justice. How much more would they have to lose before it all ended? "Promise me you'll never keep anything like that from me again."

Sam heard the hurt threading Gray's rough voice. "I didn't mean to keep her from you," she said quietly. "I always intended to tell you, but then I miscarried. When you didn't show I assumed that for you our relationship had ended the moment I left. There didn't seem much point in telling you about the baby."

Sam studied Gray's face, the light and shadow etching his features so that they seemed chiseled not from stone, but from the very essence of life. There was nothing remote about him now. She realised with a jolt of searing regret that he would have loved her child, *their* child. She had hurt him. Until she'd seen his grief it hadn't occurred to her that she could do so. "I should have—"

"No," he said roughly. "No more regrets. The past has taken enough." His hands settled on her upper arms.

"It's nearly over, Sam. Just a few more days. If I know you're safe with my family in Sydney, I can finish this without having to worry about your safety."

Sam stiffened. "I'll go to Sydney. I'll be safe, but you won't be." Even though she knew the question was useless, she still had to ask it. "Why does it have to be you, Gray? Why can't someone take your place like Farrell took mine?"

He picked up one of her hands, which she absently noticed was knotted into a fist, and enclosed it in his warm grip. "You look so fierce," he whispered, "like a cornered tigress. Maybe you do love me."

"Answer my question."

He released her hand. "Harper is my mistake."

"So you're the only one who can fix it." Her fists thudded into his chest, and he trapped them there. "It wasn't *your* fault! Harper was the one who pulled the trigger."

"I didn't pull the trigger," he agreed flatly, "but I may as well have done. Jake and Rafaella died because of *my* carelessness. Their future, the family they had planned, died with them. Instead of a wedding, my family had to endure a double funeral. But I was still alive. Do you know how that felt? I *wanted* to live, I was glad to be alive, and Jake was dead because I screwed up."

As if a veil had been ripped aside, she saw the grief and fury that ate at him, consuming him piece by piece, even as he strove to overcome his feelings with the relentless hunt for Harper.

The coldness, the remoteness, had become necessary for Gray simply to function. His body carried the scars of the battle he still fought, but those scars were as nothing when compared with his inner wounds. He was clenched tight around that hurt, held in thrall to pressures that would crush a weaker man.

His strength and will took her breath, made her ache inside with the need to ease the burden. He had hurt her, but his pain was beyond bearing. "You can't bring Jake back." Her mouth twisted in bittersweet memory of her own struggle with death. "He's gone. You can't reach him, and he wouldn't thank you for putting your own life on hold for him. Jake loved you. He would want you to *live,* not spend your life trailing death.'

Gray flinched. "The cold fact remains that when Harper was moving in on the family I'd sworn to protect, I wasn't doing my job well enough to stop him."

Sam drew a startled breath. "You were with me." Her stomach clenched with cold dread. "Is that why you walked away from me in the park? Because every time you looked at me I would have reminded—"

"No." His voice was hoarse. "If you understand only one thing about this whole twisted mess, it has to be that I've always wanted you."

But he had chosen to keep her separate and apart from the most traumatic event of his life. He was closing her off from what she needed most—him—and stashing her neatly out of the way, where she could be safe.

Sam pulled away from Gray's hold. He loved his family, and he had loved his brother. She understood that emotion very well, just as she understood his fierce depth of loyalty, but she was only just coming to understand the rest.

Gray blamed himself for those deaths.

The blood drained from her face, leaving her feeling chilled, slightly dizzy in the hot sunlight that now blazed down. The sheer force of his will had dismayed her, but now she could see exactly where the iron had been forged.

And that didn't change her wild need to protect him, both from the external dangers that had already scored his flesh and altered his voice, and from the shadowy internal danger that she was only now beginning to understand. He was a master at closing himself off, at walking away. In some ways they were terribly alike, except that she had learned, finally, how empty walking away could be.

The necessity that drove his actions was clear, but that didn't change the central problem. Gray had only ever talked about want and need, never love. She had to wonder if the very iron that tempered his will hadn't also encased his heart.

"Oh, yeah," she said softly. "I understand. Completely. You're so big and strong, you have to take the whole weight on your shoulders. Well, lighten up, Lombard! How could you—or anyone—have guarded against a man like Harper? By your own admission, he's stalking your family! If he hadn't killed when he did, he would have bided his time and killed later. Read the papers! Watch the evening news. These guys make the headlines on a regular basis. If you had kept Jake and Rafaella safe, who would he have got on a second attempt, before you finally realised what he was all about? Tell me who might have died in their place? And who would have got the blame for it?"

Chapter 14

After Gray left, it was eerily quiet. Sam unpacked, then made herself a sandwich. Carter had moved his gear into one of the bedrooms and was now out in the garage checking something to do with alarms.

Her hands shook as she sipped an ice-cool glass of milk to help the small bite of peanut butter sandwich she'd just swallowed go down. The tremor was half exhaustion and half a growing tension over what she knew she had to do before she turned her life completely over to Gray.

Doggedly she worked her way through the sandwich and the milk, and gradually the tremor subsided. The food steadied her, easing the faintly sick feeling in her stomach.

She was leaving tomorrow. Gray had organised her flight before he had left. It was close to Christmas, so he hadn't been able to book a seat on any of the airlines, because they were all full. That hadn't been a problem. Gray was a Lombard; he had simply chartered a private jet. Carter would fly with her to Sydney, then return to

Auckland once she was handed over to whoever was assigned to bodyguard her.

Tomorrow she would meet Gray's family, make her home with them while Gray stayed here and...

She went cold at the thought of how many times he must have put himself in harm's way, as he was doing now. A stubborn part of her couldn't believe that everything would turn out all right, that after all this time there would be any kind of a fairy-tale ending.

She gave herself a mental shake. This was the kind of thinking that had sent her running once before. Loving Gray might terrify her, leaving the Royal, her friends, everything she knew and had clung to, might hurt, but even hurting, she wasn't willing to go back.

She took a deep breath. In order for her to go forward, there was one thing she had to do. Alone. Without Carter dogging her footsteps—or perhaps vetoing her decision altogether—without the possibility of the presshounds finding her and uncovering the most private piece of her past. Something she should have done a long time ago. Gray hadn't left her time for much in his light speed schedule; if she was going to act, it had to be now.

Just the thought of what she had to do made her heart race. She wasn't foolish enough to discount the risk she would be taking, even if she knew that risk to be minimal. When she had unintentionally eavesdropped on Gray's plans for her earlier on in the day, she hadn't missed Carter's relief at being released from what he termed "babysitting" duty when Sam was eventually handed over in Sydney.

No one knew where she was, except Gray and his men. If anyone *was* watching her, they would be watching the policewoman at the hotel.

Methodically Sam rinsed her dishes and placed them in

the dishwasher, then wiped up the crumbs she had made, forcing herself not to hurry, to keep her movements controlled—if she gave way to the panic that beat inside her, Carter would know something was wrong, and he wouldn't let her out of his sight. When the kitchen was clean, she went in search of Carter's truck keys, praying he didn't have them on him.

He had left his truck keys on the dresser. She slipped them into her pocket. Next she collected her handbag and stored it in a cupboard in the kitchen, where she could grab it quickly on her way out. She scribbled a note informing Carter that she would be back in a couple of hours and left that in the cupboard with her handbag. She would leave the note in plain sight on the table when she left.

When she had done everything she could to ensure a speedy exit from the house, she hunted amongst her belongings for a couple of old T-shirts she wouldn't miss and jammed them down into the S-bend of the toilet bowl until they were out of sight. She washed her hands, then pulled the flush until water spilled over onto the tiled floor. When she was satisfied that the situation looked dire enough to keep Carter occupied for the few minutes it would take her to make a clean getaway, she went to find him.

Sam slipped into the kitchen while Carter was unblocking the toilet. After grabbing her handbag, she anchored the note beneath a glass on the dining table and walked quickly to Carter's truck, which was parked in the drive. Her heart was pounding, and her mouth was dry. The truck was pointing toward the garage doors, which meant she would have to reverse out. Ruthlessly she forced that complication to the back of her mind. Reversing would slow her down, but she would manage.

She climbed into the cab, jammed the keys into the ignition and pulled the door closed as gently as she could. Her feet didn't reach the pedals.

Frantically Sam searched for the lever that would adjust the seat and eventually found it. Heart still slamming so hard in her chest that she could actually hear it, she propelled the seat forward until she could comfortably reach the accelerator. There was no sound from the house, but as a precaution she locked the truck doors, then turned to study the stick shift.

She was momentarily bamboozled by the twin set of gears. It was a four-wheel drive truck. She had never driven a truck, let alone a four-wheel drive.

For a moment her brain simply wouldn't work. She was used to an automatic shift; it had been years since she had driven a stick shift, and she had never driven anything as big and unwieldy as this extended-cab truck. Taking a deep breath and praying she was doing the right thing in leaving the smaller lever completely alone, she chose the larger of the gear-shifts and checked that it was in neutral. Whispering another prayer, she turned the key in the ignition.

The truck engine jumped to life, turning over with a vibrating rumble that made her shoot another glance at the house. Carter would have to be deaf not to have heard that!

Awkwardly she depressed the clutch and set the gear in reverse. As she was backing out, the front door of the house burst open and Carter sprinted toward her.

Sam stamped on the accelerator. The truck shot out into the empty suburban road. She braked, then wrenched the gear stick into first. The truck jerked forward, almost stalling.

The flat of Carter's hand hit the window. "Sam!" he roared, and jerked at the door. "Dammit, let me in!"

He was reaching into his pocket. He pulled out a set of keys. The set she had found in his room must have been a spare!

Sam cast him an imploring glance and shook her head. They were travelling down the street, but slowly. She didn't want to hurt Carter, but she wasn't going to let him in, either. She pumped the accelerator enough to make the truck leap forward.

Carter's fist thumped on the window; then he was left behind, keys in his hand. Sam sucked in a breath and accelerated down the street. The truck felt heavy, unwieldy, as she rounded a corner. She hauled on the wheel, barely missing a dark blue sedan parked on the side of the road. She was sweating, her heart racing, reaction shuddering through her in hot and cold waves.

Shoving hair from her face, she wound the window down and gulped draughts of cooling air. It had been worse than she had thought, but she had done it. She felt ashamed at the deception, the worry she was going to cause, but it was only for a couple of hours. She liked Carter and regretted pulling Gray's wrath down on his head, but this was one issue she wouldn't, couldn't, budge on.

In just a few hours she would be leaving everything she knew, walking into a future that was at best uncertain, and she didn't know when she would be back. She would do whatever it took to make her relationship with Gray work, give up whatever she must. She would fit in with *his* family, but not without cost.

What she had to do now would be painful and very,

very private. She had to cut loose of the past—relinquish ties that had defined her life from childhood. She had clung to the grief as a way of holding on to her family. As long as she felt pain, they were *real*.

It was past time to say goodbye to her family, her baby, to finally accept that they were gone and she was on her own—utterly alone in the world except for a man who might never allow himself to feel anything for her beyond the searing physical attraction that presently bound them—and she couldn't bear for anyone to witness that moment.

Gray found Jack in the dining room of the Royal, arguing with Milly about the cracking plaster. He had taken his jacket off, his tie was jerked down, and his sleeves were rolled up. His hair was tousled, as if he had been running his fingers through it repeatedly.

Gray had never seen Jack actually argue before, although they'd had plenty of "discussions." He had never seen Jack lose his cool over a building before—a column of figures maybe, but not a building.

Milly leaned closer, practically stabbing his chest with her finger to make her point. They were nose-to-nose, toe-to-toe, and Gray decided that what they were arguing about was incidental to what was really happening.

Jack spotted him and jerked back from Milly, a flush darkening his lean face.

Gray killed any hint of a smile as he met Milly's incensed gaze. "Mind if I steal him from you?"

"He's not mine," she said shortly. "And if he was, you wouldn't have to steal him, I'd give him to you. Gladly."

Milly turned on her heel and stormed from the room.

Jack let out a breath. He looked hunted. "What's wrong now?"

"I want you to alter the construction schedule of the new hotel. We'll go ahead with the plans, but start construction where the parking building is first. Eventually we'll knock it all down, but instead of doing it all in one hit, we'll do it by degrees."

"I'm almost afraid to ask why."

"So no one loses their accommodation, or their job."

"You want to keep the staff on?"

"Yeah. When the place is shut down they can go for training."

Jack's hunted expression turned incredulous. "You want me to make over the *staff?*"

"Why not?" Gray murmured. "We have the technology. We can make them better than before, stronger than before...."

Jack groaned. "We must be crazy. What is it about this place? You don't know the half of it. The barman has one leg and an eye that pops out when he gets excited. The chef used to be in the navy, and he's got more tattoos than he's got skin. He runs a soup kitchen for street kids when the restaurant closes. Hell, sometimes he even closes up early on paying customers so he can give our food away for free! The only reason we bought this joint was so we could knock it down. The odds are that it'll fall down before we ever bring the demolition crew in. Now look at what we're doing!"

"Maybe the chef would like to run a soup kitchen for real? Look into the tax write off—we're probably going to need one anyway. And, Jack?"

Jack groaned. "This is gonna be bad, I just know it."

"Did you know the fourth floor used to be called Belle's Palace."

"Yeah. Some hooker used to hang out there."

"Sam likes the idea of that hooker." Gray gauged Jack's frustration level and decided to sweeten the pill. "Milly probably does, too," he said blandly. "Baroness Belle, her name was. Why don't you get hold of that fancy architect who bills us six figures every time he picks up the phone and make him work for his money? I think he should investigate the history of this place and incorporate it into the new design, maybe use some of the original materials."

Jack sank back in his chair and jerked at his tie, which was already badly askew. "Have you any idea what doing that kind of thing costs?" He grunted in resignation. "I suppose you can afford it."

Gray had a vivid mental picture of Sam's desolation when he'd said they wouldn't be repairing the roof, her blank expression as he'd driven her to the safe house, the stark sense of betrayal she couldn't hide when she had realised he had set up this whole situation. Her grief when she'd told him about losing their baby.

Frustration and a deep-seated inner fear filled him because he had to walk away from her *now,* when there was still so much unresolved between them. "I can't afford not to do it."

Jack slumped in a chair and morosely pulled his tie down even further. He looked like he'd been dragged backward through a haystack. "I know what you're saying. There's something about the women in this place— they're beautiful, but mouthy. Every time Milly looks at me, I feel knee high to a slug."

"That high?"

"Okay, then, an ant."

Gray had just showered and changed into fresh clothing when someone knocked on the door to his suite. He shrugged into the shoulder holster and a jacket, checked the clip on the Glock and holstered it, then went to answer the door. The restless sense of urgency he hadn't been able to shake eased slightly when he recognised Sadie Carson.

"Have there been any more break-ins?" she demanded.

Gray's gaze sharpened. "What break-ins?"

"Well, I'm not talking about that sleek devil who shinnied up my drainpipe last night. Knew he was one of yours right off. Sam had a break-in a couple of weeks ago. Thought you would already know about that, since you're so hot on security.'

A cold trickle of sensation travelled down Gray's spine. Every hair at his nape lifted in animal-sharp awareness of danger. "No," Gray said from between his teeth. "She didn't tell me."

So that was why she had locked up so tightly, with not even a window cracked to let in a breeze. He hadn't questioned the stuffiness of her flat, because at the time it had pleased him; he had wanted her securely locked in.

Frustrating as it was, one of the things that had always attracted him to Sam was that cat-like, walk-alone independence; he could identify with it, because he was that way himself. She didn't cling or demand, and she had no problem telling him when to back off. But in this instance, he wished she had told him instead of coping alone with a situation that must have alarmed and frightened her.

Sadie glanced down the corridor, as if afraid of being overheard, then leaned in closer. "If I were you, I'd keep an eye on that Leroy," she said bluntly. "He was pumping Addie for information about that policewoman you've got posing as Sam. He's up to something."

Gray didn't bother asking Sadie how *she* had found out

so much. Those two old ladies were all over the hotel and so sharp they didn't miss a trick, even though the take-over of the hotel had provided a convenient smokescreen for the substitution. Sam was supposed to be sick and confined to her flat while Jack took over the day-to-day running of the hotel. Officer Farrell was supposed to stay out of sight as much as possible. The bulk of their sur-veillance was directed at Sam's quarters, because that was the logical place for any attempt to happen. Staff who had daily contact with Sam had been given a sanitised version of events, just enough to keep the hotel running smoothly and to scotch rumours.

He fastened his gaze on the whipcord lean woman who was waiting patiently for his response. ''What do you know?''

Sadie's expression was satisfied. ''I followed Leroy. He met a man in one of those fancy little wine bars two streets across. I've seen the same man in here once before, about the same time you arrived. He's medium height, medium build, brown hair, no distinguishing features ex-cept for a gammy arm—the left one, and too much co-logne. Calls himself Soames.'' She snorted in disbelief. ''May as well have called himself Smith.''

The unsettled feeling in Gray's gut, the prickling at the base of his neck, resolved into certain knowledge.

Harper was here.

He had been here all along, and he was watching them.

Fear slammed into him like a mailed fist, shaking him to his core. If Harper had been watching, he knew where Sam was.

Gray hardly noticed when Sadie said a brisk goodbye and strode away.

Sam. She was in danger. And he had put her there.

He didn't know how Harper had done it, how he could have penetrated the operation so swiftly or so deeply.

A low curse grated from his throat as everything fell into place. Harper hadn't penetrated the operation, he had been following his *own* strategy, and he had formulated that strategy the same way Gray had, with gut instinct, knowledge of his opponent and simple logic.

They had both known Sam was an important link, and they had both used her to arrange the confrontation each had hungered for, for reasons that were as different as night and day, yet as alike as darkness and shadow.

Harper had always been coming after Sam. He had homed in on her with the unerring instinct of a predator, unable to ignore the opportunity, the simplicity, the sheer perfection, of using her to lure Gray in.

There was a bleak symmetry to that reasoning, a sense of coming full circle. Seven years ago Gray had gone after Harper in the mistaken belief that he was holding Sam. The bastard would no doubt enjoy the irony.

He slipped his mobile phone from his pocket, but before he could dial, it buzzed.

"Carter," the caller identified himself. "She's gone. Took the truck and left."

Gray swore. "How long ago?"

"About thirty seconds. If I could reach my ass, I'd kick it. She had it all planned, blocked the toilet up with a couple of T-shirts, then, while my head was in the john, she swiped my spare set of truck keys and took off. She left a note on the kitchen table saying she'd be back in two hours."

Gray's hand tightened on the phone. He wondered what else could go wrong. "I think Harper's here," he said curtly. "And that he knows about the safe house. Get out—now."

It was Carter's turn to swear.

Gray thought coldly and quickly, running through everything he knew about Sam, her habits, the people she knew. She was completely isolated except for the Royal and the people who lived and worked here. He knew she wouldn't come near the Royal. That left one place she was known to frequent. The cemetery.

Instantly he knew that was where she had gone. Another small piece of the puzzle that was Sam fell into place—too late. She had told him about losing the baby, but he hadn't been able to see beyond his own fury that she'd run from him, that she hadn't even let him know she was pregnant. Their baby would be buried at the cemetery.

No wonder she had spent so long staring at those gravestones. She had a lot more grieving to do than he had ever imagined. "Get out of the house and phone your new location in to Ben. I'll send him out to pick you up. West will stay here to give Farrell back-up. I'm going after Sam. I'm pretty sure she's gone to the cemetery. I'll call Blade and let him know what's happening. And, Carter...watch your back. If the man I just had described to me *is* Harper, he's been here all along. The bastard got here before we did."

He strode through to the bedroom they had turned into a temporary operations centre. West was seated in front of a sophisticated array of surveillance equipment, methodically checking each of the security cameras and maintaining communications with the SAS unit and the police team. Tersely Gray told West what he'd just learned, leaving him to mobilise the teams. They would have to split the operation between the Royal and the cemetery, just in case he was wrong about Harper.

As he loped down the stairs and out into the car park,

he could only hope that Sam had gone to the cemetery. And that the man Sadie Carson had described wasn't Egan Harper.

Sam parked the truck, locked up and pocketed the keys.

The cemetery drowsed under the weighty heat of the early-afternoon sun. The warm scent of freshly cut grass combined with the scents of honeysuckle and roses as she picked her way among the graves to the corner plot. Two mynah birds squabbled in a nearby oak tree, almost drowning out the distant crunch of gravel as a car, followed by a van, pulled into the parking lot.

Sam didn't recognise either vehicle. With a sense of reprieve, ridiculous under the circumstances, because she knew Carter hadn't been able to follow her, she touched her parents' gravestone. The stone was slightly grainy in texture, encrusted with lichen and warm with the heat it had collected from several hours of exposure to the sun. Tears sheened her eyes, blurring the bare facts engraved into the stone, facts that had changed her life when she was barely seven years old—too young to lose her parents, and too old to ever forget them. But the grief she felt was distant, more a sadness for what the child she had been had had to go through.

Gramps' grave was still mounded, the stone bright and fresh, warm to the touch, too, and as sharply cut as his humour had been. Her fingers drifted over the smooth surface, and she found it within herself to smile. Gramps had clocked up eighty-two years, and he hadn't wasted one of them. He had been ready to die, even if Sam hadn't wanted to let him go. She could see now that she had been selfish, trying to hold on to him when, in the most natural of cycles, his time had been up.

He had known, she realised wryly, but he had let her

have her way with treatments that he had said in his gruff voice were, "No use, just throwing good money after bad." It had been his final gift to her, holding on so that she could feel that she was winning, if not the war, then a small skirmish against death.

The baby's grave was different. Her hand shook as it settled on the stone, and all the strength went out of her legs. She sank to her knees on the soft, damp ground, uncaring that her jeans were soaking through. This good-bye was the most difficult.

She pressed on the stone, both hands now, and the impervious surface mocked her, as it had always done. Her baby had been tiny, delicate—in legal terms, she had never lived. In human terms, the abyss between life and death had never seemed so broad and dark and complete.

Gray signalled and changed lanes, accelerating past a lumbering goods truck. Traffic was light, but that didn't change the fact that he was still long minutes away from the cemetery. Every instinct he had told him that those minutes were important.

He thumbed the redial on Blade's number for the third time, relieved that this time he didn't get an engaged signal. Impatiently he waited for the pick-up, his gaze sweeping the highway signs, searching for the off-ramp.

Sam's summation of events kept hammering at him. She had said Harper had always wanted revenge and would find a way to take it no matter what. Was she right? Had he got too close to the situation and failed to see what was under his nose? If he had protected Jake and Rafaella better that day, would Harper have picked out some other member of his family? His mother and father? Blade? His baby sister, Roma?

He frowned, deliberately shutting the thought from his

mind. One fact was inescapable; it hadn't changed for seven years and it wouldn't change until he had Harper under wraps: this was his damn mess, and it was his responsibility to clean it up.

Blade finally picked up, answering with a terse, "Yo."

Gray supplied his location.

Blade swore. "I've just finished talking to West. We're en route. Wait for us."

"Have you got clearance?"

"Not yet."

Gray let go of a breath. The operation was a joint one with the police, which worked smoothly as long as it was just surveillance, but for the SAS to operate as a counter-terrorist force on home soil, they needed an actual transfer of authority. Without a positive ID on Harper, the bureaucratic decision making would take time he couldn't afford. If they'd spotted Harper on any of their surveillance cameras, there would be no problem. "I can't wait for you."

"Dammit, Gray. Don't do this."

Gray spotted the off-ramp sign and signalled the turn. "There's no time, and I'm armed. If they've got her, I have to try."

Chapter 15

A heavy hand landed on Sam's shoulder. She was hauled to her feet, her arms wrenched behind her back, and something cold and hard was pressed against the side of her neck.

A gun, she thought with an odd sense of inevitability as a second man stepped into view.

"Very touching," he said.

Sam stared into blue eyes as bland as that light, cultured voice and shuddered. She had no doubt that this was Egan Harper. He wasn't a big man, barely making average height, but with the sinewy leanness of a striking snake. "Harper."

"Ah. I see you know who I am. How excellent. I recognised *you* immediately. You photograph extremely well, Miss Munro. I should know. I've taken several over the last few days. May I say that none of the photographs do you justice. But then, Lombard always did have good taste in women."

A third man came into sight, and Sam's stomach sank. Even without the gun, the odds were heavily against her. She lifted her chin and glared at Harper. "Why are you doing this?"

The man holding her stroked the gun coldly along the curve of her throat.

Harper smiled. "I don't believe you're that naive. Lombard and I are old adversaries, but, as entertaining as the game has been, it had to end sometime."

She pulled at her captor's hold on her wrists, and he replied by exerting enough pressure to make her cry out.

Harper lifted a hand, and despite her resolve not to show fear, she flinched. But he didn't hit her; he stroked her cheek. "Such lovely skin. A pity to damage you, but I will if I have to. Think about it, Miss Munro. Now, shall we proceed to the church? Not for a wedding, of course." He chuckled at his joke, then checked his watch. "We don't have much time to waste. According to my sources, Lombard should be here in approximately five minutes."

Sam was pushed across the lawn, up the steps and into the dim interior of the church. Harper issued terse instructions, not bothering to glance at her as he did so. One man was going to watch the car park, Harper would position himself in the cemetery and she was to be kept in the church with the third man as a guard.

One of the men had an accent; he was lean and dark with bad acne scars, and it was a good bet that he was South American. The man guarding her was a New Zealander. Compared to Harper and the man with the accent, he was solidly built, his arms and shoulders brawny. Evidently he was at the bottom of this particular power pyramid—hired muscle, as opposed to the hardened professional that the Latin man appeared to be. It also appeared that he didn't like being left out of the action. His movements were edgy, his muddy hazel eyes simmering with resentment.

The enormity of what was happening hit her. Up until now, she had been too shocked to do much more than react to instructions. She didn't doubt she was behaving exactly as they expected her to do. They were all armed, and she had never even handled a gun.

Within seconds, Harper and his man had melted away and Sam was left with Hazel Eyes.

He gestured with the gun while craning to look out the small window. "Into that room," he ordered tersely.

Sam walked into the dim little side room he indicated, taking note of the contents. It smelled musty and appeared to be a storage place for hymn books and odds and ends of furniture. Light struck through a narrow window, catching swirling dust motes.

A meaty hand shoved her between her shoulder blades, sending her stumbling against the wall at the rear of the room. Sam spun to face him. Her captor, evidently convinced that she was completely cowed, slipped the gun in the waistband of his jeans and pulled some kind of cotton wadding and adhesive tape from his pocket.

Sam settled her back firmly against the wall and mentally counted off the seconds as rough hands stuffed her mouth with the wadding.

She knew what these men were going to do to her, that they wouldn't let her live. This was her own stupid fault. She had slipped away from Gray's security and in doing so had exposed him to risk. Harper was counting on Gray coming to her rescue, as he'd done seven years ago, and Gray would do it. He would risk himself for her again, walk into the trap, and she couldn't allow that to happen.

Grimly she eyed her Neanderthal captor, mentally calculating his weight, the quickness of his reflexes.

When he peeled a length of tape from the roll, she took a deep breath through her nose, grabbed handfuls of his shirt and jerked downward with all her strength as she dropped to the floor.

He grunted, his head smacked into the wall, and he crumpled. Sam crawled from beneath his buckling frame, spitting out wadding as she went, but his dead weight sprawled sideways and back, and he ended up slumped across her legs. Panic spiralled through her when she tried to scramble free and couldn't. She strained, and finally, with a twist of her hips, she managed to drag first one leg free, then the other, but she'd wasted valuable seconds and he was already groaning, stirring.

Sam staggered to her feet, reeling to one side, sending a three-legged chair crashing to the floor. Her hip caught on the corner of a table. Hot pain burst up one side as she stumbled to the door.

A roar sounded behind her. Adrenaline slammed through her system, anaesthetising the pain in her hip as she ran from the dim shadow of the church into blazing daylight. She could hear Hazel Eyes coming after her, the heavy pounding of his boots on the wooden floor. Her spine crawled, and her skin tightened with anticipation and dread; she expected to feel a bullet ripping into her flesh at any moment.

Time seemed to alter, slow, as she ran, almost as if she was an actor in a movie and somehow reality had shifted and she had got caught up in a slow motion sequence. No matter how fast she ran, it wouldn't be fast enough. Her breath was coming in choking pants. The residue of the wadding caught in her throat, making her cough, depriving her of precious oxygen.

"Gray!" she cried out, her voice husky and hollow

with panic, not caring who heard her or if she was caught again.

She opened her mouth to call again. Her gaze skimmed the vehicles in the car park as she ran, and the cry died in her throat. Gray's truck wasn't there.

A sense of futility gripped her. She had failed. She was too early. Gray wasn't here yet.

Something heavy hit her on the back of the head, sending her crashing to the ground in a shocked daze.

"Don't kill her, idiot!" a voice rapped out.

Hard hands hauled her into a sitting position. Her head spun sickeningly.

Harper swore virulently. "Help me get her back inside. Lombard's not here yet."

"Get your hands off her and drop your gun," a low voice commanded. Gray stepped into view, legs spread, both hands curled around the grip of a handgun.

Cold metal jabbed into the sensitive flesh just below her ear. An arm whipped around her neck, jerking her head back so that pain jagged through her skull again.

"What's she worth to you, my friend?" Harper said softly. "If you shoot me, she dies. There's also the little matter of Nico."

"That would be the dark, lean guy with the acne scars."

"Ah," Harper said. "A pity. He was a good man. We seem to be at an impasse. What's it going to be, Lombard? Me or the woman?"

Gray didn't take his eyes off Harper. "Let her go, Egan."

"Five seconds, or I'll make the choice for you."

"You know it's me you want, and alive. That won't happen if she's harmed any further. Take her into the church and leave her there, and I'll lay down my weapon.''

Harper smiled. ''Nice try, but you're a lousy liar. You're obsessed with the lovely Miss Munro. You always have been. I'm only sorry it took me so long to realise that fact. We could have got around to this charming little scene so much more quickly. Drop the weapon, or I'll blow her brains out.''

Silence stretched, taut and loaded with menace.

Harper began to count.

With a blank look on his face, Gray tossed his weapon on the ground.

Harper's henchman retrieved the gun. Sam was pulled to her feet and half dragged, half herded toward a dark van. For the second time she found her mouth full of the foul, moisture-sapping wadding. Tape was strapped across her mouth, and her hands were tied with cord.

Gray's jacket was stripped from him, his gun removed along with the holster. He was searched, his pockets emptied, and the contents, including his phone, tossed on the ground. His hands were tied behind his back. As soon as Gray was vulnerable, Hazel Eyes stepped forward and punched him in the stomach.

He drew his arm back for another punch, and fury boiled up in Sam. She launched herself at Gray's attacker, only to be summarily jerked back by Harper. Gray grunted as the punch landed. His head lifted and their eyes met— his calm and remote. He shook his head, an infinitesimal movement, and Sam had to swallow her rage and anguish.

Gray had walked into this trap of his own accord, to save her. He was being beaten, yet still he was trying to give her reassurance.

''We don't have time for this,'' Harper snapped. ''Lombard has people following. Get them into the van.''

They were pushed in to sprawl on the bare metal floor
of the van. The doors were slammed and secured, and the
two men climbed in the front. Hazel Eyes, or Billy, as
Harper called him, was driving.

The van moved off with a jerk that threw her against
Gray. For several minutes the van careened along city
streets, and Sam had to brace herself as best she could.

Harper said something soft, his voice laden with threat.
Billy slammed on the brakes, and the van fish-tailed, tyres
squealing, before he reduced his speed.

They travelled for what seemed like hours, but it
couldn't have been more than three or four in the afternoon. There was only one stop, so the driver could relieve
himself at the side of the road. By late afternoon they
were winding their way through steep hill country. The
sealed surface ran out, and they bumped along on a dirt
road.

Billy uttered an oath and swerved, swearing about live-
stock on the road and the wet, muddy conditions. He accelerated, swore again and braked.

The van slewed violently, almost righted itself as Billy
corrected, then hit a pothole and went sideways across the
road and onto the grass verge. Gray flung himself over
her, the heavy weight of his body anchoring her in place
as the van bumped, lurched, hit a ditch and careened over.

They rolled, tumbled, then everything went black.

When Sam came to, she was lying on the grass, still
bound and gagged. Every bone in her body was aching,
and she could taste blood in her mouth. Her head was
pounding; one arm and a shoulder throbbed. She turned
her head. Gray was propped against a tree, watching her.
The van was only metres away, teetering on the edge of
a drop-off, its roof and the side that she could see crumpled in. There was no sign of Billy. Harper was seated

directly opposite, a gun trained on the both of them, a knapsack slung on his back. He didn't seem to have a scratch on him.

"Ah, you're awake," he said as smoothly, as if she had just risen from an afternoon nap.

He noticed the direction of her gaze. "Billy ran away. He was bright enough to realise his usefulness had just come to an end. It seems I overestimated his driving ability and underestimated his cunning."

He came to stand over her, and she tensed, certain he was going to hurt her in some way, perhaps shoot her. He did neither. He bent and tore the gag from her mouth.

"Sit up," he commanded.

Sam gasped at the burning sensation and spat the sodden wadding from her mouth, coughing and choking as she drew a startled breath of air. Harper jerked her into a sitting position, and she felt the cold kiss of a blade against her skin. Alarm punched through her again, successfully clearing the dizziness the abrupt movement had caused, but he hadn't cut her, he had cut the cord binding her wrists.

For long moments she couldn't move her arms. They had been kept in the same position for so long that they were frozen in place. Inch by inch, she first straightened them, then brought them to her side, working her protesting shoulder and elbow joints.

The sight of her hands shocked her. They were swollen, a reddish purple, and her wrists were ringed with dark bruises. She clenched her jaw as the pain burning in her joints speared down her arms and into her hands, a hot rain of needles through her veins, as circulation reasserted itself.

"Take Lombard's gag off."

Sam's head jerked up at the order.

She shuffled on her knees to where Gray sat. She lifted her hands to Gray's face, trying to ignore the excruciating sting of pins and needles. Her fingers felt useless, weighted, too clumsy to accomplish the task of grasping a corner of the tape and tearing it loose from his mouth. She caught the end of the tape. The very act of squeezing her fingertips together made sweat break out on her brow. She gritted her teeth and pulled, trying to be as gentle as she could.

Eventually the tape was off, and she turned to glare at Harper. "Are you going to free his hands?"

Harper smiled mirthlessly. "Why would I want to do that? Get up. Thanks to my friend's poor driving skills, we're going to have to walk the rest of the way."

Harper gestured toward the dark, impenetrable rain forest edging the road. "Not exactly the kind of exercise you're used to Lombard—the going is a little rougher than a golf course." He smiled in apparent delight at his quip, but Sam noticed he walked a wide circle around Gray as if, even bound and gagged, he feared the bigger man. He brandished his weapon. "Oh, and if you're thinking of playing hero, the Sig has fifteen rounds, as I'm sure you must remember from your time with the military. The first round has your charming fiancée's name on it."

Gray tracked Harper's every movement, fury burning with a cold flame deep in the pit of his stomach. Harper jerked his head at the bush line, indicating that Gray was to go first.

Gray hadn't been knocked out when the van rolled. He had seen Billy grab a black briefcase and run. Harper had almost gone crazy, but he had been dazed by the crash and slow to react. Billy had got away. Evidently there had been something in the briefcase that was either valuable or that Harper needed badly, because he was still agitated.

Cold satisfaction put an icy lid on Gray's temper as he eased to his feet, wincing at the pounding in his head. The bastard was savvy enough to make him break the track through the bush, while he strolled behind Sam with his gun at her back, using Sam as insurance to keep him in line. Gray would have to expend double the effort that Harper did, but he would get his chance.

Harper had made two mistakes.

The first was an error that Gray himself had fallen head-long into—that of underestimating the opposition.

The second was in not killing him outright.

Gray caught Sam's gaze, holding it until she was out of sight behind him, trying to infuse her with some level of comfort, instead, she gave it to him. *She smiled.* The smile was shaky and incredible. She was pale and bruised, probably suffering from shock, but her chin was up, and her heart was in her eyes.

She loved him.

The simple truth of her love hit Gray hard, triggering a moment of disorientation so great he actually stumbled. She *loved* him, and for the first time he allowed himself to feel the depth and completeness of that love, let the soft flames lick at the darkest corners of his soul. It brought something inside him to painful life—a part of himself he'd thought had died with Jake. The agony was sweet and complete, complicated by the threat of imminent death that Harper carried with him like a second, darker shadow.

They could die. Sam could die, and Gray wouldn't allow that to happen. He couldn't.

He loved her.

The magnitude of the deceit he had practiced on himself stunned him. He had always loved Sam.

A shudder coursed through him. The sweetness of the

simple act of breathing had never seemed so wondrous, or so threatened.

For years he had lived on the edge, risked himself time and again, evaded death by a hairsbreadth. He had even worried Blade, who spent more than a little time on the edge himself. Now he wanted life with a fierceness that poured like hot lava through his veins. And he would have it. With Sam.

He moved his hands experimentally. Billy hadn't tied him as tightly as he could have done, but the knots he'd used were good; he would have difficulty freeing himself. His hands were swelling, but with judicious flexing he was able to assist the flow of blood, staving off complete numbness. His face was caked with dried blood from a cut over his forehead. The cut was little more than a scratch, but he could imagine how bad he looked. He was banking on it.

For the past half hour he'd hung his head and not responded to Harper's taunts in an effort to project defeat and a half-dazed state. It had worked, probably because Harper had made the basic mistake of discounting his military service, writing him off as a commissioned officer in some cushy desk job.

SAS Command used "plausible deniability" to its fullest extent. Their covert people couldn't be traced through any available official records. That shadowy secrecy was now Gray's best asset. He'd fought in more hellholes than he could comfortably remember, his specialty was jungle warfare. Harper couldn't have chosen a better arena for this final showdown, because final it would be. Gray's last active codename had been a little dramatic for his tastes—he would have been happy with a letter from the Greek alphabet and a number—but that kind of call sign was recognisably SAS. Perhaps the code name some desk-bound career officer had given him was prophetic: Jaguar.

A ripple of black humour surfaced. For Harper, he was willing to go for a little drama.

For Harper, he would be one with the jungle.

Chapter 16

Nightfall came quickly in the bush, heralded by the swiftly fading light beneath the dark shroud of the forest canopy, the abrupt cessation of birdsong, and the mournful hoot of moreporks readying for the hunt.

Despite the subtropical lushness of the forest, there were no snakes, no large natural predators aside from wild pigs to worry about. The danger lay in the terrain: steep, bony hills covered with a slippery layer of decomposing vegetation, streams and waterfalls lined with algae-slick boulders, sudden drop-offs and massive granite cliffs.

Gray kept a steady pace, his ears attuned to Sam and Harper, who were directly behind him as they climbed ever upward. With every step he had to use his shoulders to push aside tree branches and fern fronds. His face was repeatedly stung by whipping branches, and sweat channelled into the myriad small scratches, making them sting.

They came out on an old abandoned logging skid, a raw flattened area gradually being reclaimed by a forest that was now apparently protected from all logging. A break in the massively tall stand of ancient kauri gave a sweeping view of the dark valley they'd spent the last few hours traversing. There was a glimpse of a road slashed out of the wilderness, and higher still the regular lines of a building—a cabin, perhaps—straddling the curve of a broad spur.

Harper pointed at the distant hut. ''That's where we're going.'' He waved his gun at the centre of the skid. ''But this is where we stop for now. Lombard. Over there!''

Gray walked to the centre of the skid, his gaze coldly assessing as he studied Harper, fear and rage eating at his restraint like acid searing through metal.

The gun jerked in Harper's hand, as if he had actually considered pulling the trigger, then hauled himself back from the brink. ''Sit down,'' he snarled.

Gray sank down, not shifting his gaze from Harper. If he did, he would look at Sam, and that would probably break his heart. Worse, he would do something stupid and get them both killed.

Harper sank onto a tree stump on the perimeter of the skid and eased off his pack. He didn't look good. He was limping and sweating profusely, and his skin was greyish, his eyes fever-bright.

Gray gave in to the compulsion and allowed his gaze to settle on Sam. She was hollow-eyed, weaving with exhaustion, but she hadn't collapsed—she was watching Harper, her hands clenched into fists, and Gray tensed.

''Sam,'' he warned in a voice so rough it sounded like gravel breaking.

Sam flinched, startled by the sound of Gray's voice when she had been so concentrated on Harper. Her eyes fastened on Gray. She had been watching his back for hours—watching his muscles bunch with exertion, his clothes plaster to his skin with sweat, the trickle of blood from the cut on his head. With every step she had taken, at times pushed along by the sharp nudge of that gun on her spine, rage had built inside her. Harper had *hurt* Gray.

But even hurt and bound, vitality had radiated from him, flowed in the sleek shift of those muscles, the relentless rhythm of the pace he'd set.

And Harper wanted to kill him.

Somehow she couldn't be frightened by her own death, but Gray's... Anguish and fury pumped renewed vigour into her tired muscles. Her hands balled into even tighter fists. Harper would have to go through her first.

"Sit down, Sam," Gray warned softly.

Sam was caught and held by the low, even timbre of his voice, the staggering force of his will even across the desolate width of the clearing. His reassurance was a tangible thing, as real as if he'd reached out and touched her. Slowly her hands relaxed. Wearily she reached up and wiped sweat-dampened tendrils of hair from her face. There was something else in Gray's gaze, something that made her heart leap with wild hope.

Harper tossed an empty water container at her feet, rudely breaking the spell. "She doesn't have time to sit down." He jerked his head in the direction of the small stream that rippled between steep, fern-covered banks. "Fill that with water, then you can start a fire. And don't try anything stupid," he warned gently. "If you do, I'll shoot Lombard, then I'll shoot you."

Sam stared into Harper's burning gaze as she retrieved the plastic container from the sparsely grassed, hard-packed clay pan of the clearing. If he wanted a fire, that meant they would be spending the night here. Relief flowed through her, as cool as the water she could glimpse drifting over the shallow, broken stream bed below.

The hut they were heading for lay high up in the hills, too far to reach before nightfall, which meant they had the hours of darkness to catch him off guard. Anticipation made her heart pound. An opportunity would present itself; it had to. She would bide her time until it did.

The first stars appeared, wheeling in a sky washed from buttery gold on the horizon to the clearest, darkest, midnight-blue. The air had taken on a refreshing edge, already heavy with condensation as the temperature cooled.

Harper motioned with the gun. Sam started down the bank, clutching the container in one hand and using her free hand to grab at the coarse ferns to hold herself steady. The brief moments of rest seemed to have destroyed her coordination. Her legs wobbled with exhaustion, and the clay bank crumbled beneath each cautious step. Her heels stung, and she noted numbly that the blisters that had formed over the last couple of hours must have lost their skin. She half scrambled, half fell the rest of the way down the bank, ending up hard on her knees in the water.

Sucking in a shaky breath, Sam sat back on her haunches. Blood welled on one palm where she had cut herself on a sharp rock.

A sharp rock.

She stared at the bright well of blood, then down at the whitish, sharp-edged rock. The water was as cool as she had thought it would be, and it smelled delicious, laced with the tangy, woodsy scent of the bush. Her mouth instantly felt as dry as a desert; she longed for a drink. Harper had kept the water for himself through the long, hot afternoon, and she was dehydrated, but her need for water was instantly shoved aside in favour of another more urgent need. Survival.

Harper bit out a harsh phrase, and she hurriedly began filling the water container. In the same movement, she plunged her bleeding hand into the water and let her fingers close around the rock. It was slightly rounded where it nestled into the stream bed, narrow and jagged on top. As she got to her feet she scooped the rock up and slipped it into the pocket of her jeans, jerking her shirt from the waistband so that it concealed the bulge. She was wet to her knees and her shirt was splashed with water; surely he wouldn't notice the wet patch spreading down from her pocket.

Harper drank greedily when she handed over the water, then watched coldly as she gathered wood for a fire. When she had finished, he tossed her a lighter. He had several candy bars in the knapsack and proceeded to eat them while she tried to get the fire going.

After her third attempt, a small blaze flared up. Harper pushed the water container in her direction, indicating that she could drink first, then offer what was left to Gray.

Sam lifted the container to her lips. The water was cool and brackish and tasted like heaven. She took several swallows, careful not to drink too quickly or too much, then walked over to Gray.

His gaze was on her, dark and coolly assessing as she approached. Sam knelt, leaning close and angling her body so she could ease the rock from her pocket without Harper seeing what she was doing.

"You're limping," Gray said softly.

"It's noth—"

Harper reared to his feet and advanced a few steps, stopping just short of the fire. "No talking!"

Sam flinched, water spilled down Gray's chest, and the rock flipped to the ground with a small thud. Breathing fast, she tilted the container to Gray's lips, at the same time nudging the rock around where he could reach it with his hands. His gaze flickered as he drank deeply and rhythmically. When she glanced down, the rock had disappeared from sight.

Gray watched grimly as Sam returned to her crosslegged position several metres from him. The risk she had taken in bringing him that rock made him break out in a cold sweat. If Harper had caught her, he would have been merciless.

Harper didn't need Sam except as a prod to get Gray to do what he wanted while they hiked to the cabin. When they reached their destination, he would have no use for her at all. His eyes slitted with barely controlled fury as Harper brought out a length of rope and tied Sam's wrists and ankles.

Harper resumed his position. This time he sat on the ground, his back resting against the stump, his legs sprawled out in front of him.

Gray felt the jagged edge of the rock with his almost numb fingers, and suppressed a fierce grin. Turning the crude blade against the cord that bound his wrists, he began to saw, careful not to betray by even the smallest movement of his shoulders, what he was doing.

Dusk deepened to a crystalline blackness pierced by the subtle glitter of stars and the rich, full-bellied glow of a rising moon. Leaves shivered in a faint breeze, and a morepork drifted overhead, its call echoing eerily.

Harper tossed a piece of wood on the fire. Sparks leaped in the air as the flames curled hungrily around the new fuel. "Do you remember," he muttered harshly, "in the warehouse? I almost killed you."

Gray didn't reply. His shoulders ached from the sheer restraint of holding still while he continued to saw at the rope, and his swollen fingers burned with the exquisite agony of simply gripping the rock.

Minutes passed as he concentrated on sawing. His

hands were slippery with sweat and blood; he was slicing into his own flesh as often as he managed to connect with the nylon.

The rock slipped from his fingers. Sweat beaded Gray's forehead as he began to search with fingers that were growing increasingly numb, increasingly useless.

Harper got to his feet, his movements jerky, his breathing rapid. He strolled over to Sam.

"Son of a bitch," Gray snarled beneath his breath as he recognised the wildness in Harper's eyes and finally understood what was happening to the man.

Gray began working systematically through all his muscle groupings, flexing and releasing, improving the blood-flow, readying himself to spring if he had to. His window of opportunity would be small. He would have to get Harper off guard, then take him down hard and fast before he could use his gun or the knife he had concealed up his sleeve.

In close-quarter battle terms, it would be one wild-ass move, but in his favour was the fact that Harper wasn't stable. He had a habit, and he'd been separated from his supply. Cocaine, most probably. That would account for the paranoia, the shaking hands, the hay fever-like symptoms.

"So easy to kill," Harper muttered. "It's a wonder more people don't take it up."

Gray's jaw locked. "Any fool can pull a trigger. Why don't you pick on someone more your size?"

Harper swung toward him. "The bigger they are, the harder they fall," he snapped. "Do you know how long I've waited for this moment?"

"Seven years, at a guess," Gray drawled in a deliberately goading tone, relieved that he'd succeeded in drawing Harper's attention away from Sam. His fingers found the stone, and once more he clumsily forced the jagged edge up against the rope.

Harper advanced another step. The sudden rage drained from his face. "You've got balls, Lombard, I'll give you that."

"And you're a gutless weasel, even with a gun."

Gray heard Sam's swiftly indrawn breath. She was behind Harper now, and struggling to her knees, but Gray didn't dare take his eyes off Harper.

Harper lifted the gun, sighted. "I could kill you."

"Yeah, you could kill me, but that won't stop what's going to happen."

Harper rubbed fiercely at his nose, the gun shaking in his hand. "What are you talking about?"

Gray named a series of locations from Costa Rica to Ecuador and the upper reaches of the Amazon Basin, giving the precise map coordinates of every bolt-hole they'd raided, every arm of the terrorist network they had systematically destroyed.

Harper moved another step closer, the gun now held in a two-handed grip. The full moon had lifted behind him, outlining his head and shoulders, darkening his face so that his eyes glittered. "How do you know about those places?" he demanded hoarsely.

A section of cord gave way. Gray sucked in a breath, forcing himself to stillness while he tested his bonds. "I know about them because I was there. His voice dropped to a cool whisper, drawing Harper in closer, closer, as the other man strained to hear. "I got close to you, Harper. That day you killed that prostitute in Bogota, I almost had you then. How old was she? As old as your mother when she was pregnant with you?"

"What do you know about my mother?"

Gray flexed and tensed. The cord went slack, he eased

his hands free. He stayed in position, working his hands and fingers. Sam was on her knees swaying, her gaze fixed on Harper's back.

Gray suppressed a violent curse. She had risked herself by bursting out of that church to warn him. She was going to try something similar now. But if she distracted Harper, and he spun... "I know your mother didn't want you," he answered softly. "She was young and pretty and ambitious, and she married a British peer. She had another baby two years after you, only this one had a last name. I heard your half-brother came into his title a couple of months ago."

"That title should have been mine!"

"Is that why you killed Jake? He stumbled across your gun running operation, uncovered your half-assed attempt at building a terrorist empire from beneath a raft of paper companies. You couldn't stand being exposed by a man so similar to your legitimate half-brother."

For a moment Harper didn't seem to hear, then he jerked. "What?"

"Is that why you killed Jake, you son of a bitch?"

Harper sucked in a sharp breath and shook his head, as if disoriented. "What do you know about the prostitute?"

"Carmita Chavez. Eighteen, no dependants. Worked for a scumbag called Tito Garcia."

The gun jerked in Harper's hands; his voice dropped to a harsh whisper. "You can't know about her. Nobody knows, except..."

"The agent who's been dogging your trail for years, getting so close that sometimes he could almost reach out and touch you. Take a real good look, Harper, because I'm that agent—your shadow. Every time you looked over your shoulder, *I* was there."

"You can't be *him.*"

''Say the name, Egan. You know it almost as well as your own. You heard it whispered in bars and back rooms, from San Salvador to Quito.''

''Lombard,'' he muttered. *''I killed you!''*

''In the brothel? You didn't kill me, you killed your own man.'' Gray's voice flattened with contempt. ''Always screwing up, Egan. You screwed up again. Maybe you should look at kicking that nasty little habit you've got. How long's it been since you snorted your last line? The man who ran away from the van—Billy—he took your supply with him, didn't he? You must be hurting by now.''

''I don't *need* it!''

''What are the symptoms?'' Gray continued in a conversational tone. ''Although you don't have to tell me. You're shaking. You can hardly hold that gun straight. And you're sweating— I can smell you from here. Your nose must be on fire. I've heard that white powder eats you from the inside out.''

''Shut up!'' Harper lowered the wavering gun, centering it on Gray's chest.

''No!'' Sam surged to her feet and hurled herself at Harper's back.

Gray sprang, a hoarse cry ripping from his throat. Harper spun, already firing. Gray crashed into him, sending him spinning. The gun discharged again and again, the popping detonations distinct in the stillness of the night.

Gray rolled, surged to his feet and threw himself bodily over Sam, protecting her as best he could from the wild shooting. He didn't know if she had been hit. All he knew was that she was lying still beneath him. Too still.

The silence that followed was as deafening in its own way as the shots had been. The scent of cordite lay heavy on the air, sharply acrid against the richer, softer scents of bush and river.

Gray lifted his head, expecting to see Harper, the gun once more pointed directly at him. There was…nothing, nothing except the rustling of leaves, a distant curse, the sound of a crack—a branch breaking—something heavy sliding down a hillside.

Harper. He had run, blundering into the bush.

Sam moved beneath him, making an odd gasping sound. "You can…get off me…now."

For a frozen eternity Gray couldn't move; then he clambered off Sam. The flickering embers of the fire and the bright wash of the moon were enough for him to see the dark stain all down the front of her shirt. She tried to get up. He put his hands on her shoulders, pushing her back down. "You're hurt," he said hoarsely. "Stay still."

"Harper?" Sam drew another shuddering, gasping lungful of air.

Gray tried to unfasten her shirt, but his fingers were still swollen and clumsy. He was sweating, shaking, panic making his fingers even more useless. There was so much blood he couldn't see where exactly it was coming from. She was having difficulty breathing. He shuddered under the lash of a wild fear. He had goaded Harper, reeled him in, exploiting the unexpected advantage of his shakiness, driving him to the point where he would be vulnerable enough for Gray to try for the gun. Instead, Sam had made her move, and Harper had used the gun.

If Sam was hit in the chest, he wouldn't be able to stabilise her; he would lose her. The shoulder he could handle, the stomach, maybe, as long as nothing vital had been nicked….

Dammit, how could Sam ask about Harper when she…

"I'm all right, Gray——I'm…'' She gasped, struggling for air.

"Shh, don't talk,'' Gray said, trying to keep his voice low and soothing. Trying not to transfer his panic to Sam. "I'll take care of you, baby, just—'' She tried to roll away from him, impeded by the rope tying her wrists and ankles. "Dammit,'' he muttered, incensed. "Lie still!''

A button flew off, then another. He tore the shirt open and found…nothing. Nothing but gleaming white skin, tinted a pinkish shade in places where the blood had seeped through the shirt.

"I'm only winded,'' Sam gasped.

Gray stared at her in disbelief. He ran his hands feverishly over her torso, pulled her into a sitting position, untied her hands and stripped the shirt off altogether. Not satisfied with that, he unclipped her bra and tossed that aside. Her breasts were full and round and perfect, the centres peaking in the slightly chilly air, her flesh deliciously soft and cool against his hands.

Sam was still breathing jerkily. Her hair was a wild tangle, her cheek smudged with dirt, her eyes dark and faintly gleaming in the moonlight. "Find anything interesting?''

"Yeah.'' His hands tightened on the silky perfection of her breasts. He still couldn't believe she was unharmed. "I was sure he'd shot you.''

"He didn't shoot me.'' Sam reached out and touched his arm, and the clammy wetness of the blood streaming down. "You're the one who's bleeding.''

Chapter 17

Sam untied the rope at her ankles, slapping Gray's hands away when he tried to help. She surged to her knees. "Let me see," she demanded.

Gray barely glanced at his bicep, where a bullet had ploughed a raw furrow. "It's just a scratch."

Just a scratch. Sam's jaw locked up as she gently pulled his arm around so that the glow from the embers illuminated the wound. It was ugly, but the bleeding was already slowing. "Can you use your arm?"

"Of course I can use it." He pulled free of her grasp to demonstrate. "I'll tend to it later. We need to go. If Harper keeps blundering around in the bush like he is, with our luck he'll probably run in a circle and end up back here. And I'm pretty sure he's still got the gun."

"We're not leaving until I've bandaged your arm."

Gray ignored her, moving to get up.

Sam caught hold of his shoulders and hauled him back

down into a kneeling position. "Are you deaf? Don't move until I'm finished!"

He resisted. "You can bandage it later." Then, more gently, as if he'd only just noticed her distress, he said, "I'm all right, Sam."

"Says who?" Picking up her shirt, she put the material between her teeth.

"What are you doing?"

She jerked at the cloth, starting a tear, then ripped the whole arm off. She did the same with the other sleeve. "I'm finishing the demolition job you started on my shirt."

"Sam—"

"Shut up!" she said fiercely. "You saved my life twice today, and Harper shot you. Just a few more inches to one side and he would have killed you." She folded one sleeve into a pad. "Hold this over the wound."

Sam bound the pad in place as firmly as she could, then sat back to survey her handiwork. The bloody furrow was neatly covered by the ruins of her shirt. Abruptly the adrenaline that had bucked through her veins when Harper had aimed that gun at Gray's chest faded. She began to shake.

"Ah, Sam…" Gray pulled her close, pushing her face into the dark, muscular curve of his neck, banding his arms around her naked back, his arms and hands searingly hot in contrast to her skin.

Sam wrapped her arms around his waist and sagged against him, soaking in his heat, which she suddenly needed desperately. She was cold and exhausted. Shivers wracked her, rising from somewhere deep inside and rolling outward in deep, shuddering waves. Gray held her closer, rocking her gently, pressing on the small of her back and forcing her closer still, letting her absorb his heat. He felt and smelled delicious, hotly male, sweaty and *alive*. She could scarcely believe they were both alive.

She lifted her head, seeking his gaze. "I couldn't let him shoot you."

"So you tried to make him shoot you instead."

"I was distracting him. There's a difference."

"And you won't do it ever again. Not that I'm going to give you the chance," he muttered, easing her away from him, hands cupping her shoulders. "That's twice today you've nearly got yourself shot. Lady, you draw trouble like a magnet draws iron filings. Once we get out of here, I doubt I'll ever let you out of my sight again."

He jerked his T-shirt over his head and began dressing her in it as if she were a child and needed his help. "We need to go."

"What about your arm?"

"My arm feels fine. Now that you've bandaged it, I can hardly feel a thing."

"Liar."

"Yeah," he murmured, tilting her head back. "It stings like hell, but I've had worse." He bent and brushed her mouth with his, the touch soft and oddly sweet. "C'mon, baby," he coaxed, "on your feet. Harper left his pack behind. With any luck, he left you a candy bar."

Before they left, Gray did a quick search of the camp site, just in case Harper *had* dropped the gun. No such luck, although Gray did find Sam's bra. He picked up the delicate lacy garment, slipping it into his pocket before going to fill the water container in the stream. While he was about it, he washed the blood from his arm and rinsed his torso and face, ridding himself of dried blood and sweat and soothing his hands, which were still swollen and awkward. The wound on his arm was still seeping, but Sam's bandage had stemmed most of the flow.

His jaw tightened when he remembered the way she had flung herself at Harper's back in a desperate attempt to save him. Fury at the way she had risked herself mixed with disbelief and awe that she had done so. When he got her out of here, he wasn't sure what he would do to her first, shake her for giving him one of the worst moments of his life, or shackle her to his side so she could never scare him like that again. The breath hissed from between his teeth. As panicked as he had been, he had still noticed the way her breasts had looked in the moonlight, how they had felt against the rough skin of his palms.

Who was he trying to kid? he thought as he recapped the container and picked his way back up the bank. When they got out of here, there was only going to be one thing on his mind: holding Sam close and never letting her go.

Sam had laid the contents of the pack out next to the almost extinguished fire. Evidently it hadn't belonged to Harper but to the driver of the van, Billy, who had left it behind in his rush to escape with the briefcase, which had no doubt held a small fortune in cocaine. There was a driver's licence, a lighter, a crumpled pack of cigarettes and a grubby cell phone. There was also one candy bar left.

Gray tried the phone, then shoved it back into the pack. "We'll have to go higher before we can get a signal."

Sam split the chocolate bar with Gray; then he strapped the small pack in place, and they started cautiously into the night.

"Hold on to the back of the pack," he told Sam softly. "I don't want to lose you in the dark. We'll be going slowly. The last thing we want to do now is break our necks tumbling into a gully."

Gray could feel Sam's grip on the pack as a light resistance against his shoulders. They had only walked a few metres beneath the canopy of the trees when the transition from moonlight to darkness was complete. Gray stopped, reaching a hand back to steady Sam when she bumped softly against him. He could hear her breathing, still a little fast, and abruptly remembered those moments when they were stuck in the elevator. She had been frightened by the dark, but she hadn't said a word, simply endured.

He found her hand and squeezed it; she squeezed back. "Move closer to me," he said in a low voice. "We'll stay here until our eyes adjust."

She shuffled closer, slipping her arms around his waist and leaning into him. Gray remained motionless, waiting for his night-vision to kick in, using the time to listen for any sound that might indicate that Harper had somehow found his way back to them.

He didn't think it would happen. Harper had been barely capable of sustaining his two-handed grip on the Sig; Gray doubted his capacity to do more than stumble blindly through the bush, but he would leave nothing to chance.

The clarity of his senses increased until they were animal-sharp; outlines became visible, but he could have done with some night-vision goggles. It was as black as sin, and twice as dangerous. If they tumbled down into a steep gully, or walked over the edge of one of the sheer granite cliffs he had seen from the logging skid, it was game over, no matter what Harper did.

An hour later they stopped. They hadn't covered more than half a mile since leaving the skid site, but it would have to be enough. Gray sat down, propped his back against a tree, using the pack as a cushion, and pulled

Sam down between his legs and in close against his chest. "Try and sleep. We'll stay here until it gets light."

Sam's breathing gradually slowed, evened out. Gray felt it the moment she went to sleep, the warm slackness of her body pressing against his. A rough wave of tenderness swept him, and he cuddled her closer, trying to ease her awkward position so she would sleep better. They had made love, but they hadn't actually slept together yet. This was a hell of a place to start.

The almost forgotten intimacy of sleeping with a woman—with Sam—enfolded him, making him forget all his aches and pains, making him forget Harper was wandering, armed, through the forest, half-crazed from his cocaine addiction and as likely to shoot a tree as anything living.

With a distant feeling of incredulity, he felt himself sliding toward sleep, utterly seduced by the warm weight of Sam's head on his chest, the silky brush of her hair on his bare arm. As he drifted, lost in the relaxed, meditative state before true sleep, he became aware that something that usually happened right about now *wasn't* happening.

Relief shuddered through him. The stark images that had haunted these moments before sleep for years, making his muscles cord and his pulse pound, hadn't come. Instead his mind was filled with other images: fiercely protective blue eyes with a cat-like gleam; a delicately sensual face smudged with dirt and lit with a cool courage any soldier would envy; a sultry, stubborn mouth that only hinted at the passionate, stubborn woman inside. He should have taken note of that mouth seven years ago, because he knew now that it was going to drive him crazy in all the ways that mattered.

His final thought as he let his head rest against the rough bole of the tree was a pleasant one; if he was going to be haunted by anything, he couldn't have chosen a more alluring demon.

They moved on at first light, stiff and cramped, but surprisingly rested. Breakfast was cool water from a stream and a hurried wash.

An hour later they stopped for a drink on a rocky outcrop that offered a breathtaking view of the valley they had just walked through.

While Sam sipped the brackish water, Gray tried the cell phone again, grunted with disgust then slipped it back into the knapsack. "We'll have to go even higher to get a signal."

"What about Harper?"

A cold grin bared his teeth, and Sam suddenly had the sensation of time shifting, time lost. In the primeval bowl of the valley, they could have belonged to another, much more ancient, time. The sun slanted down, lighting Gray's torso with a radiance that burnished his skin to hot gold. With the makeshift bandage knotted around one gleaming bicep, the battle scars scoring his flesh, he looked both powerful and wild, and completely at home in this environment.

"Harper will keep. He won't be moving higher. He'll be panicking and walking in streams, trying to get out. When I can get a call through to Blade, he'll be able to pinpoint our position by triangulating our signal with the nearest repeater. All I have to do is keep the channel open and hope that our 'friend' Billy kept the batteries charged."

A few minutes later, Gray got a call through.

An hour later, the sound of a helicopter beat rhythmically, receded, then grew stronger.

Gray paused, his head up. "They're in," he said coldly.

An eerie silence fell, as if even the birds were waiting for the drama unfolding to reach its deadly conclusion. Time passed as they trudged ever higher. Finally they stumbled out onto the raw dirt road. A cooling breeze dispersed the building heat of the day and blew Sam's hair around her cheeks. Gray stood, silent and remote, a grim sentinel standing watch over the hunt below.

Sam sank wearily to the ground. Her legs felt like pieces of limp noodle, and her heels burned like fire. "You could have left me and gone after him."

Gray turned, and the controlled remoteness of his expression made her flinch. He *did* want to be hunting Harper. Maybe he still would.

Weariness washed through her. There was no maybe about it. Gray had been hunting the man for seven years; why would he give up now, when Harper was so close and so vulnerable? The hut was only a short distance away. Once he had her safe, he would go.

His gaze dropped to her feet; he studied them as if they fascinated him. "Take off your shoes," he said softly.

Sam blinked, for a moment unable to understand what he had said, because the words didn't fit what she had expected him to say.

Gray went down on his haunches beside her and gently unlaced and removed her shoes. She couldn't prevent herself from making a small noise as the first sneaker came off, rubbing her abraded heel. He held up first one foot, then the other, surveying the raw patches. He was silent for so long that she began to think he wasn't going to say anything. Finally, he asked, "Why didn't you tell me?"

"You didn't complain about your arm."

He was silent again—ominously silent, she decided.

Abruptly he swung her up into his arms, leaving the shoes where they lay. "Why should I expect you to tell me anything?'' he muttered, seemingly to himself. "You were so damned quiet, I should have guessed something was wrong.''

''It was only bl—''

''I don't care if it's blisters,'' he cut in, silkily soft. "I don't care if it's a broken nail. From now on, you will tell me everything that happens to you.''

Sam eyed the square set of his jaw. "That could mean a lot of talking.''

He drew a breath that sounded strangely impeded, almost strangled. "I should have carried you the whole damn way.''

''I'm too heavy.''

''One more word, Sam,'' Gray said from between clenched teeth.

Sam examined the cabin, which, according to the notices on the wall, belonged to the Department of Conservation and was now used as a goat culler's hut. There was a large flat area outside, with a windsock and ground lighting, which was obviously used as a helipad. No doubt that was why Harper had wanted the place as a hideout. The hut itself was small and compact inside, only one room, which contained four built-in bunks, a dusty table and chairs, and a crude counter with a large, chipped enamel basin that served as a sink sitting on top. There were no taps. Outside, next to the hut, Sam found a water tank with a tap at its base.

Gray had taken a cursory look inside, then strode back out to stand on the edge of the rough outcropping, staring across the valley. His eyes had been curiously blank, his expression, once again, remote. After his outburst on the road, Sam was confused. He was brooding and taciturn, snapping at every word she said, and she'd had enough.

If he wanted to go after Harper, she wished he would just go.

After opening several cupboards in the kitchen, Sam found various kitchen utensils, tin plates and mugs inhabited by dead insects, an odd assortment of freeze-dried and tinned food—obviously left behind by various inhabitants of the hut—a selection of can openers, a tiny solid fuel cooker and a rusted first-aid box.

She had just finished dressing her heels when a shadow darkened the door. She eyed Gray coolly. She hadn't expected him to come back inside; he had been so focussed on what was happening down in the valley.

"If you sit down," she said briskly, "I'll clean your wound."

To her surprise, Gray sat. Sam untied the bloodied bandage and peeled it gently from his arm. She drew a sharp breath. In the light of day, the bloody gouge on his biceps looked even more painful.

Gray's voice was infuriatingly calm. "It looks worse than it is."

Sam opened the first-aid box with a snap and extracted a miniature bottle of disinfectant. "Then you won't mind if I use some disinfectant."

He followed her movements warily. Sam decided to tip the disinfectant directly over the wound. She didn't want to risk introducing any more foreign tissue into the raw welt.

Gray's breath hissed from between his teeth.

Sam recapped the bottle and returned it to the box. "Since it's just a scratch, I won't attempt to stitch it."

His startled gaze connected with hers.

Sam eyed him levelly. "What's one more scar among so many?"

"You're angry," he said neutrally.

Her hands shook as she applied a dressing. "That man was going to kill you."

"He didn't succeed."

She fastened the bandage and stepped back to survey her handiwork. The white bandage glowed against the sleek copper of his skin, adding a dangerous edge to all that steely control.

"You can go now," she said abruptly.

Gray flowed to his feet. If he was in pain from his arm, he didn't show it, but instead of shouldering the pack and walking out the door, he came to stand in front of her.

"What do you mean, go?"

She gestured toward the door of the hut. "Out *there*. Where he is."

"Trying to get rid of me so soon?"

An incandescent rage filled her. She wanted to stop Gray, but she didn't know how. She didn't know what she had to offer that was more exciting than the cat and mouse game he played with death. She didn't know if what he felt for her had the strength to overcome that remote core of grimness that was such a part of him. He had brought her to safety, but he had done so out of duty; every step of the way, his attention had been on Harper. She understood his obsession; she even approved of it, despite the fact that it hurt her, hurt *Gray,* so much. "It's what you want, isn't it?"

His jaw shifted, and his expression darkened until she felt she was being drawn into him, drowned in black heat and loneliness. "No. That isn't what I want."

"Don't you need to phone someone?"

His dark gaze swept over her face. "Jack was right," he drawled. "Beautiful, but mouthy."

Sam's gaze narrowed. She had been used as bait, deceived, kidnapped, tumbled around in a rolling van, bound and gagged, frog-marched through a steaming rain forest by a madman. Her head hurt from who knew which bang it had received, and she had been scared to within an inch of her life by the amount of blood that had streamed from Gray's arm. He insisted the ugly gash on his arm was just a scratch. That was like calling the Pacific Ocean a puddle.

The cold-eyed warrior standing in front of her had done his duty by her. He wanted Harper. He would go after him.

She lifted her chin and eyed him coolly, preparing herself the only way she knew how for the hurt that would follow. The only defence she had left was her pride. "I told you before that I understand…what you need. You can send someone to get me when it's all over. I'll be perfectly safe here while you go after Harper. I don't need you to baby-sit me."

Gray watched the fierce gleam in Sam's eyes fade to that opaque blue that said the door had once again been slammed in his face. She was shutting him out, pulling back behind that wall of reserve.

The control he had been exercising for hours broke.

He had almost gone crazy when he had found out that Sam had probably fallen into Harper's clutches. He'd had to watch her risk herself for him not once, but three times: outside the church, by the van, then at the logging skid. She had trekked through the bush with a gun jammed in her back, her heels blistered and raw. She hadn't complained once. Gray was beginning to understand the depth and strength of Sam's will, and the uncomfortable fact that the woman facing him was just as stubborn, just as single-minded in her own quiet way, as he was. Now she was closing up on him, pulling that ladylike reserve into place as neatly as if she were rearranging the fall of her

skirt at a tea party. She was saying she didn't need him.
She was telling him to go.

The hell he would go.

Sam eyed Gray warily as he advanced on her. There
was something heated and reckless in his eyes, and his
jaw was set. Her confusion increased as he caught the
edge of her T-shirt and began pulling it over her head.
"What are you doing?"

"There's blood on it. It needs washing."

He tossed the T-shirt on the counter, then started working on her jeans. Sam automatically shielded her breasts
as he stripped denim and panties from her. "I don't understand."

When she was naked, he began undressing himself.
"You will."

He extracted what she recognised as her bra from the
pocket of his pants, before tossing them aside and strolling, naked, to the sink. He tipped water from the bucket
he'd brought in earlier over the clothes and began washing
them.

"You're wasting time," she said a little desperately.

He cocked his head to one side, and his lids lowered
lazily, shading the hot glitter in his eyes. "Bite me," he
drawled.

Suddenly the room was overheated and way too small.
Sam swallowed, wondering what he would do if she did
just that.

This obviously wasn't a good time to pick a fight with
him. He was edgy, and he was naked. They were both
naked. She glanced down, her gaze drawn against her will.

Gray snagged her gaze, holding it effortlessly as he
prowled toward her, the T-shirt in hand. When he reached
her, he began stroking the cool, wet cloth across her skin,

her breasts, cleaning the last remnants of his blood from her, she realised.

"I have more important things to do than go after Harper."

The movement of the cloth was unintentionally arousing. Or was it? A moan slipped from her lips as the cloth lingered on her breasts, and they tightened, her nipples peaking almost painfully hard. She was tired and bruised; all she should want to do was sleep.

Her breath released slowly, softly. "Such as?"

"Make sure you don't tackle any more terrorists. If you turn up at the altar with a bullet hole in you, my mother will have my hide."

The cloth glided down her belly, stroking, caressing, the gentle pressure sending tingling hot streamers of sensation through her.

"If I had wanted Harper," Gray continued slowly and deliberately, as if it was important that she understand every word, "I could have had him last night. I could have had him within half an hour, probably sooner. I'm good at that kind of thing. Do you understand what I'm saying?"

The cloth slipped between her legs. Her knees threatened to buckle. "You're very good at your job."

"Going after Harper's sorry butt would have meant leaving you, and that wasn't an option. I didn't save your life so you could rush off and try to get killed again the second I turned my back."

Gray tossed the T-shirt back in the basin and ran his hands over her arms. "I don't intend to make the same mistake I made seven years ago. I was young and arrogant, and I let you get away. Now I'm older, and I'm probably still arrogant, but I'm sure as hell not letting you out of my sight."

He bent and kissed her gently on the mouth. "I'm not much good at this stuff," he said, low and taut. "I love you, baby. I'm sorry it took me so long to figure it out, and I'm sorry you've been hurt, but I'll take care that nothing hurts you ever again." He eased her closer, dropped his forehead on hers. "I'm not perfect. I can't ever promise to be. I let Harper go for one reason, and one reason only: I wasn't capable of leaving you. In case you haven't noticed, ever since we got here, I haven't been able to leave you alone."

Sam stared, dazed, into Gray's fierce glare. "You've been outside."

"Yeah. Trying to keep my hands off you. It didn't work."

She shook her head, even more confused. *That* was why he had been so taciturn? "Why would you want to keep your hands off me?"

Gray's eyes narrowed. "Damned if I know. I thought you might be in shock, exhausted, bruised, traumatised…little things like that."

Sam fixed on the most startling thing he had yet said, the thing she couldn't quite believe yet. "You…*love* me?"

His hands came up, cradling her face, rough and warm and gentle. "I'm crazy about you. I always have been." He dipped and kissed her with a sweetness that made her ache.

Sam wound her arms around his neck, stunned and still not quite believing she'd heard right. She wanted him to love her so much it was hard to take in that he actually did. A tremor rocked him as she fitted herself against him.

He lifted his head. "If you don't want to be made love to up against the wall, you'll have to let me pull some mattresses on the floor. I can't fit on one of those sardine-sleepers.''

He dragged all four squabs off the narrow bunks, lined them up on the floor, then pulled her down with him.

Sam snuggled against him, mindful of his sore arm. "Are you sure you should—"

"Have I got a pulse?" he growled.

Sam slipped her palms up over his torso, feeling the heavy slam of his heart, then down further to a piece of his anatomy that also had a pulse but was hotter, and much smoother, much silkier, than his chest. "I don't think you're in any danger of suffering from heart failure."

A rough sound was torn from his throat as she cupped and gently stroked him. "I'm not wearing a condom again. Do you mind?"

Sam gave him a bemused look. "Who, me?"

Gray reversed positions, kneeing her legs apart and settling himself between them. "Yeah, you," he said deliberately, "and nobody else. I don't have a condom with me, and even if I did, I still wouldn't want to wear one. I don't want to be separated from you by anything. I want to feel *you* around me, and I want to know that I could make you pregnant." His voice dropped, shook slightly. "We didn't use a condom the last time we made love, so you could already be pregnant. I want you pregnant, Sam. If you don't want my baby, you'd better say so now."

Why would she want to argue about what she had always wanted? Sam smiled, tears blurring her eyes at the same time. Sheer happiness burst inside her, rippling outward on a shimmering wave that swamped the empty places inside her. All she had ever wanted was a chance at happiness, a beginning, and this was it. "I'm not arguing."

"Good." His voice was tight with strain. He didn't know if he could have stopped now in any case; his control was debatable.

Drawing in a breath, he began to move, gloving himself with exquisite slowness, every muscle corded as he held himself in check. It seemed incredible that they had made love only the day before. It felt like a week, a lifetime, ago. Relief shuddered the length of his frame as he withdrew, then drove deep again. Sam clung to him, lifting her hips to meet each thrust. Her response made his throat tighten. He couldn't bring the baby they had lost back, but they had both had their season of grieving. It was time, past time, to move on, and he was fiercely eager to do so. The sheer hope in the simple act of lovemaking flooded him. It was life, pure and simple—the opposite of death—and he gloried in this simple act of mating, and of creation.

Sam was his. He would never let her go. They belonged together, and he was prepared to do whatever it took to convince her of that fact. If he had to keep her beneath him for a month, he would do so. The thought made him light-headed, and he instantly decided they needed a honeymoon. A long one. At least a month.

Sam arched and clung, and he felt the moment she shivered and turned to sleek, hot liquid around him; then the dark magic took him, too, slamming into him with all the power of an iron fist, ripping a hoarse cry from his throat as he plunged deep and poured his very essence into the sweet, warm crucible of her womb.

They had just finished a meal. Sam opened the window over the counter a little wider and tossed the basin of water she'd used to rinse their plates out onto the struggling shrubs outside. The T-shirt she was now wearing flapped around her thighs. It was still slightly damp, and so large it was like wearing a tent, but it was all she had.

"Come here," Gray said lazily from their makeshift bed.

Sam padded back toward him, a delicious glow suffusing her, anticipation shivering down her spine. They had made love, gone to sleep, then made love again.

Gray was sprawled on the mattresses, and finally decent now that he'd pulled on his pants. His bronzed torso, the dark hair clinging to his chest and muscled abdomen, was primitively beautiful in the mellow light of late afternoon.

Sam smiled, eluding his grasp. "Don't think you're going to get treated like this all the time."

"I cooked."

"You poured hot water on some dried lumpy stuff and waited for it to congeal."

A slow smile curled his mouth. "Like I said, I cooked."

He held out his hand again, and this time she took it, still giddy with delight that he had said he loved her, that he had stayed with her, that he intended to stay with her.

He pulled her down beside him, not taking his alert, heavily lidded gaze from the door. A dark shadow coalesced in the opening. The shadow was dripping.

Sam tensed. Gray's arm stroked down her arm in reassurance. "Blade," he said softly.

Sam had never met Gray's younger brother before, but she would have recognised him anywhere. They were of a similar height and build, and had the same high, exotic cheekbones and deep-set black eyes, the same rock-hard jaws and sinful mouths. Blade also had a ponytail and a rueful edge to his smile.

He acknowledged Gray; then his gaze cut straight to

Sam. "You any relation to that crazy old lady at the Royal?"

"Are you talking about Sadie or Addie?"

His mouth curled whimsically. "Yeah."

"In that case, yes. They're honorary aunts."

"Figures." Blade transferred his gaze back to Gray. "Does that mean they'll be related to us?"

"'Fraid so."

"Hell's teeth."

Gray pulled Sam closer. "Is it done?"

Blade's expression turned icy. "Yeah. Crazy son of a bitch did himself—ran right over a cliff screaming something about some big wild cat coming after him. Have to say, I'm damn disappointed. I was looking forward to doing the honours. They're air lifting the body and the team out, then they'll come back and pick us up."

Gray drew a deep, shuddering breath and pulled Sam close.

She knew then that much of his composure had been the steely restraint that would always be a part of him. She wouldn't want that to change; she loved him because he was so strong. Perhaps subconsciously she had always been so attracted to him specifically because of his iron will, even though it had kept them apart for so many years. She needed a strong mate, one who could give her reassurance that he would survive, even against terrible odds. He had given her that reassurance, and he had given her the gift of choosing her over Harper, choosing love and life over the obsession that hunting the terrorist had become. Nothing could completely obliterate the purgatory of the last seven years, but they had made a start—a beginning.

It would take time, but now they had all the time in the world.

Sam heard the distant beat of rotor blades.

"Here come the cavalry," Blade drawled. He consulted his watch. "With any luck, we'll still make it home for Christmas."

"Christmas? What's the date?" Sam asked, then shook her head in disbelief when she got her answer. "It's Christmas Eve."

Gray's arms tightened around her; she sensed his smile rather than saw it. "Merry Christmas, baby," he rumbled lazily. "Turn your head so I can give you your present."

"What's my present?"

The smile glittered deep in his eyes as he bent to her mouth. "Me," he said simply.

Epilogue

Gray had one minor detail to clear up before they caught their flight out to Sydney.

Leroy was just closing up when Gray stepped into the claustrophobic confines of the trendy black and white salon. Leroy was dressed to match his elegant little bolt-hole in a loose black shirt tucked into white linen trousers. Jewellery winked from his ears. A medallion lay against the V of smooth tanned chest that was on display.

Leroy eyed him uneasily as he shoved items into a sleek, black briefcase. "I'm just closing."

"I don't want a haircut."

Leroy went still, then tried for a professional smile. "I heard on the news that there was some terrorist guy on the loose. Something to do with your family. Did they catch him?"

"Yeah. We caught him. No thanks to you."

"Me?"

''That's right, Leroy, *you*. I heard you were keeping company with a certain gentleman. A Mr. Soames.''

Leroy's golden tan faded to a sickly yellow. ''Mr. Soames was the terrorist?''

Gray knotted his hand in Leroy's pristine collar and jerked just enough that he had to come up on his toes. ''Mr. Soames,'' he repeated neutrally. ''Harper was his real name. Egan Harper. He's wanted in a dozen countries for various crimes, including rape and murder. You told the bad guy that the woman managing the Royal wasn't Sam.''

Gray felt the bulge of Leroy's Adam's apple rippling against his knuckles as he tried to swallow.

''I didn't know,'' he gasped as Gray tightened his hold.

''No,'' Gray agreed smoothly. ''You didn't know, but you managed to cause trouble anyway.''

''He—he really was a bad guy?''

''The worst.''

''A killer?''

''He liked knives, Leroy. He was a real artist. If I had time, I could show you pictures of just how artistic he could be. I've lost count of the number of people he's killed.''

Leroy's eyes went wide. ''He could have killed *me*.''

''You're not out of danger yet. *I* could kill you.''

The Adam's apple did its little trick again. Disgusted, Gray let Leroy's collar go.

He crumpled back against the wall, hands automatically smoothing his clothes, setting his medallion to rights. ''Is Harper locked up?''

Gray toyed with the idea of letting Leroy think that Harper was still on the loose, and that he might be looking for Leroy next, but he would learn the truth soon enough.

A sanitised version of Harper's demise would be in the news.

"He's dead."

Relief flooded Leroy's features. "Then he can't get me."

Gray's eyes slitted. "You don't get it, do you, Leroy? Sam nearly died because of the information you supplied Harper."

Leroy finally seemed to realise where the real danger lay. He licked his lips, edging sideways. "So...what do you want?"

Gray could think of a number of things he wanted quite badly, but Sam had made him promise to give up violence. He was trying, but Leroy just wasn't helping. "I want you where you'll never come into contact with my wife again. I don't want her to see you, or even remember you. I don't want one single thing to bring back the horror of what she has just been through. That means you have to leave town."

"This is my business. I can't leave!"

"How much?"

Leroy's eyes narrowed. He named a figure.

Gray's jaw clenched, the violence was looking better and better. "I wouldn't be too greedy, Leroy," he said softly. "You've stepped on a lot of toes recently, Sadie and Addie Carson's included. Those two ladies have a real fondness for Sam, and they aren't exactly the retiring kind. If they thought you were being difficult, I wouldn't put it past them to leak your name to the press."

Leroy shuddered and quoted a lower figure.

Gray smiled coldly. "My solicitor will be in touch. I don't care where you move. After this, I don't want to ever so much as think about you again. Just make sure you move to a city that doesn't have a Lombard hotel in it and is never likely to have one. And the next time you get the urge to get involved in international terrorism, Leroy,'' Gray said, letting his voice drop to a menacing purr, ''squash it. You're better at blue rinses.''

Ten months later

Gray Lombard was asleep.

Four-year-old Bunny McCabe gave her uncle Gray a considering look. He was lying on the grass, in the sun, in her back yard, and he just didn't have time to be sleeping. He had work to do.

She poked his chest. One eye opened a slit, and she giggled. ''You're hairy.''

Gray peered up at the chubby four-year-old. Her dark pigtails swung silkily against her cheeks, and her McCabe-blue eyes were fixed on him like a couple of lasers. ''Your dad's hairy,'' he rumbled in justifiable defence.

Ben stifled a snort of laughter from his lounging position on the porch hammock, where he had retired after the Sunday lunch that had sent them all, except for Bunny, into lazy-afternoon-sleep mode.

Bunny regarded Gray with a level, unblinking stare, and in her completely feminine way chose to ignore his comment. She plonked a naked baby doll on his bare stomach to punctuate the change in subject. ''Get up, Uncle Gray, you gotta *practice*.''

Gray knew an order when he heard one. ''Yes, ma'am,'' he said, and saluted.

Bunny giggled again and pulled on one of his hands, helping him up. When he was sitting, she thrust the doll at him. It was a faithful rendition of a male newborn, complete with landing gear.

''Watch,'' Bunny instructed, as she spread out a frayed

and slightly grubby diaper and began folding it in an intricate, totally mystifying shape that Gray decided would
probably stump an origami master. She summarily
snatched the doll from his incompetent hands and proceeded to truss the doll's lower parts up tight. When she
was finished she jammed a safety pin through the front of
the diaper with a satisfied grunt.

Bunny surveyed her handiwork, brushed her hands off
on her overalls, then turned her laser gaze on him. "That's
what ya gotta do. Now you try."

Gray was almost getting the hang of it when Sam
stepped out on the porch. She was in her ninth month of
pregnancy and had been napping in the cool of Ben's
spare room.

"Gray."

Gray looked up from the wreck of the diaper. He had
bent the safety pin that time and was trying to hide that
fact from Bunny's critical gaze. He was also pretty certain
that, if the doll had been a real baby, his reproductive
future would have been sadly curtailed.

Sam's face was flushed with excitement; her eyes were
sparkling. "I'm in labour," she stated baldly.

Gray's heart stopped, then just as abruptly pounded
back to life. A hot rush of adrenaline flooded his system.
For a second he thought he was having a heart attack.

Ben sat bolt upright in the hammock—a difficult feat
at the best of times.

Gray sprang to his feet and eased Sam into the rocking
chair that was set out on the porch.

Sam didn't even try to protest. She had long since
learned that sometimes it was best to simply let Gray have
his way, then calmly continue on with what she wanted.

"You can't be in labour," he insisted, a hint of panic in his gravelly voice. "It's too early."

Sam couldn't understand the panic in Gray's eyes. She had had a wonderful pregnancy. Apart from a little morning sickness in the first months, she had never felt so well or so happy. Gray had looked after her like she was a piece of precious porcelain, but for the most part she had been quite capable of living a normal, energetic life. The only reason she had let Gray coddle her so much, aside from the fact that she just plain enjoyed it, was that *he* had needed to do so.

They had honeymooned on one of the remote Fijian islands, and when he had found out she was pregnant, he had taken her back for a second honeymoon. Ever since they had gotten home, he had all but carried her around on a satin cushion. He hadn't wanted her to travel after that, but Sam had put her foot down. This trip was special.

The day before they had attended Jack and Milly's wedding, and there had been no way she was going to miss out on that event. Besides, she had wanted to catch up with everyone at the new Lombard hotel, which was still under construction, and see for herself how happy and content they all were with the new premises and their new jobs.

It had also been an opportunity for them both to finally come to terms with the miscarriage she'd had all those years ago.

While they were at the graveside, Sam had had the oddest notion that they had their daughter back, that they were being given a second chance with this pregnancy, just as she and Gray had had a second chance.

Gray had watched her like a hawk this whole trip—as if he fully expected her to do something wild and unpredictable, like give birth without providing him with due notice.

She had got used to his concentrated attention, although not without adjustment. He loved with a single-minded intensity that was formidable and, at times, could be a little uncomfortable. They had their moments, like when she had to explain that she was quite capable of doing simple tasks like lifting a casserole dish from the oven to the table, or hanging curtains in the nursery.

She was learning to live with Gray's natural instinct to control and protect, because she knew it would take him a while to shed the insecurity of everything that had happened between them, and with Harper. If he was dictatorial at times, it was only because he needed her as much as she needed him.

She took his hand and laid it against her stomach so he could feel the strength of the next contraction.

His black eyes glittered over her, and she could almost see the gears shifting in his mind as he began formulating his plan of action. He would try to run this birth like a military operation, the same way he had tried to run her pregnancy.

"How long?" he muttered.

Sam smiled serenely. "Now."

Gray walked out into the waiting room in a daze. He was still wearing denim cut-offs, although he had taken the time to pull a T-shirt on. God help him, there hadn't been time for much else.

"Is the baby here yet, Uncle Gray?"

Ben was sitting with Bunny snuggled on his lap. Bunny had her doll pressed close to her cheek while she listened to the story Ben had been reading her. They had all been at the hospital for a total of thirty minutes.

Thirty minutes.

So much for planning this birth as if it was a military operation. Sam had blown every plan and contingency to hell, just as she had always done.

His wife was early, and she was fast.

If they had been held up in traffic, he would have had to play midwife in the back seat. Gray broke out in a fresh sweat at the thought of that eventuality. No point in buying trouble, they had made it—just—even if the speed of the delivery still stunned him.

"She wants you to come in," he said hoarsely, then held the door while Ben carried Bunny through to the delivery suite.

Sam was sitting up in bed. The nurse had sponged her down, and she was wearing a delicate blue nightie she just happened to have packed in her handbag, along with various other items needed for an overnight stay.

Gray was still in a state of shock. Sam looked as fresh as a daisy.

Gray realised that while he hadn't been prepared for any of this, Sam had quietly been carrying around everything she needed in her handbag. He would never again question why women carried handbags; he now knew the answer: it was because they were organised.

A thin, reedy cry sounded. Gray went stock still, his heart beginning to hammer almost as fast as it had during the hell-on-wheels ordeal of labour and birth. Just the thought of it brought back the panicky feelings; he had never felt so helpless, so out of control.

He picked up the tiny bundle, his stomach tightening on a rush of awe and tenderness. His hands were so big and rough, his baby daughter so soft and fragile. Rheumy eyes fastened on his; then the little head turned, and she began nuzzling his thumb. The crying stopped.

The breath shuddered from Gray's lungs. Carefully, supporting the baby's head, he cuddled her on his shoulder, dipping his head to breathe in her sweet scent.

The reality of what had happened struck him anew as he reluctantly handed his baby daughter over to Sam for feeding. He eased himself behind Sam, pulling her in against the support of his chest and enfolding both her and the baby with his arms as the baby's tiny fist kneaded the plump roundness of Sam's breast. A tremor started deep in his belly, rippled through his big frame as emotion built and broke over him with the rolling power of a big ocean wave. The last of the darkness that had held him in thrall for too many years was extinguished by the sheer, blazing joy of his family.

Sweet heaven. He was a daddy.

"Welcome to the club," Ben murmured drily, letting Bunny's wriggling little body down so he could shake Gray's hand and bend to kiss Sam on the cheek.

Bunny leaned on Gray's thigh and watched, absorbed, as the baby fed with a single-minded, ferocious hunger, then, in the blink of an eye, fell asleep. Fascinated, she plunked her baby doll in her daddy's hands. Dolls were okay to practice on, but she knew the difference between a doll and the real thing, and this was *definitely* the real thing.

"Yep," Bunny said matter-of-factly, as she surveyed the second baby just waking up in his crib, his little face screwing up while he got ready to holler. "Just as well I gave you training, Uncle Gray. You're gonna be *busy*."

* * * * *

Don't miss Silhouette's newest cross-line promotion,

Four royal sisters find their own Prince Charmings as they embark on separate journeys to find their missing brother, the Crown Prince!

The search begins in October 1999 and continues through February 2000:

On sale October 1999: **A ROYAL BABY ON THE WAY** by award-winning author **Susan Mallery** (Special Edition)

On sale November 1999: **UNDERCOVER PRINCESS** by bestselling author **Suzanne Brockmann** (Intimate Moments)

On sale December 1999: **THE PRINCESS'S WHITE KNIGHT** by popular author **Carla Cassidy** (Romance)

On sale January 2000: **THE PREGNANT PRINCESS** by rising star **Anne Marie Winston** (Desire)

On sale February 2000: **MAN...MERCENARY...MONARCH** by top-notch talent **Joan Elliott Pickart** (Special Edition)

ROYALLY WED
Only in—
SILHOUETTE BOOKS

Available at your favorite retail outlet.

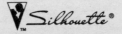

Visit us at www.romance.net

SSERW

If you enjoyed what you just read,
then we've got an offer you can't resist!

Take 2 bestselling love stories FREE!
Plus get a FREE surprise gift!

Clip this page and mail it to Silhouette Reader Service™

IN U.S.A.	**IN CANADA**
3010 Walden Ave.	P.O. Box 609
P.O. Box 1867	Fort Erie, Ontario
Buffalo, N.Y. 14240-1867	L2A 5X3

YES! Please send me 2 free Silhouette Intimate Moments® novels and my free surprise gift. Then send me 6 brand-new novels every month, which I will receive months before they're available in stores. In the U.S.A., bill me at the bargain price of $3.57 plus 25¢ delivery per book and applicable sales tax, if any*. In Canada, bill me at the bargain price of $3.96 plus 25¢ delivery per book and applicable taxes**. That's the complete price and a savings of over 10% off the cover prices—what a great deal! I understand that accepting the 2 free books and gift places me under no obligation ever to buy any books. I can always return a shipment and cancel at any time. Even if I never buy another book from Silhouette, the 2 free books and gift are mine to keep forever. So why not take us up on our invitation. You'll be glad you did!

245 SEN CNFF
345 SEN CNFG

Name		(PLEASE PRINT)	
Address		Apt.#	
City		State/Prov.	Zip/Postal Code

* Terms and prices subject to change without notice. Sales tax applicable in N.Y.
** Canadian residents will be charged applicable provincial taxes and GST.
All orders subject to approval. Offer limited to one per household.
® are registered trademarks of Harlequin Enterprises Limited.

INMOM99   ©1998 Harlequin Enterprises Limited

MONTANA MAVERICKS
Big Sky Brides

Legendary love comes to Whitehorn, Montana,
once more as beloved authors

Christine Rimmer, Jennifer Greene and Cheryl St.John

present three brand-new stories in this exciting anthology!

Meet the Brennan women:
SUZANNA, DIANA and ISABELLE

Strong-willed beauties who find unexpected
love in these irresistible marriage of
covnenience stories.

Don't miss
MONTANA MAVERICKS: BIG SKY BRIDES
On sale in February 2000,
only from Silhouette Books!

Available at your favorite retail outlet.

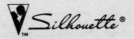

SUZANNE BROCKMANN

continues her popular,
heart-stopping miniseries

*They're who you call to get you out of
a tight spot—or into one!*

Coming in November 1999
THE ADMIRAL'S BRIDE, IM #962

Be sure to catch Mitch's story,
IDENTITY: UNKNOWN, IM #974,
in January 2000.

And **Lucky's story** in April 2000.

And in December 1999 be sure to pick up a
copy of Suzanne's powerful installment
in the **Royally Wed** miniseries,
UNDERCOVER PRINCESS, IM #968.

Available at your favorite retail outlet.

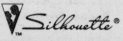

SIMTDD2

Start celebrating Silhouette's 20th anniversary
with these 4 special titles by
New York Times **bestselling authors**

Fire and Rain*
by Elizabeth Lowell

King of the Castle
by Heather Graham Pozzessere

State Secrets*
by Linda Lael Miller

Paint Me Rainbows*
by Fern Michaels

On sale in December 1999

Plus, a special free book offer inside each title!

Available at your favorite retail outlet
*Also available on audio from Brilliance.

Silhouette®
Where love comes alive™

Special Edition is celebrating Silhouette's 20th anniversary!

Special Edition brings you:

• brand-new LONG, TALL TEXANS
Matt Caldwell: Texas Tycoon by **Diana Palmer**
(January 2000)

• a bestselling miniseries
PRESCRIPTION: MARRIAGE
(December 1999-February 2000)
Marriage may be just what the doctor ordered!

• a brand-new miniseries SO MANY BABIES
(January-April 2000)
At the Buttonwood Baby Clinic,
lots of babies—and love—abound

• the exciting conclusion of ROYALLY WED!
(February 2000)

• the new AND BABY MAKES THREE:
THE DELACOURTS OF TEXAS
by **Sherryl Woods**
(December 1999, March & July 2000)

And on sale in June 2000, don't miss
Nora Roberts' brand-new story
Irish Rebel
in **Special Edition**.

Available at your favorite retail outlet.

Where love comes alive™